A portentous picture . . .

"There, done!" declared Lady Meriton.

Cecilia Waddley and Sir Branstoke turned toward Lady Meriton. The lady proudly held up her completed silhouette. It was not solely of Sir Branstoke. The dark red paper featured Cecilia as well. Lady Meriton had captured them close together, moments before Sir Branstoke wiped the sugar from her chin. The poses relayed a magnetism between the two figures without recourse to expressions. Cut of vibrant red paper, it was a hauntingly intimate picture.

Cecilia's heart beat faster. Proud of her cutting, Jessamine evidently detected none of the undercurrents she did. Cecilia stole a look at Sir Branstoke.

Branstoke caught her eye. A smile flickered on his lips. He raised an eyebrow in amused inquiry, his brown eyes dancing.

Cecilia groaned softly and flopped back against her pillows, closing her eyes. Now she knew she was in trouble.

BAY MEADOW FARMS

The Waylaid Heart

The Waylaid Heart

HOLLY NEWMAN

CHARTER/DIAMOND BOOKS, NEW YORK

THE WAYLAID HEART

A Charter/Diamond Book / published by arrangement
with the author

PRINTING HISTORY
Charter/Diamond edition / August 1990

ISBN: 1-55773-377-5

Charter/Diamond Books are published by
The Berkley Publishing Group,
200 Madison Avenue, New York, New York 10016.
The name "CHARTER/DIAMOND" and its logo are trademarks
belonging to Charter Communications, Inc.

PRINTED IN THE UNITED STATES OF AMERICA

10 9 8 7 6 5 4 3 2 1

Chapter One

SNUBBED! It hardly seemed possible.

Intrigued, Sir James Branstoke raised his gold-rimmed quizzing glass to observe the slender yet shapely form of Mrs. Cecilia Haukstrom Waddley. He mentally reviewed his brief encounter with the renowned ninnyhammer.

If the woman had been any other than Mrs. Waddley, her actions would have fallen into the category of a snub, to the point of a direct cut. However, Mrs. Waddley's eccentric reputation preceded her, and he found he was loath to grant her the sophisticated subtlety of manner necessary for the proper delivery and timing of an effective snub. No, something sent her scurrying off, slipping through the crush by the music room door.

Branstoke rubbed the rim of the quizzing glass thoughtfully against his cheek. He'd greeted the infamous widow with comments designed to flatter and draw a blush, thereby avoiding a recital of her most recent afflictions. He swiftly perceived she was not attending him.

Her head tilted and her dark blue eyes sparkled strangely. Suddenly her eyes widened and she left, going off in a flurry of gossamer layers of muslin and trailing lavender ribbons, leaving him without a word. He doubted she was the slightest bit aware of her social gaff. Ruefully, he wondered whether it would have mattered to her. Her attitude was that of a hound flying to a scent and totally out of character for the woman all society considered a beautiful yet charmingly featherbrained creature.

Despite her youthful marriage into trade, society eagerly welcomed her back into its august ranks upon her widowhood—as much for her elevated purse as for the elevated positions of her grandfather, the notorious Duke of Houghton, and her uncle, the Marquis of Nye. At five and twenty, she was no longer in the first bloom of youth; yet with hair the color of moonlight and large, twilight-blue eyes, she possessed an ethereal beauty and fragility. It was her ethereal appearance that gave credence

1

to her complaints of the various and sundry illnesses afflicting her body.

Absently, Branstoke twirled the quizzing glass by its black riband. He'd endeavored to engage Mrs. Waddley in conversation as a refreshing diversion from his attentions to Miss Philomel Cresswell, the current London beauty and society darling. Though a diamond of the first water in appearance, Miss Cresswell lamentably possessed the hardness of that particular stone. Mrs. Waddley, with her childlike chatter, he deemed a pleasant counterpoint—and would provide a subtle message to Miss Cresswell that he was not a man to be manipulated, as she was wont to try. However, from his brief observation, he doubted Mrs. Waddley was as simple as everyone thought.

He glanced at the circle of gentlemen surrounding the laughing Miss Cresswell. He was in no hurry to rejoin their ranks. It would be more entertaining to discover the true nature of Mrs. Waddley—if there was anything to discover. Somehow, his intuition told him there was. A slight smile playing upon his lips, Branstoke stuck the end of the quizzing glass into his waistcoat pocket and sauntered off in the same direction his quarry had taken, his curiosity piqued.

Cecilia heard a chorus of raucous masculine laughter before she reached the arched entrance to the card room. She groaned softly. Fearing the worst, she tentatively peeked around the corner. Her brother stood in the middle of the room in boisterous conversation with eight or ten other gentlemen. A frown of annoyance twisted her bow-shaped lips. She leaned back, out of sight of the open doorway, rapidly tapping her foot in frustration as she contemplated this turn of events.

She wondered which—if any—of those gentlemen had been the recipient of the words she heard fall from her brother's lips not five minutes earlier. They were the precise words she'd been waiting and hoping to hear since she read them in her late husband's journal eight long months ago! They were the words that pitched her willy-nilly into the same society that eight years ago had closed ranks against her.

Cecilia lightly gnawed on the soft inner tissue of her lower lip. Never would she have expected to hear those words coming from her brother! Randolph Haukstrom may be a ne'er-do-well gamester; nonetheless, he was also heir to his grandfather and uncle. And though he would not bear their titles, he'd have their money and property. He was already comfortably living off these expectations—not forgetting the allowance they granted him. What reason could there be for him to become involved in anything illegal? For thrills and adventure? That was hardly Randolph's style. He was too much the dandy. Worse! He was a veritable coxcomb! Hardly the sort to go skulking about on a dirty, dank wharf at night—or any time! Besides, he was her brother. It was ridiculous to imagine him involved in George Waddley's death.

Death. Disgust at her own hesitation to name his demise for what it was swelled within Cecilia. It was murder. Premeditated, cold-blooded murder. Not that anyone believed her; nonetheless, murder it was and murder she would prove.

But, could Randolph be involved? she asked herself again.

Cecilia bit her lower lip harder as she pondered the mystery. Of course, she determinedly conceded, just because Randolph was her brother, she mustn't dismiss him out of hand. After all, it had been his chicanery that had seen her married to George Waddley in the first place. Not that she regretted her marriage to Mr. Waddley—God bless his soul—for he had been the gentlest and sweetest man she'd ever met. She counted herself luckier than many young women married off to save their families' fortunes. A decent, hard-working man, George Waddley had not deserved to die.

Another burst of rowdy laughter drew her attention back to the card room, warning her of the tenuousness of her present position. It would be difficult to justify her presence outside this exclusively male haunt. Besides, she rationalized, she wouldn't learn anything more from Randolph this evening, so involved was he with his cronies. If only she hadn't been delayed by Lady Amblethorp as she left the music room, she could have discovered her brother's companion! Well, it made no sense to ponder what might have been. At least she now had a possible lead, a glimmer of light to pierce the dark mystery of Mr. Waddley's death. The question was, how to use it?

Stealthily, Cecilia stepped backward, slowly distancing herself from the card room entrance. Her attention remained riveted on the doorway as she listened intently for signs of any gentleman leaving the room. Satisfied that no one was coming and that she was far enough from the doorway, she whirled around to make her escape back to the music room.

Her face abruptly met a broad masculine chest and the snowy white folds of an intricately tied cravat. Her breath went out in a whoosh, her eyes fixating on the milky white pearl nestled in the folds. She sagged against him, her senses aroused by the sharp smell of soap and clean linen mingled with the musky scent of the man. Her nose itched. She moved sideways, stumbling on the toes of his highly polished shoes. Idiotically she wondered if he used champagne in his blacking. Strong arms came around her waist to steady her.

"Oh! Oh my, I'm truly sorry," she babbled, her senses swirling. *Of all the stupid mistakes,* she chastised herself as she gathered her wits and tilted her head up. "So clumsy, I'm—*Sir Branstoke!*"

Cecilia choked, blushed, and stumbled backward into his still supportive arms. Belatedly she realized it was this gentleman she had left in the music room without so much as a by-your-leave. A bright wave of color swept up her face again. "Oh, I'm—I don't know what to say! Please forgive—"

"Are you all right?" he inquired calmly. Seeing that she had recovered her balance, he politely dropped his hold and stepped away, though his gaze remained fixed on her flustered countenance.

Cecilia's slender fingers unconsciously twisted a knot of ribbons trailing from a nosegay of violets pinned to her bodice. "What? Oh, yes—" she said weakly. Her normally quick mind was not focussing. Frantically she sought an explanation that would pacify this man. Sir Branstoke was an enigma in society. He was the image of a social gadder: handsome, frivolous, and lazy. Yet he also had the whispered reputation of being a canny gentleman.

"I mean, *no!*" she amended shrilly. She winced, beginning again breathily: "No, I feel a trifle dizzy and—and my heart is pounding," she continued, warming rapidly to her role. "Oh, you cannot know sir! I pray you will forgive my clumsiness. I am not well, you know. No, no, not at all. That is why I' here. I came to find my brother to see if he might escort me home, but he is otherwise engaged."

She broke off and looked back toward the card room, letting a look of confusion cross her features. "Jessamine. Yes, yes, I must find my Aunt Jessamine," she said vaguely. She turned to walk past Sir Branstoke as if she had already forgotten his existence.

Branstoke fell into step beside her. "If you are ill, perhaps you would like to sit out here while I send a servant for your aunt." He took her elbow and gently, but firmly, guided her to a secluded alcove in the hall.

A wave of panic swept over Cecilia, leaving her skin prickling, her senses strangely heightened toward the man at her side. What was his purpose? They were scarcely acquainted, and he was known for being one of the entourage for whatever dewy fresh London belle was considered the catch of the season. She didn't trust him.

Truthfully, she didn't trust easily. "You are all solicitation, sir. It is not necessary. La! I am better now already, I assure you. It is just my nerves, you know. I have terrible nerves. My physician tells me he never saw such terrible nerves!"

"You are to be consoled," Sir Branstoke murmured conversationally.

Cecilia shot him a sharp glance through the veil of her pale lashes, wondering if she'd overplayed her hand. She did not know if she was relieved or chagrined to see his urbane countenance remain unchanged. Furthermore, she wondered at the firm grasp he retained on her elbow.

"You are too kind. I'm sure I have quite recovered," she said with false brightness while gently attempting to free her arm. The feel of his fingers on her arm sent a tingling up it, a tingling that ended in the vicinity of her heart which sent shock waves throughout her body. This gentleman was dangerous in ways she hesitated to contemplate.

"But I insist," he persevered, steering her adroitly to the alcove settee. With his free hand he signaled a passing footman.

"Please find Viscountess Meriton in the main music room. She will be the woman madly wielding a pair of scissors and carelessly dropping snippets of paper on the floor. Tell her that her niece is feeling a trifle unwell and desires her presence here—discreetly, of course." He settled her down on the settee. "Mrs. Waddley does not need her unfortunate ill-health bandied about in company."

Cecilia lowered her head to hide the humor she felt at this last statement. Her health was a constant source of amusement to the ton, though they clucked and commiserated in her presence. She looked up in time to see Sir Branstoke slip a coin into the footman's palm. The man grinned cheekily and trotted off down the corridor.

Sir Branstoke reached into his pocket, drawing out a gold-enameled snuffbox. "The lack of proper decorum found in servants these days is appalling," he drawled. He opened the box with a deft, one-handed motion and took a small pinch of its contents. "Don't you agree?"

"Oh, well yes, I suppose," Cecilia answered meekly, carefully schooling her expression to childlike confusion. She looked up at him, her eyes wide, revealing purple rims around their royal blue color.

Sir James Branstoke paused and stared down at her upturned face, a speculative gleam lurking in his lazily hooded brown eyes.

Under his steady regard, tiny moths began to flutter in Cecilia's stomach. She found she could not turn her eyes from his intent gaze. He had a pleasant, good-looking face without being handsome in the current Adonis fashion. His features were regular, his hair a wavy thick pelt that echoed the rich, variegated brown of his eyes. Nonetheless, there was something about those sleepy, world-weary eyes that caught her attention, something that made her breath come a little faster. A slow blush crept up her neck to her cheeks, staining them a rose color. She opened her mouth to speak, but no words came.

Suddenly, the lid of the snuffbox snapped shut. The small sharp sound was like a pistol shot in the silence between them. Cecilia jumped. Sir Branstoke raised his eyes from hers. He looked in the direction of the card room where a renewed chorus of laughter could be heard. He looked back at her, a slight smile playing upon his lips.

"Sir?" Cecilia ventured, uncertain as to the proper response. In all her playacting, never had she felt as uncomfortable as she did before this enigmatic gentleman. "Please don't feel you must wait upon me until my aunt's arrival. I assure you I am recovered from that dreadful pounding in my chest. It was the music and the crush of people, I dare say. I do suffer from an irritation of the nerves, you know, to say nothing of the spasms that sometimes grip me in a most terrifying fashion." She prattled on artlessly, hoping to rout the gentleman by her complaints.

"I imagine that opera sung by such incompetents as Signora Casteneletti might have that effect. I do not know whether to be grateful or not for possessing a stronger constitution," he observed drily.

Cecilia nodded vaguely while pondering the advisability of allowing a touch of a whine to color her voice. *That would be doing it too brown,* she concluded. She cast about in her mind for some other venue.

"Cecilia, my dear!" Lady Jessamine Meriton called as she entered the hallway.

Cecilia turned toward her aunt, quickly masking her relief.

"I am sorry. I was so involved cutting a silhouette of Signora Casteneletti that I did not notice you leave," Lady Meriton said contritely. She gracefully sank onto the settee and raised a cool hand to Cecilia's brow.

"It was nothing, more my fears than actuality, as I've tried to convince Sir Branstoke," Cecilia said, indicating the gentleman with a small inclination of her head.

Lady Meriton turned to look up at Branstoke, one finely chiseled eyebrow arching quizzically.

Branstoke appeared mildly amused. "I assured Mrs. Waddley it was no bother to keep her company." He looked back toward Cecilia, tipping his head slightly in her direction. "I leave you now in good company. Ladies—" he said, bowing elegantly before turning to saunter down the hall in the direction of the card room.

"What has been going on? How did you keep Branstoke so attentively at your side?" Jessamine hissed.

Cecilia wrinkled her nose and shook her head. "I really do not know. *Especially* since I walked away from him in the music room without so much as a by-your-leave."

"Cecilia!"

"I know, I know that was careless." She pushed back wisps of white-blond hair that had managed to slide out of their confining pins to create a halo effect about her face. "—But wait until I tell you what I heard. Then you'll understand how the gentleman's presence could completely vanish from my mind." She glanced up and down the hall. "I suggest you pretend to administer to me a *sal volatile* while we talk. That should suffice to keep others away. You may find need of it yourself when I tell you I have heard the words Mr. Waddley recorded in his journal!" Cecilia said, trying to keep her voice hushed and her excitement from creeping out as she pulled a small bottle of restorative from her reticule and handed it to her aunt. She grabbed Jessamine's hand as she placed the bottle in it and squeezed it. "I almost despaired, you know, of ever hearing anything of its like."

"Well, tell me, please. Don't keep me on tenterhooks!"

"I was, as I said, exchanging empty pleasantries with Sir James Branstoke, when I heard the words: '*Talkers are no good doers,*' "

"Is that all?"

"Well, then there was a laugh, and a pause, before the voice went on to wonder whether that extended to singers as well," Cecilia admitted. "But that is not relevant."

Her aunt looked at her askance. "You must have a tin ear, my dear."

"Jessamine! Be serious. *Talkers are no good doers* is the exact phrase Mr. Waddley wrote down, and that is not a phrase to come trippingly off of anyone's tongue."

Jessamine sighed and shook her head. "All right," she relented, "who did you hear, do you know?"

Cecilia nodded sadly. "Only too well, though the speaker was behind a column—it was Randolph."

"Your brother?"

Cecilia pursed her lips and nodded again. "I'll own I was shocked. I swear I stood as still as one of Elgin's marbles for several seconds after the voice moved on. When the full measure of what I'd heard filtered to me, I turned without a thought to Sir Branstoke and headed in the direction of the voice." She paused, frowning. "Lady Amblethorp delayed me at the doorway. I believe she wanted to assure herself I was not running out because of the music. I told her I was not, but by then, too much time had passed and Randolph was comfortably ensconced amid a large group of gentleman in the card room."

"But Randolph? You must be mistaken, Cecilia. He could not possibly—"

Cecilia lifted her shoulders in the barest suggestion of a shrug.

"For what reason? I'll own he might have once had cause, thinking to make you a wealthy widow and thereby sponging funds from you."

"Which I never would have given him!"

Jessamine smiled. "Be that as it may, dear, being a man, I'm sure he thought he could appeal to your womanly nature. Anyway," she went on, ignoring the look of disgust Cecilia cast in her direction, "once Carlton's sons died, he became heir to the properties of the Marquis of Nye *and* the Duke of Houghton."

"And under those circumstances tradesmen extended him credit based upon his expectations and promises of payment," Cecilia finished for her. "Yes, I know. It was a practice Mr. Waddley considered extremely foolish. Besides, grandfather and Uncle Carlton now grant him an allowance far greater than I think he could spend, though I grant you he does somehow manage to do so."

"Regardless, the point is he does have money of his own without recourse to Mr. Waddley's."

"True. But I don't believe Mr. Waddley was killed for money. I told you there appeared to have been some irregular dealings at the warehouse and on the wharf that Mr. Waddley found out about and was killed for knowing."

"Precisely, Cecilia. And what, I ask you, would Randolph be doing that could concern the dockyards? I can't imagine him setting foot in such a location, let alone dealing with individuals who might. If he did, he might smudge his Hessians or soil his snowy white cravat!"

Cecilia giggled, then sobered lest anyone notice. "Upon first consideration I suppose it does seem ridiculous. But Jessamine, somehow I know it isn't. I must investigate further. This is the only clue I've ever received beyond the journal! Gracious, the journal! Of course! In the journal there are several references to *H*. It must be *H* for *Haukstrom*. Now wait a moment, while I think—" She ran her tongue across her top lip as her eyes narrowed in thought.

Her shoulders sagged. "No, I'm grasping straws of hay. In the journal, Mr. Waddley wrote he was disgusted at *H's* need for signs and symbols. That can't have had anything to do with Randolph."

Jessamine nodded, smiling sadly. "Come, we've sat here long enough," she said matter-of-factly, rising to her feet. She extended a hand toward Cecilia who rose gracefully to stand beside her.

"Let's bid Lady Amblethorp good-bye and return home," Cecilia suggested wearily as they neared the music room. From inside mediocre applause followed another aria sung by Signora Casteneletti.

"Why ever did Lady Amblethorp hire her?" Jessamine asked as they watched the singer take her last bow.

"I believe she came highly recommended by her ladyship's brother," Cecilia said drily, a crooked smile curling up one corner of her lips. "Somehow I don't think she knew precisely what her brother recommended the woman for."

"Cecilia!" Jessamine exclaimed.

"Don't attempt to feign shock, you haven't the constitution for an effective deception of that nature. Stick with lying," Cecilia advised breezily while looking about the room for their hostess.

Jessamine sighed. "Sometimes you make me wonder how I let you talk me into helping you."

"Simple, with Meriton out of the country on a diplomatic mission and Franklin away at school, you were bored."

Jessamine frowned at her summation causing Cecilia to laugh spontaneously. Quickly she covered her mouth with a handkerchief and began to cough.

"By the way," she added softly, "if anyone asks, my illnesses this evening are pounding in the chest and dizziness with a touch of disorientation. That last is in case Sir Branstoke should chance to question anyone. I would like him to believe that my behavior this evening stemmed from one of my illnesses."

Lady Jessamine Meriton laughed and patted her niece's hand. "With your reputation, how could he believe otherwise?"

Cecilia frowned and shook her head. "I don't know," she said slowly. "He is an odd gentleman. His manners are languid, but something about his eyes—there is a shrewd glint in their depths that makes me nervous. The man sends shivers through my body when he looks my way."

"Sir Branstoke? Well, I just hope those shivers are not a sign of a growing tendre for the man, for I tell you straight out that it is common knowledge he only courts the current catch of the season—who in turn would like to catch him."

Cecilia raised the lace-edged handkerchief to her lips to smother another laugh. "I am well aware of that. Do not be alarmed. I have no intention of setting my cap for him. In fact, I believe it would be wise to avoid his company."

"Now you are being fanciful!"

"I'm not so sure," Cecilia murmured, looking back over her shoulder.

There, at the entrance to the music room stood Sir James Branstoke. At her regard, he cocked his head and bowed slightly. A blush rose to suffuse Cecilia's pale cheeks. For the first time in her life, she felt light-headed and dizzy—without recourse to artifice. She turned jerkily toward Lady Amblethorp, effusively complimenting her hostess for the musicale while apologizing for leaving early, the high color tinting Cecilia's complexion giving credence to her claim of sudden, feverish ill-health. Quickly Lady Meriton retrieved her lap desk from a chair near the door, and the two ladies departed.

Sir James Ruger Branstoke watched Mrs. Waddley and Lady Meriton take their leave of Lady Amblethorp. Idly, he wondered if anyone else noticed how beautiful Mrs. Waddley looked with a blush upon her pale cheeks, or how in confusion her deep blue eyes darkened to purple.

He smiled slightly, his thin lips curling in sardonic amusement. Society was decidedly obtuse. There was no trace of illness that he could detect in her radiant countenance. So why did she feign a sickly constitution? Branstock didn't know, but he intended to find out.

Chapter Two

CECILIA GENTLY PUSHED ONE PANEL of the swagged, rose-colored damask draperies to the edge of the window. Cold air trapped next to the glass panes by the heavy drapery material grazed her pale cheeks. She shivered slightly. Each warm breath she exhaled swirled visibly in the air, frosting the window. Soon she'd have to move or the growing circle of condensation on the glass would obscure her view. She'd need to move to see the clear blue sky dotted with scudding, billowy clouds; to see the red clay chimney tops in contrast to the sky and the soot-streaked roofs; or to look down the street at the pale green foliage on trees and bushes. The beauty and freshness of spring, all sights Mr. Waddley loved. They brought out the hidden poet in that dedicated merchant's heart. Cecilia smiled wistfully.

The marriage of Mr. George Waddley, merchant, to Miss Cecilia Haukstrom, arranged by her father and brother solely for the hefty financial settlement they would gain, had not been a love match. Nonetheless, eight years of marriage had brought George Waddley and his young wife close. She even came to think that the respect she held for him was a form of love. George Waddley treated her like she was someone special, a queen in his realm. More important, he told her he considered her his greatest friend. To Cecilia that was the highest accolade he could bestow.

Her head tilted to rest against the frosted glass. She remembered how they would talk for hours—oh, how they would talk! He introduced her to the wonders of trade and the mysteries of finance. He gave her an understanding of politics and an appreciation for newspapers. Her bright mind and ready wit pleased him, he said. He told her he hadn't understood what he was doing until she came into his life.

Now he was dead. A victim, society decreed, of the teeming London underworld that owed its life to thievery. He simply walked in the wrong place at the wrong time. How trite. And oh, Cecilia knew, how wrong.

Cecilia clenched her fist, her nails grating against the damask material. Mr. Waddley was murdered. Murdered because he discovered illegal activities occurring at his warehouses and wharf. Before the night he went out, never to return, Cecilia's husband confided he had uncovered something, something that distressed him. He wouldn't say precisely what, though she inferred some form of late-night illegal activity on his wharf. He told her he wasn't certain of his facts, and until he was there was no profit in conjecture. His face rigid with anger and indignation, he said he hoped he was wrong about his suspicions.

Mr. Waddley was restless that entire day. More than once Cecilia caught him staring at her with an intense frown pulling his shaggy eyebrows together. What had been behind that frown? Why couldn't Mr. Waddley be more forthcoming with her? They talked of everything else. Why his strange reticence in this matter? Did he have an inkling of her brother's involvement in the occurrences at Waddley Spice and Tea? Was he trying to save her pain at the knowledge of some nefarious dealings on her brother's part? If that were so, she wished he hadn't. The thought of Randolph's possible involvement in illegal activities was repugnant, but not unexpected. He was a wastrel and often vulgar—bloodlines notwithstanding. In truth, any love she bore her brother came solely from duty.

Still, Randolph was displaying a rare attentiveness. He'd offered to act as her escort on numerous occasions. That very evening he was to take her to the Italian Opera. When he began extending his services as escort, Cecilia believed his motives stemmed from a belated guilt at the marriage he'd arranged for her. A guilt he decided he had the luxury to indulge in since he became his uncle's and grandfather's heir.

Now she couldn't help but wonder if he harbored a different form of guilt. Try as she would to banish that thought, it insidiously wound its way through her mind and imagination, tying her beleaguered brain in knots until all she was aware of was the echo of his voice within her mind. Like a chant in time to the endless beat of a metronome, her memory replayed those hated words. *Talkers are no good doers.*

The strange thing about the phrase was that, heard spoken, it had a familiar ring to it, like it was something she'd heard before. Her pale brow furrowed as she tried to recall where she might have heard the phrase. Unfortunately, she could not place the elusive memory. She sighed.

"Cecilia? Are you all right?"

Cecilia turned toward the soft, concerned voice of her aunt, her hand falling from the drapery at her side. "Yes, I'm all right." She smiled and a slight laugh escaped her parted lips. "Much better, actually, than society would have me."

Expressions of doubt and concern captured her aunt's face and that of the gentleman, a certain Mr. Thornbridge, seated near her. Lady Meriton pursed her lips, refraining from further comment on the subject. She elected instead to wave her niece to a seat by her side. "Come. Have a pastry with us. Cook has outdone herself."

"No, thank you. I'm not hungry," Cecilia returned instantly in habitual response. She did, however, cross the room to join her aunt on the elegant sofa.

Lady Meriton studied her niece critically. "Yours is presently a sylph-like figure. I fear it will soon be skeletal if you persist with your current eating habits. Should that happen, those illnesses you feign may well become more real than imagined." She poured a cup of tea for Cecilia.

Cecilia laughed, accepted the cup, then patted her aunt's hand. "Should that occur we shall have to depend on my erstwhile physician here," she said, inclining her head in Mr. David Thornbridge's direction, "to see that I recover."

Mr. Thornbridge started at his benefactress's sally, his cup rattling in it's saucer. He placed the cup and saucer carefully on the inlaid table at his side. "Mrs. Waddley, I must protest," the young gentleman declared, his face suffused with embarrassed color.

"Oh, Cecilia, be serious," Lady Meriton abjured, thrusting a small plate bearing a sugared tart into her niece's hands. "Pay no attention to her, Mr. Thornbridge. My niece is as healthy as a horse and more than likely shall remain that way, skeletal or not. I should know better than to request she eat," her aunt said briskly while watching with complacency as Cecilia took a bite of the confection. "It is best to just put the food before her and allow her own nervous habits to guide it to her mouth."

Cecilia paused in the act of raising the pastry to her lips. She stared at the tart, ruefully smiling. *"Touché, ma tante,"* she murmured before taking another bite. She absently brushed sugar from her cheek. "Mr. Thornbridge, I apologize for my melancholy demeanor today."

"Please, Mrs. Waddley, there is no need."

Cecilia waved his hurried assurances aside. "Yes, there is. You see, last evening I heard someone repeat the phrase my husband recorded in his journal. The phrase that he felt confident is the password for whatever group is illegally using the Waddley Spice and Tea properties. It is the first real break we've had!" She popped the last morsel of tart into her mouth and set her plate on the tea tray. Her slender fingers, free of encumbrances, fluttered, echoing her words.

"So Lady Meriton has explained."

"I own," Cecilia continued earnestly, "I should be merry as a grig to have some new direction for our investigation. Unfortunately, to my mind, it has been like a dam breaking. I find myself remembering too much."

"I'm certain that given the situation, it is a perfectly natural happenstance."

"That is true, dear," Lady Meriton said, her troubled pale blue eyes expressing concern for her niece.

"Where did you hear this phrase? I'll own I've been wracking my inept brain to understand it or its genesis!" the young Waddley's manager exclaimed.

"Now that is the crux of the matter," Cecilia said, a wry smile twisting her lips. "I heard it last evening during an exceedingly boring musicale given by Lady Amblethorp."

"Almost all *Society* was there," added Lady Meriton, "though why, I do not know. Lady Amblethorp is an indifferent hostess. For some curious reason, last night there was a paucity of entertainments on the calendar."

"Everyone who is anyone was at the Amblethorp musicale," Cecilia said drily.

"Yes, and the spate of entertainments Julia Amblethorp has offered this season stem solely from desperation. She's afraid the season will end with Janine unbetrothed. This is the poor child's second season."

Cecilia smiled and shook her head. "Be careful you do not write off Janine so easily. I see rebellion brewing in that quiet little mouse." Her eyes sparkled at a private vision of the future. "But we digress. Mr. Thornbridge's question should not be where did I hear the phrase, but on the lips of whom."

"You identified the speaker?"

Cecilia sighed and looked away a moment. "It was Randolph Haukstrom."

"Your brother?" Incredulity cracked his voice.

She turned back toward him and nodded. "Now you understand why my mind has been tied in knots. At first it did not seem probable, or even conceivable. Further reflection allows me to own it is possible." She looked down at her clenched hands. She took a deep breath and slowly uncurled her fingers one at a time until they lay flat in her lap.

"My father, Baron Lionel Haukstrom, is a gamester." Each word was drawn out then bitten off sharply like it was some foul tasting food. "By the time I was twelve, he'd run through his own inheritance. He would have run through mother's portion as well if grandfather hadn't had the wherewithal to place a clause in my parent's marriage contract that withheld direct control of the principal from my father. My brother Randolph was bitter at the family financial straits. It prevented him from cutting a swath through Society, you see. For several years he planned and schemed at ways to reverse the family fortunes. Then he heard of a wealthy merchant who was unmarried. Randolph contrived to meet this merchant and put the idea in his head that he needed a wife—an aristocratic wife. Me."

Cecilia rose and began pacing the room. "I was sixteen at the time and still a resident at a Bath seminary for young ladies. My grandfather paid for my education and invited me to Oastley Hall for the holidays as a way to insure I *not* become soiled by my father's and brother's machinations. Unfortunately, he was not successful. To make a long story short, Mr. Waddley bought me—" Her voice rising in shrillness, she broke off and turned away to compose herself.

"E'gad," murmured Mr. Thornbridge.

Cecilia took a deep breath and began again, her voice low but steady. "There really can be no other term for it. Father fetched me from school, informed me of my good fortune, and took me to a small church where my brother and Mr. Waddley waited."

"I would not have thought Mr. Waddley to behave in such a ramshackle manner."

Cecilia smiled ruefully. "I should add that father had the forethought to provide me with a veil. Mr. Waddley's first look at me did not occur until after our vows were exchanged. Randolph led him to believe I was older and a teacher at the school, reduced to those circumstances by our poverty and therefore unlikely to enjoy a respectable marriage. Moved by my supposed plight, Mr. Waddley offered marriage."

Mr. Thornbridge nodded in understanding. "That I readily believe."

She laughed, her dark blue eyes sparkling. "Knowing my husband, Mr. Thornbridge, can you imagine his reaction when he discovered he'd been gulled?"

"He would have been furious."

"He was." Cecilia sat down on the sofa again, some of the tenseness leaving her body. "But his fury was not directed at how he'd been fooled. He was furious at the use my father and brother made of me. Being a man who's word was his bond, he honored the contract he made with my father. Afterward, he made certain they understood that our marriage did not give them license to run tame with his fortune. He would see to it that London tradesmen did not issue them credit backed by his wealth."

Mr. Thornbridge's eyes gleamed. "I can well imagine! Did your family actually think your marriage would be a *carte blanche* to his pocketbook?"

"Oh, yes! Particularly Randolph. It is my belief he felt we should continue to thank him remuneratively for arranging our marriage. In his mind he was not responsible for decimating the Haukstrom fortune; therefore, he should not be penalized. The irony is that he would have run through the money in half the time it took father."

"Only because Prinny and his set are so spendthrift. They set a standard that others rush to follow," interjected Lady Meriton, her voice thick with disgust.

"Like lemmings rushing to the sea, they seek their own destruction," quipped Cecilia.

"Precisely. I only hope I have adequately educated Franklin to avoid the excesses of his peers."

Cecilia laughed and reached over to pat her aunt's hand. "I should not worry unduly. Franklin is a shrewd lad. If he wasn't, I'm certain Meriton would pack him off to one of England's colonies, or even to the United States."

Lady Meriton smiled. "Yes. He would call it *seasoning*. Much more educational than a Grand Tour. That reminds me, my dear—and do not let me forget again—Franklin has written that he's again in need of new clothes. I swear I used to worry he would never grow. Now I worry he shall never stop! Oh, forgive me, Mr. Thornbridge, prattling on like this on personal matters. So ill-conceived."

Mr. Thornbridge nodded understanding, then frowned in thought. "Excuse me, Mrs. Waddley. I fear I am confused. Didn't Mr. Haukstrom come into a sizable allowance *before* Mr. Waddley's death?"

"Yes. From my grandfather, the Duke of Houghton and my uncle, the Marquis of Nye. My uncle had twin sons, Trenton and Sheridan. Sheridan was killed in Spain during the peninsular wars. Trenton died in 1814."

"After engaging in that silly duel with Lord Welville," Lady Meriton added, her lips pursed in sour disapproval. "Everyone knows Lady Welville is no better than she should be. Trenton was not the only gentleman with whom she played fast and loose."

"But he was the only one Lord Welville challenged to a duel— to their mutual misfortune."

"I've always contended that it was unfortunate he was born first. Sheridan was worth ten Trentons."

"Jessamine, we are rambling again. Mr. Thornbridge has no interest in the skeletons rattling about in our family closet." Cecilia's head tilted, a thoughtful expression narrowing her blue eyes to slits. She tapped a fingernail against her chin. "Though I must admit, thinking of those skeletons does affirm my fears that Randolph may be involved with my husband's death. The family tree is not filled with the most upright and honest of relations, despite our so-called aristocratic blood."

"Yes, and when one considers that father was once a highway-man—"

Mr. Thornbridge choked and sputtered on a sip of tea. "A highwayman? The Duke of Houghton?"

Laughter burbled from Cecilia. "And a smuggler. Jessamine, I believe we have shocked poor Mr. Thornbridge! Do not worry, sir. Grandmother claims the history is more dramatic than the actuality. She refers to that time in the duke's life as a minor indiscretion. Now he is the model of straitlaced propriety. If anyone challenges him on the contradiction of his life, he calls it the luxury of old age. But my point is, Mr. Thornbridge, that it would not be singular for my brother to be involved in illegal activities. It *is* in his blood." She leaned forward to pick up her cup. She sipped the tepid brew as she watched conflicting emotions chase across Mr. Thornbridge's face.

"I admit, Mrs. Waddley, a certain astonishment at your revelations. Nonetheless, if Mr. Haukstrom did begin receiving a healthy allowance as the next heir to the Marquis of Nye and the Duke of Houghton before Mr. Waddley's death, why would he continue engaging in nefarious activities?"

"That I cannot answer. What I can suppose is that there was some sort of adventure attached to his activities or perhaps the depths of his involvement prevented his extrication. But we are getting ahead of ourselves. We have no proof, only surmises. What I would like you to do, Mr. Thornbridge, is to investigate my brother's financial situation. How does he spend his money? Does he owe anyone? Is he involved in any unusual investments or business ventures? What about his cronies, what are their financial states?"

"I understand, Mrs. Waddley."

"But, Mr. Thornbridge, please be careful. I suspect additional involvement by someone within Waddley Spice and Tea, though I have no idea who that person could be."

"If you are speaking of involvement among the managers, that is only a handful of men—myself included."

"And we satisfied ourselves in regards to you weeks ago. It is a moot concern. But tell me, do you have any trouble among the other managers at Waddley's with visiting me?"

"No, quite the reverse, actually. As the manager possessing the least seniority, I handle the dirtiest jobs. Calling upon you— or *pandering to the bereaved widow,* as it is known in the company—is considered one of those jobs," he drawled, the gleam of shared secrets in his eyes.

Lady Meriton pursed her lips and ducked her head to hide a smile. Spotting her lap desk on the floor, she reached down to pick it up.

Cecilia was temporarily nonplussed. Then she smiled ruefully and nodded. "The idea that you are forced to dance attendance upon a silly ninnyhammer should give you freedom to come and go as you please. Excellent."

"Particularly a ninnyhammer who is forever relating to anyone unfortunate enough to be at hand the sad state of her health.

It would drive most men to distraction," offered Lady Meriton as she rummaged through her lap desk.

"Yes, I believe I have become quite imaginative in that regard."

A sharp knock on the drawing room door drew the startled attention of its occupants. Quickly Cecilia slouched back on the sofa adopting a languid posture. Lady Meriton called out her permission to enter.

At the sight of the thinning pate of Loudon, her aunt's sad-eyed butler, Cecilia relaxed. He was one of the few servants aware of her dissembling.

"Excuse me, my lady, but there is a gentleman below who begs a visit with Mrs. Waddley."

Cecilia sat up straight, her features animated again. "A gentleman? Who is it, Loudon?"

Silently the butler held out a small white card to his mistress. Lady Meriton fixed her butler with a frown as she fumbled to adjust the small rimmed glasses she wore on her nose, then she glanced down at the card. "Cecilia! It's Sir James Branstoke!"

"What? I knew the man was trouble! I can't see him. I don't dare." Cecilia's hands fluttered about her, her complexion growing paler than usual without recourse to rice powder. She turned to glare mockingly at her aunt. "I thought you said my blue megrims would drive any man to distraction."

"*Most* men," corrected Lady Meriton. "But you are getting frantic without cause. I have known Sir Branstoke these many years. Allow me to assure you that he is a veritable walking somnambulist. The man does not see beyond the end of his nose unless he is looking at someone's attire. He is a tyro for sartorial elegance."

"Who is Sir Branstoke?" asked Mr. Thornbridge.

"He is merely a gentleman who came to Cecilia's aid last evening when he thought she was ill. My niece now would have it that he doubts her ill health."

"He does, and I swear he is not the quintessential dandy he appears. Trust one artificer to recognize another, Jessamine. Loudon, send him away, say I am indisposed. Yes! That's it, I am indisposed and closeted with my physician."

The butler cleared his throat and looked sheepishly at Mrs. Waddley. "Begging your pardon, ma'am, but I took the liberty of informing the gentleman of your visit with your—ahem, *doc-*

tor. He informed me he would wait. A most courteous gentleman, but rather implacable, I would say."

"I'm afraid that is a very proper summation, Loudon." Cecilia sighed then determinedly compressed her lips. "All right. You may show him up, Loudon. Mr. Thornbridge, quickly fetch the blanket folded on the settee over there while I douse a handkerchief in lavender water to bathe my feverish brow. I shall probably need it in actuality before this interview is over."

"Cecilia, you are refining too much on last evening's occurrence," protested Lady Meriton.

"I hope you are correct, Jessamine. Oh, blast! I've spilled lavender water on my dress. I dare say I shall reek for hours. No matter. Spread that blanket across my legs, Mr. Thornbridge, then hover over me like you are checking my pulse, or fever, or something."

"I must protest, Mrs. Waddley. To feign a doctor's position for the servants' benefit is a dashed nuisance; but to portray one to a member of *Society*—"

"Is no different. Do not turn squeamish on me, Mr. Thornbridge. I would not believe it. Any man willingly engaging in nocturnal forays to a black dock on which another man has been murdered cannot be easily daunted," Cecilia admonished before slapping a lavender-water drenched handkerchief against her forehead, dribbling more of the liquid down the front of her gown.

"Let me assure you, Mrs. Waddley, there is an immense difference between the two tasks," Mr. Thornbridge said fervently, clasping her wrist as the drawing room door opened.

"Sir Branstoke, my lady," announced Loudon, standing in front of the man while he ascertained that the room's occupants were ready to receive their guest. Satisfied at Mrs. Waddley's invalid position, he stood aside and allowed Sir Branstoke to enter.

The butler's maneuver did not go unregarded by Sir Branstoke. Nonetheless, his visage remained impassive to the point of bored. He lifted his quizzing glass to his eyes and surveyed the drawing room.

"Lady Meriton, forgive this intrusion at this impossible hour of the morning. It is not my desire to discommode you. I told your man I would wait, but leave I could not without first ascertaining Mrs. Waddley's condition."

His heavily lidded brown eyes turned to Mrs. Waddley. Gowned in an ethereal-looking pale blue and gray confection and sporting a lacy matron's cap over her white-blond hair, she was artistically posed in a nest of pink and rose-colored satin pillows. A blanket was tucked around her legs and at her elbow stood a small table covered with medicinal bottles and vials. With one hand she held a lace-edged handkerchief to her forehead. Her other was held by the gentleman standing at her side. For some reason, the entire scene reminded Branstoke of some Rowlandson cartoon. He wondered why. He stepped toward Cecilia. "My dear lady, I am devastated to see you as yet unrecovered from the exigencies of yesterday evening. Cannot your medical man do anything to relieve your suffering?" he asked languidly, his sleepy-eyed gaze resting on David Thornbridge.

The young Waddley's manager dropped her hand abruptly as he fought a tide of red threatening to sweep up his neck. He coughed to clear his throat and ran nervous fingers through his hair.

Cecilia limply removed the saturated handkerchief from her forehead and waved Mr. Thornbridge away. "You are mistaken, sir, I am much better today, just tired. *Doctor* Thornbridge is a veritable miracle worker. Oh, forgive me," she tittered, raising a slender hand to cover her lips in contrition. "So silly. My wits have gone begging. You gentlemen have not been introduced. Sir Branstoke, allow me to present my dear physician and pillar of strength, Dr. David Thornbridge."

A soft, strangling sound came from Mr. Thornbridge. Cecilia shot him an admonishing glance. "Your modesty is commendable, but totally unnecessary. I neither flatter nor lie," she said sweetly.

Lady Meriton's pale blue eyes widened and her mouth opened and closed spasmodically. She did not know where to look lest she reveal her knowledge of her niece's bouncers.

"Now I am rambling again. Dr. Thornbridge, this is Sir James Branstoke," Cecilia serenely continued, apparently oblivious to the reactions of her confederates.

The gentlemen exchanged greetings.

"I will be going now, Mrs. Waddley," Mr. Thornbridge said gravely.

"Oh, yes, I know. You have your rounds to make."

"My wha—? Ah, yes indeed, my *rounds* to make. Umm—uh,

get plenty of rest today. You should feel much better by tomorrow," Mr. Thornbridge finished in a rush while backing toward the door. "Lady Meriton, Sir Branstoke," he said bowing in their directions, "good day."

"A rather young man for a physician, isn't he?" Branstoke drawled after the white double door closed behind Mr. Thornbridge. He turned to look at Mrs. Waddley, one dark eyebrow raised in lazy inquiry.

"He is gifted beyond his years," Cecilia said serenely, her dark blue eyes guilelessly opening wide.

"To be sure, my niece is quite fortunate in his attentions," Lady Meriton added brightly. "Please, Sir Branstoke, won't you be seated?" She waved her hand toward the chair recently vacated by Mr. Thornbridge. "Would you mind terribly if I cut your silhouette while we visit, Sir Branstoke?"

"Not at all, Lady Meriton. I would deem it an honor. You are a noted silhouettist."

Lady Meriton blushed prettily at his grave response. Cecilia stared, amused.

"Can we offer you something by way of refreshment? Some Oastley estate-brewed ale, perhaps?" Lady Meriton asked as she drew a sheet of black paper from her lap desk. She glared at it a moment then replaced it, drawing out a dark red sheet instead.

"Thank you, Lady Meriton. I should like that. The Duke of Houghton's ale is legendary."

"Mr. Waddley often said the duke should market his ale; but of course, grandfather would have nothing to do with trade," Cecilia said as her aunt rang for the butler and requested ale for Sir Branstoke.

"Yet he countenanced your marriage into trade."

Sir Branstoke's demeanor irritated Cecilia, though she couldn't precisely define the reason. "Come now, sir, if you think to disturb me by that remark, you are well out," she said more sharply than she'd intended. She looked down at the handkerchief she held while consciously relaxing and ridding her face of any irritation. She was acting out of character and this would never do.

"Disturb?" he inquired blandly.

She laughed brightly, hoping he didn't detect any brittleness in the sound. "La, sir! It is commonly known my marriage was arranged by my father and brother as a means to recover the family fortunes."

"Ah yes, now I do seem to recall a time when your brother was sadly purse-pinched," Sir Branstoke said vaguely, leaning back in his chair.

He did appear the languid gentleman of her aunt's description. Why did that bother her? And why did she feel he was baiting her? She was mentally composing a properly featherbrained response to him when a soft knock on the door announced Loudon with the ale.

"I have taken the liberty of bringing you a fresh pot of tea as well, my lady," Loudon said as he set the tray down on a table. He picked up a pitcher and poured frothing ale into a tankard for Sir Branstoke. He handed it to him then turned to Lady Meriton. "Do you require anything else, my lady?"

"I do not believe so." She glanced up from her scissors and paper to look at her niece. "Cecilia?" she asked.

A pained expression crossed Cecilia's face. "The mere thought of food nauseates me dreadfully."

Her aunt nodded vaguely, her attention returning to the paper she held in her hand. Loudon, used to his mistress's unorthodox dismissals, bowed and left the room.

Sir Branstoke pulled a white linen handkerchief from a vest pocket and leaned toward Cecilia. He wiped her chin. "There was probably too much sugar in the last pastry you ate," he drawled, displaying to her the remnants of sugar on his handkerchief.

She pulled sharply back, coloring deeply as embarrassment and discomfort chased fleetingly across her face. His nearness reminded her of when she collided with him last night: his solidity, his scent, the prickling of her senses. She was *aware* of him. She'd never felt that heady sense of awareness before. It frightened and excited.

Quickly, angrily, she had herself in hand. She tittered. "I—I dare say you're correct. Jessamine—" She turned toward her aunt, uncomfortable under Sir Branstoke's regard. "I believe I should stick with water and soda crackers after one of my turns. The sugar is most likely aggravating my condition. No wonder my heart sometimes pounds so!"

"If I may say so, Mrs. Waddley, perhaps the ah—abundant

use of lavender water could be a contributor as well," suggested Sir Branstoke, the ghost of a smile tightening his thin lips.

Cecilia turned back to look at Sir Branstoke. She wrinkled her nose and had the grace to look chagrined. "That was an accident. I was hoping the pungent odor was noticeable only to myself."

"I regret to tell you it is not," he said solemnly though his eyes twinkled at her.

Cecilia wanted to respond in jest, but dared not. She pursed her lips and cast her eyes down. Her fingers plaited the fringe of the blanket thrown over her legs. She sighed. "I don't know what is wrong with me lately. I am so fidgety I constantly drop and spill things quite in the manner of the Countess of Seaverness."

"Rest assured, madame, no one could be in the countess's league," he said drily. "The woman is a walking disaster—most of the time to the detriment of others. Perhaps you are, as your physician suggested, in need of rest."

"I believe you are correct," Cecilia said, leaning back against the pillows. If that was what he would believe, then that is what she would pretend. She allowed her body to relax visibly, and her eyes to droop in a sleepy manner. "Every day since Mr. Waddley died I've discovered my energies flagging. I tell you, sir, it causes me no end of suffering, to be without strength. I confess that sometimes I fear I shall fade away." Her voice died away to a mere thread. She looked at him wanly and allowed the tiniest hint of a smile to grace her lips. She sighed, her eyelids fluttering.

"I understand that you and Mr. Waddley lived quiet lives. Perhaps you are merely unused to racketing about London during the season," suggested Sir Branstoke. He sipped his ale and watched her over the rim of the tankard.

That was not the idea she wished to give him! Racketing—as he called it—about London was necessary to her plans for discovering Mr. Waddley's murderer. She opened her eyes wider to mitigate the idea that she was exhausted. "You may be correct," she conceded, "nonetheless, I refuse to give in to weakness of any kind. I would not care to be an invalid. Also, I believe activity fosters energy and good health later. If I do not push myself unduly, I shall daily improve my health."

"A commendable philosophy, Mrs. Waddley. Are you perhaps husbanding your energies today in order to expend them this evening?"

"As it happens, I am. My brother has very kindly engaged to take me to King's Theater this evening."

"You are an Italian Opera enthusiast?"

"Why, yes, Sir Branstoke, I am."

"I enjoy it also. It is infinitely preferable to the English translations staged at Covent Garden."

"I have no experience of opera at Covent Garden, but I have heard it is lacking."

"Sadly."

"There, done!" declared Lady Meriton.

Cecilia Waddley and Sir Branstoke turned toward Lady Meriton. That lady proudly held up her completed silhouette. It was not solely of Sir Branstoke. The dark red paper featured Cecilia as well. Lady Meriton had captured them close together, moments before Sir Branstoke wiped the sugar from her chin. The poses relayed a magnetism between the two figures without recourse to expressions. Cut of vibrant red paper, it was a hauntingly intimate picture.

Cecilia's heart beat faster. Proud of her cutting, Jessamine evidently detected none of the undercurrents she did. Cecilia stole a look at Sir Branstoke.

Branstoke caught her eye. A smile flickered on his lips. He raised an eyebrow in amused inquiry, his brown eyes dancing.

Cecilia groaned softly and flopped back against her pillows, closing her eyes. Now she knew she was in trouble.

Chapter Three

"BRAVO!" Randolph shouted. He clapped wildly and rose from his seat as the opera company took their bows. He tossed his head to flick back a shock of dark blond hair from his brow and yelled his approval again, a broad grin lighting his handsome, dissipated features.

Cecilia looked askance at her elder brother. She wondered acidly if perhaps he shouldn't be on the stage below. Randolph's enthusiasm was markedly at odds with the behavior he displayed during the performance. His interest in the proceedings on stage had been erratic. For most of the opera he sat slumped in his chair, an expression of boredom on his face. Only on three occasions that she recalled did he take any interest in the entertainment. That was when the stage was crowded with chorus members. Shrewdly, Cecilia thought he must have a *cher amie* amongst the cast. Otherwise, his only reasons for attending the Nonsensical Screechings, as he called opera sung in Italian, would be to view society and strut about to be seen in return. Most likely he would not be in a box either, preferring the pit and the company of other dandies. She believed she recognized one or two of his friends in that milling throng of sartorial elegance mixed with lesser lights.

She was a trifle surprised that none of his friends visited their box during the interval. How was she to proceed with her investigations if Randolph's cronies never came around? Had she played her part too well in the past? It might do well to decrease the frequency of attacks of illness in favor of excessive silliness. After all, the goal she set herself when she adopted the sickly mien was to become someone people took for granted and talked around, almost as if she didn't exist. Like people do around children. It would not suit her purposes to be avoided by others.

Randolph abruptly broke off clapping and swung around to gather his greatcoat and curly brimmed beaver hat from an empty chair. "No sense you bestirring yourself, sister dear. Press of people leaving. Bound to make you feverish or fidgety, or something. I'll just pop on down to watch for John with the carriage. I'll return to get you," he said jovially, though he curiously avoided Cecilia's questioning gaze. He backed out of the box without waiting to hear her response.

Cecilia compressed her lips in exasperation; then the humor of her brother's behavior forced her to smile and shake her head in wonderment. Ruefully, she decided she'd wager her best diamond earrings that Randolph went in search of whatever barque of frailty in the chorus was the current recipient of his ardent regard.

No matter. Randolph made the offer to attend the opera, she did not ask him to serve as her escort. Over the past six months since she'd entered society she'd only occasionally availed herself of Randolph's company. She little dreamed that any of his crowd could possibly aid her in the investigation, let alone be involved; therefore she did not waste her time cultivating their acquaintance. She would use this invitation as open permission to expect Randolph to dance attendance on her and thereby introduce her to his friends. They would not avoid his company forever! Poor Randolph, he was about to find her exceedingly demanding.

A shout from below drew her attention to the pit. Several elegantly dressed gentlemen still strolled about that area, ogling the orange girls and the other bits of muslin that invested in the price of a ticket in hopes of greater evening returns. The shout came from a nattily attired young man who was looking up at the boxes. Seeing he'd drawn Cecilia's attention, he grinned cheekily and pantomimed an invitation to join him.

Cecilia frowned and shook her head, looking determinedly away. Her gaze traveled around the horseshoe tiers of boxes, most of which were now empty. Halfway around the horseshoe and one level up her gaze stopped. Sir Branstoke sat in that box. And he was staring at her! She knew he was, though, as always, his eyes appeared nearly closed. What had she done to warrant his attention? A flare of unreasoning anger burned through her. Perhaps if she knew, she thought caustically, she'd be more successful in drawing Randolph and his friends to her side.

His gaze didn't waiver. Under his steady, unnerving regard, vivid red swept up her neck. Quickly she raised her handkerchief to her lips and began coughing, mentally damning her unwanted reaction and ducking her head down to hide the tell-tale color.

A slight smile curved Sir James Branstoke's thin lips as he observed Mrs. Waddley's antics. He wondered where that boor of a brother of hers had gone to. He saw Randolph with her during the performance. Now he was gone, leaving her haplessly open to undesirable attentions from young bucks on the prowl. From his limited experience of Mrs. Waddley, he'd wager she thought herself equal to any situation. The woman was confident in her charade, and he owned she did it skillfully. Nonetheless that brand of confidence was ripe for a fall. He couldn't help question the rationale for her behavior. There was some mystery there, something other than discomfort in society. She struck him as a determined woman. He wondered at the focus of that determination.

"I cannot help noticing the direction of your attention. Have you met Mrs. Waddley?" a soft voice asked him, humor underlying the words.

Sir Branstoke turned to his hostess, nodding slowly. "A most interesting woman. Do you know her, Lady St. Ryne?"

"I've only met her briefly. Unfortunately, at the time she was suffering from, I believe, palpitations of her heart. Or so she said."

Her husband, the Viscount St. Ryne laughed. "When I was introduced she was recovering from a severe headache, one that left her weak and fretful, she said. She is the most tiresome woman I have ever had the misfortune to meet. And when my mother was in the throws of matchmaking, I met many. Mrs. Waddley is a complete ninnyhammer," he said dismissively.

Sir Branstoke's lips twisted wryly. "So you really think so. Interesting."

Lady St. Ryne laughed. "Our friend is being enigmatic again, my love."

Her husband smirked. "This time we'll find the astute Sir James Branstoke has made an error if he sees aught behind her behavior other than the woman is a dashed flibbertigibbet." He turned to pick up his wife's cloak from the back of the box.

"I must confess, sir, that though we do not know Mrs. Waddley well, we do know a gentleman who is far better acquainted," the Viscountess St. Ryne said as her husband settled her cloak about her shoulders.

Branstoke raised an eyebrow, encouraging his hostess to continue as he drew a gold enameled snuffbox from his waistcoat pocket and opened it with a dextrous flick of his thumb.

She fastened the cloak at her collar. "The son of our clergyman at Larchside is employed by Waddley Spice and Tea. He is a manager there. A very personable young man. He's done well there and seems quite happy in his position. From what I've heard of Waddley Spice and Tea, I dare say Mr. Waddley must have been an extraordinary gentleman. Not at all the merchant to demand his pound of flesh."

"Really," murmured Branstoke, taking a pinch of snuff.

"Yes. Mr. Thornbridge gets down to Larchside fairly often to visit his father. Evidently the company has always been considerate of family obligations."

Branstoke stilled. "Mr. Thornbridge, you say?"

"Yes, Mr. David Thornbridge. Do you know him?"

The ghost of a smile curved Sir James Branstoke's lips, his lazy lids closing again to mere slits as he turned to look back at Mrs. Waddley. "I believe I may," he said softly.

The Viscount and Viscountess St. Ryne looked at each other quizzically. Lady St. Ryne shrugged slightly then gathered up the folds of her cloak. "Will you be coming back with us?" she asked Branstoke.

"No. Thank you anyway, Lady St. Ryne. And thank you for inviting me to join you this evening. It has been a most—ah, illuminating evening."

Lady St. Ryne pursed her lips and shook her head at the inexplicableness of Sir Branstoke. She looked up at her husband but found no help there. Sir James Branstoke was the deepest person of her acquaintance. She gave it up and exchanged courteous goodnights with their guest before leaving the box on her husband's arm.

Branstoke bowed politely as they left, then turned back to study Mrs. Waddley. A shuttered expression hardened his features. The gentleman from the pit was now in Mrs. Waddley's box. Judging by his erratic movements, Branstoke judged him to be well in his cups. Too foxed to be daunted by Mrs. Waddley's various and sundry claims to illness, he was ardently professing his enchantment with her person. Where was that fool, Haukstrom? He should be looking out for her, no matter how tiresome she might sometimes be.

Branstoke turned on his heel, hastily grabbing up his great-

coat and hat as he left the box, all the while calling down depre-
cations upon Randolph Haukstrom's head under his breath as
he went.

"Now what's a vision of beauty the likes of you doin' by your
lonesome, eh?"

Cecilia whirled around in her seat to confront the reeling figure of the nattily attired gentleman from the pit. "This is a private box. I must ask that you leave," she said quietly.

"I say, that's a fine voice you've got. Where'd ol' randy Randolph find you, my pretty? He's got the devil's own luck he has."
He stumbled toward her, laying a steadying hand on her bare
shoulder.

Cecilia jerked away and stood up in one fluid motion leaving
the gentleman unbalanced. He fell over the back of the chair,
his feet kicking up in the air. Cecilia swallowed an involuntary
laugh. As she watched the man struggle to get up, she raised
her fan and began agitatedly fanning her face. "Oh, my nerves!"
she wailed, backing away from him. "You—you brute! I can just
feel my heart pounding in my chest. I shall have one of my spells
now, I know!" She dramatically laid the back of a shaking hand
to her forehead.

"Wha'd you go and do that for?" the man said petulantly.
"You ain't the only pretty bird feathering Randolph's nest.
Angel Swafford's got a neat little place from him over by Leices-
ter Fields. He's down in the greenroom with Angel now, y'know.
Saw him myself afore I come up." He moved slowly toward Cecilia, his arms outstretched. "The blighter ain't worth it, love."
He hiccupped and stumbled, catching himself against the back
of another chair. He leered at her; but only managed to look
the jester.

Cecilia was angered—and not a little afraid—by the man's
persistence. Never before had she suffered difficulty in dissuad-
ing a gentleman's attention. Unfortunately, judging by his glassy
eyes and gin-perfumed breath, he was in no condition to assimilate her words. She had to get away. She edged toward the back
of the box, careful to keep chairs between herself and her unwel-
come visitor. *If Randolph is with his mistress, I will ring a peel
over his head he'll not long forget,* she silently vowed.

Coughing behind her fan, she made little mewing sounds.
"Please, I feel quite ill. Do not come any closer lest I—I cast

up my accounts upon your elegant person!" she threatened, nearing the exit. "I swear I am sick enough to do so! *Ohh!*" she cried, colliding against a solid object. She sagged, her knees buckling. A pair of warm, strong arms wrapped around her.

"We have to stop meeting like this," the owner of those arms murmured in her ear.

Branstoke! She struggled to regain her balance and stand free of him, but he held her fast. She turned startled, agonized eyes up at him.

He glanced briefly down at her face, pulled in by the deep purple rims of her wide open, twilight blue eyes. He was stunned by the vulnerability there. From somewhere inside him, a closed empty space cracked open. Abruptly, he set her away from him, guiding her into a chair.

"Nutley, a word in your ear," Branstoke said softly, grasping the gentleman by the elbow and firmly leading him to the back of the box.

"Dash it all, Branstoke, I saw her first," complained Jerome Nutley, hiccupping again and swaying against Branstoke.

"*I* am not in the habit of taking up with diseased ladies," he drawled.

"Diseased?" repeated Nutley. He blinked owlishly and turned to look over his shoulder at Cecilia, nearly overbalancing himself in the process. Branstoke steadied him.

Taking his cue, Cecilia closed her eyes and agitatedly fanned herself while moaning some more.

"You're right. She don't look so good. What's she got?" he asked in a stage whisper.

"Guess," Branstoke replied curtly.

"The *French Disease?*" Nutley tentatively suggested.

Branstoke shrugged faintly. "Well, you don't see any smallpox."

"E'gad. And so pretty and delicate lookin' too," Nutley said, awed.

Branstoke maneuvered him to the exit, shoving him out of the box. "You're lucky I was here to warn you," he said solemnly.

"Obliged to you, Branstoke. Does Haukstrom know?"

"I wouldn't venture to guess what Haukstrom knows."

Nutley nodded wisely, tapping his temple with his index finger. "I think he does. Why else leave her here alone? Probably trying to get rid of her. Damn if I don't have a word with him on this shabby trick he's trying to play." He turned and sauntered off down the hall, weaving and banging into the wall in the process.

Branstoke watched until Nutley rounded the curve heading toward the stairs, a half smile playing upon his lips. He turned back to the box.

Alternately infuriated and amused at her rescuer's tactics, Cecilia didn't know whether to burst into giggles or stamp her feet. She opted for anger, since it was outrageous for him to even imply that she could be so tainted! She sat up straight in her chair and glared at Branstoke. "How dare you!" she ground out through clenched teeth.

"You are looking amazingly better. Am I to infer that your illnesses are subject to sudden stops as they are to starts?" he asked with unruffled composure. He sat down in a chair near her, crossing his legs and hooking his clasped hands around his knee.

Cecilia drew her breath in sharply and began fanning herself again, as much to play the ailing woman as to hide a threatening smile. "No woman of quality likes to be accosted as a common prostitute, let alone as one with a venereal disease," she attempted pettishly.

"Do not worry, Mrs. Waddley. The one thing no one could take you to be is common," he returned unperturbedly. "Now how is it that you are here alone and therefore open to such unfortunate importunities?" he continued before she could draw breath to issue a scathing retort.

Cecilia was silent a moment as she mastered her anger in favor of her weak, sickly persona. Though she hated to admit it, Sir Branstoke's handling of the problem with Mr. Nutley was swift and sure. And contrived, she'd wager, to discomfort her brother as well. Also, not once had *he* said she had venereal disease or that she was a prostitute. He merely didn't negate Mr. Nutley's assumptions, leaving that gentleman to play the fool—which he did without help from anyone.

"Randolph suggested I wait here until our carriage comes. He knows how crowds can bring on one of my dreadful spells with which I am so sadly plagued."

"I'm certain you've guessed that your esteemed late guest,

Mr. Nutley, is most likely correct. I doubt your dear brother is watching out for your carriage," he said drily.

She sighed and closed her fan, laying it gently in her lap.

Branstoke looked consideringly at her. "As you have discovered, it is not wise to remain here unattended. I'm afraid Mr. Nutley comes by his assumptions honestly."

"I see that," she said ruefully. "May I ask you, Sir Branstoke, to go in search of my brother for me?"

"No madame, you may not. I will not expend a particle of energy on the behalf of Randolph Haukstrom. I intend to see you safely to your carriage," he said crisply, quite at odds with his normal demeanor. He stood and gave her his hand to help her rise. Gathering her cloak in his hands, he placed it about her shoulders then offered her his arm.

Cecilia was uncertain as to how to take Sir Branstoke. Glancing at him out of the corner of her eye, she deemed it wisest to refrain from comment. Gently she laid her hand on his arm and allowed him to lead her out of the box.

"Dash it all, Cecilia, what's Nutley nattering on about?" Randolph Haukstrom called out as he rushed across the lobby followed by the Honorable Reginald Rippy and Sir Harry Elsdon, two of his frequent cronies. "Mumbling something about my foisting a diseased chippy on him."

"Haukstrom, you jingle-brained gapeseed, what do you mean leaving your sister alone and prey to every lascivious character in the theater?" demanded Branstoke.

Randolph Haukstrom's chin jutted out mulishly, though physically he seemed to shrink. "I was coming back for her."

Branstoke raised a quelling eyebrow.

"Damn it, Branstoke. What business is it of yours?"

"It is the business of every *gentleman* to protect a lady," he said softly, pointedly. "Mrs. Waddley, I believe your carriage is outside. Shall we go?"

"Now just a minute, Branstoke," said Haukstrom, red color suffusing his fair complexion.

"*Lord, what fools these mortals be!*" quipped Sir Harry Elsdon, laying a hand on his friend's arm. "Hate to say it, Randy ol' boy, but Branstoke's got a point. Not the thing at all to leave a lovely young woman like your sister unattended."

"Bad Ton," agreed Rippy, his lower lip thrusting out as his head bobbed up and down in agreement.

"Thank you, gentlemen," drawled Branstoke.

Cecilia glanced at him, wondering if the faint hint of sarcasm she thought she detected in his tone rested only in her imagination. Bidding her brother an embarrassed goodnight, she allowed Sir Branstoke to lead her out of the theater and down to her carriage.

"May I be allowed to see you home?" Branstoke asked as he assisted her into the carriage.

Cecilia paused, uncertain how to respond.

"I am concerned lest you suffer another of your—ah, sudden spells," he added blandly.

Cecilia peered at him in the uncertain, flickering carriage light. His expression appeared politely neutral, telling her nothing to answer the myriad questions that swirled in her brain. His attentions were inexplicable. Worse were her reactions to the man. He sent her nerves jumping and tingling in a manner greater than any illness she feigned. How could this be? He was, as her aunt implied, an innocuous gentleman. Refined, unfailingly polite, totally unflappable. Her hesitation was ridiculous. And it was always better to travel with companionship, even in the city.

She bit her lower lip a moment then murmured her permission. One side of Branstoke's mouth lifted into a wry smile as he inclined his head. He stepped lightly into the carriage after her and seated himself opposite.

In the close confines of the carriage, her awareness of the man increased exponentially. An insidious thought curled into her consciousness. Could he be involved in Mr. Waddley's death? Was that the reason he cultivated her acquaintance? By her reactions to him, was some small portion of her mind warning he was an enemy? Truthfully, he was entirely too even-tempered. As she suggested to Jessamine, it took one artificer to recognize another. What did he want from her? She swallowed nervously.

"Is something the matter, Mrs. Waddley? Do you feel all right?" His face was in black shadows, his voice a deep rumble that echoed the metallic ring of iron-bound wheels over street cobbles. A diamond, nestled in the ruffles of his shirt, winked in the yellow light of passing street lamps.

She laughed, a high, weak sound. "It is merely my abominable nerves. I am heartily cognizant that I am in your debt. I keep recalling Mr. Nutley's inebriated countenance." She shivered. "I dare swear the backlash of memories is worse than the actuality. I shall recover presently. Do not worry, I'll not embarrass you with one of my fits."

"I am not in the least worried on that score, Mrs. Waddley." His almost disembodied voice stretched her nerves taut. If only she could see his face!

The rustle of wool and satin warned her of his movement, heightening senses and tensing muscles. He leaned forward out of the shadows and reached across the gulf between them to lay a gloved hand on hers. A shuddering breath released her tight chest. She glanced down to where his large hand covered hers then up at his face. Dimly she was aware of the carriage halting. A footman threw open the door, spilling light into dark carriage corners.

"I feel," Sir Branstoke began slowly, almost hesitantly, "you have dragons plaguing you. Know, Mrs. Waddley, it is not necessary to stand alone," he finished softly. He quickly descended the carriage steps and turned to help her down.

Stunned by his words and manner, Cecilia automatically laid her hand in his and allowed him to draw her from the carriage. She looked at him in the glowing lamplight, really seeing him for the first time.

His hair, the color of a rich West Indies coffee, was cropped short and curled around the edges of a high, intelligent brow. His eyes were wide set, heavily hooded and thickly lashed. Somnambulant eyes, as Jessamine suggested, yet possessing tiny fan lines at the outside corners attesting to heartily felt emotions—though Cecilia dared not put a name to them. His nose was straight, his chin firm and forceful, narrowly missing pointed status. He was not much above average height, though that still made him tall in comparison to herself. The top of her head scarcely brushed his chin. Of all, however, it was his eyes that caught her attention. They were tortoise in color, a rich variegated gold and brown.

He raised an amused eyebrow at her infinitesimal pause, and she realized something else. Those beautiful, seemingly sleepy eyes, held a rapier sharp understanding that whispered, *En garde.*

Chapter Four

PEN SCRATCHING and the droning ticktock of the mantel clock were the only sounds in the library. Even the outside traffic seemed to have abated for there were no sounds of carriages, horses, or street vendors to disturb the silence. Pale, straw-yellow spring sunlight streamed in matched Doric Venetian windows throwing a bright shaft of light across Sir James Branstoke's desk and the cream bond paper beneath his hand.

His lips compressed into a thin line; a thoughtful, considering expression slightly lifting one dark eyebrow as he wrote. He paused, absently groping for his coffee cup. He finished the cold dregs in a swallow as he reread his letter. Satisfied, he set down the cup and signed his name with a flourish, then he leaned back in his chair and grabbed the bell pull.

When his butler entered, Branstoke gave instructions for Romley, his groom, to be sent up along with another pot of coffee. While he waited he propped his feet up on the desk, crossed his arms, lowered his chin into his cravat, and thought about Mrs. Cecilia Haukstrom Waddley.

Her face haunted him. Or was it just those large waif-like royal blue eyes rimmed with purple and framed with pale, downy lashes that stayed in his mind? Her eyes and her reed-slender body made her appear more fragile than the finest porcelain. Was it only her striking looks that drew his attention? No, for London every year was littered with beautiful, delicate women. There was something else he saw reflected in those eyes that drew him to her like a lodestone. For all her outward appearance of fragility—both real and affected—he sensed a shining inner core of strength. It was a strength that he'd wager she'd hardly begun to tap, because as yet, she wasn't even cognizant of its existence.

He threw back his head and laughed. It was ludicrous. She was a forged Damascus steel blade sheathed in naiveté. How rich.

And how desperately needing protection. He didn't know

what dragons she was chasing or evading; but he intended to find out. And he vowed he would save her from courting disaster.

A soft knock on the library door brought him out of his reverie. He swung his feet to the floor as the door opened to usher in Charwood bearing a silver urn of fresh coffee. The butler was followed by George Romley.

Romley stood deferentially with cap in hand while Charwood served Sir Branstoke. But Romley had been with Branstoke since his Peninsular days, and while he observed the conventions around others, when the butler left the room, a lopsided grin pulled at his thick cheeks. He gave his cap a spinning toss into a nearby chair.

"You sent for me, sar? What's the lay?"

Sir Branstoke's lips quirked into a brief, crooked smile. "For a man who claims to work an honest day for an honest day's pay, your language is progressively deteriorating into thieves' cant. I positively shudder to imagine what taverns you favor with your commerce."

The groom rubbed the side of his nose with a crooked finger. "I figure a man's got to watch to his 'orizens, sar."

"Just as well, for my purposes."

"Sar?"

Branstoke's thin smile cracked to reveal straight, white teeth. "Sit down, George, and have a cup of coffee. You do drink something other than libational spirits, I presume?"

"Course I do, and I'd be right honored, guv'nor." He sat down on the edge of a chair before the desk, hands on his knees as he waited for Sir Branstoke to pour him a cup. He almost wished that Friday-faced butler, Charwood, could see him sittin' here with his nibs. Sir Branstoke weren't never one to stand on points. Treated a man fair, he did.

"I do seem to remember, George," Branstoke drawled as he handed him his cup, "with what remarkable agility you foraged in Portugal and Spain."

George grinned. "That were a trooper's art, sar. One I'll own a mite o' proficiency in."

"Yes, and I have always been of the mind that should I have failed to take you with me when I sold out in '14, you'd have ended as gallows bait. Now I find myself wondering if perhaps all my efforts were in vain. I should hate to discover at this late date that I made an error in judgment."

Indignant outrage skewered Romley's visage. "As if I would ever, sar!" He paused and shrugged philosophically. "Leastways while I were in your employ. You was always up to every rig and row. There weren't no fobbin' you off with any gammon."

"I am happy to see we understand each other so well," Branstoke said evenly, though his hooded eyes gleamed with hidden amusement.

"Well, course, sar. Now tell me, guv'nor," Romley said, leaning forward across the desk, "how come I'm gettin' the nacky notion that you've a lay for me akin to 'em Penins'lar days?"

"I suppose, George, that's because I do," Branstoke said slowly, appreciating his man's shrewdness. He'd chosen wisely.

"I knew it!" Romley crowed, slapping a hand on his knee.

"Your enthusiasm overwhelms me," he said drily. He picked up the letter he had written, absently tapping it against the blotter. "I suggest you listen intently. I want you to deliver this letter to Mr. Hewitt, Mr. Dabney Hewitt."

"Hewitt! I remembers him! Bad sort, guv'nor, very bad sort. What do you be wanting with the likes of him?"

A slight smile pulled at Branstoke's thin lips. "He was, as you say, a bad sort and would likely have been cashiered from the military if our need for men had not been so great. We were, perforce, left with the likes of men of his ilk."

"Should ha' marked him for cannon fodder," Romley grumbled.

"War never slays a bad man in its course, but the good always!" murmured Branstoke.

"Beggin' your pardon, sar?"

Branstoke smiled. "Sophocles. Never mind, George. Suffice it to say, life is never that easy, and I, for one, never held it that cheap. You see, I once had the questionable good fortune to save Mr. Hewitt's miserable life from extinction."

"Good fortune, bah!"

Branstoke stopped tapping the letter and stared blankly at it, as if seeing something else entirely. "The interesting thing about Hewitt is that he has his own sense of morality. It's a very rigid morality, in it's own way. As I saved his life, he believes that he owes me a favor. It seems he believes he must do something important for me that will wipe the slate clean between us. He is very determined in this."

George grunted. "So he said then; but guv'nor, there's promises and then there's promises. I don't hold faith with the likes of him keepin' promises."

Branstoke laid the letter down and leaned back in his chair. "So I would have thought myself. We are wrong. Truthfully, I'd forgotten all about the incident until I chanced to run into him again six months or so ago. It is not important how that occurred. Let it stand that I came away with my purse and body intact. This however, was not sufficient to Mr. Hewitt. He lamented being beholden to a *flash cove* such as myself—that is his description, not mine. He desires the slate wiped clean."

"So he can stick his chive in you 'nother time, more like."

"George, I find your abundant faith in human nature endearing. I can deal with Hewitt in the future. The nub of the matter is that I do have a favor to ask of him that is ripe for a man of his—ah, talents."

George Romley looked suspiciously at his employer. "You ain't founderin' in high seas are you, and need to bring your ship about?"

"I assure you, my purse is intact. I need you to deliver this letter to Mr. Hewitt. He informed me when last we met that he could be reached through a tavern in the City rejoicing in the name of *The Pye-Eyed Cock.*"

"Coo—guv'nor, that's a wicked address."

"I'm sure it is, but not, I believe, beyond your touch, George."

Romley fidgeted in his chair. "Now what would I be doing in a hell-hole like that, I ask you?"

Branstoke raised an eyebrow in unspoken comment. Romley fidgeted some more, rubbing his nose vigorously with his finger. "More'n likely the bloke cain't read."

"I assure you, Mr. Hewitt's education is wider than you think."

"Why me, sar?" Romley finally blurted out.

"Why, George?" Branstoke shrugged. "Consider it my feeble way to broaden your—ah, horizons."

"All right, sar, I'll take your letter. What am I to do after I delivers it?"

"You will obtain Mr. Hewitt's agreement, and between you work out a method of operation to supply me with the information I desire. I have faith, George, in your inventiveness to pursue this project properly. I am uninterested in the particulars."

George Romley was silent a moment, then he heaved a big sigh. "All right. It'll be as you say, guv'nor." He shook his head dolefully. "I jest hope you know what yur doin', sar."

An enigmatic smile curled the corners of Sir Branstoke's lips. "So do I, George, so do I."

Cecilia listlessly turned the page of the novel she'd been trying to read for the past half-hour. It was a light, pastoral romance with some finely drawn characters; unfortunately her mind refused to stay focused on the gentle humor and happenings in the story. Her thoughts drifted unerringly to the mystery she'd set herself to solve.

She wasn't certain she actually ever placed much faith in solving the crime of her husband's murder, or of bringing its perpetrators to book. Her half-formed plans had been more in the way of an impetus to break the lethargy she'd fallen into after George's death. Their marriage had been safe and comfortable, something her life had not been as a child.

Her childhood held vivid memories of plate and pictures slowly disappearing, and servants leaving for lack of pay. The sale of her beloved pony was a particularly painful memory. Truthfully, she'd outgrown Penny, but the callousness of her father and brother when they dispensed with her little copper-colored pony had been a raw wound for years. She long felt their attitude toward the pony was equivalent to their attitude toward her—only they could not get rid of her as easily nor as profitably. Until her grandfather, the Duke of Houghton, autocratically fetched her from the slowly decaying manor that was her home, she existed simply. Carefully she darned her clothes and uncomplaining ate what she and Mr. and Mrs. Crontick—the only servants to remain—could scrounge. She was always thankful, however, that her mother never lived to see their lives reduced to such circumstances.

Dispassionately, she wondered why she didn't hate her father and brother. She certainly had every right to. Maybe it was because she'd never known them to be any different. And truthfully, the male relatives on her mother's side of the family were not above reproach either. Her grandfather's history was every bit as checkered as her father's, only he was luckier—and perhaps more skillful at cards—than Baron Haukstrom. She couldn't blame her father for virtually abandoning her, for she'd been a drain on his pocketbook. Nor could she later blame him for selling her to Mr. Waddley.

She sighed, and closed the book. She really shouldn't think of herself as being sold. That was unfair to Mr. Waddley. It also displayed a lack of delicacy on her part that was unladylike and beneath her. Marrying Mr. Waddley had been a blessing. Her lot in life had been bleak—her relation to a duke not withstanding. Most likely, she would have become an unpaid companion to some relation—and made continually aware of her charity status.

But when Mr. Waddley was murdered, she felt cut adrift. And though she no longer felt the pangs of financial hardship, all the lonely memories of childhood rushed back to haunt her.

She blinked back the unshed tears that memory called forward. What she'd had to come to terms with after her husband's death was the fact she was no longer a child who must suffer the whims of another. She was older, wiser, and financially independent. She smiled weakly, deprecatingly. She was more than independent, she was wealthy. And wealth meant power. That was something she had learned from her grandfather and that was something she was using now.

She set the novel on the table by the sofa and deliberately turned her mind from maudlin memories to the memories of the past evening. How could she become better acquainted with Randolph's cronies? It was obvious to her that she'd been naive in her assumption that her mere presence at Randolph's side would enable her to better her acquaintance with his crowd. A hypochondriac female was viewed by the bloods with a jaundiced eye. She made a grave tactical error when she'd subscribed to this role. The question was, how to recover without raising suspicion? It would have to be with increasingly good health, if at all. Unfortunately she feared she didn't have the patience for the proper degree of slow improvement necessary to allay the suspicious natures of people like Sir James Branstoke.

Now that was odd. Why did she instinctively feel there was threat of discovery from that quarter? He should be the last person anyone would consider as having a suspicious nature. That is, if one went by appearances alone, and Cecilia didn't. She remembered only too clearly the strange, almost frightening feeling in the dark carriage. She'd been too aware of his presence, his closeness. Then there was that last, strange comment he made before he bid her a casual good-night. What did he guess? No, what did he *know* of dragons? There were depths to that man that few could plummet. Just thinking of him sent flitting feelings through her stomach, like a host of butterflies suddenly taking flight.

She bit her lip as again the odd flutterings assailed her. She rose from the sofa to pace the room, as if trying to outrun the butterflies. What was it about the man? Was it possible that she could be following the wrong lead in pursuing her brother and his associates? Could Sir James Branstoke be the key she searched for and dreamed to find? What did she know about him? What did anyone know about him? He was as enigmatic in personality as was his lazy, devastating smile.

"Jessamine, how long have you known Sir Branstoke?" Cecilia Waddley casually asked as she paced back and forth across her aunt's small, private parlor.

"What's that, dear?" Lady Meriton shuffled through a sheaf of papers lying on a small ebony and gilt writing desk, a thoughtful, distracted frown pulling down the corners of her pale lips.

Cecilia paused in her restless pacing. She stared, unfocused, as she wrestled with herself. She swung around to face her aunt. "I was just wondering how long you've known Sir Branstoke?" she said slowly, with thin lightness.

Lady Meriton pushed her glasses up her nose as she looked at her niece. "I don't really know. Three or four years, I suppose—no, it's three years since he sold out—"

"Sold out? He was in the military?"

"Oh, dear me, yes. In the Peninsular campaign, like Sheridan. He's been on the town since he returned. I vaguely recall meeting him earlier; however, I cannot place when. Is it important?"

"Yes—I mean, *no!*" Cecilia compressed her lips. "I'm just curious. He seems to know everyone and to be invited everywhere."

"That's true enough. He is a perfect guest, and just the ticket for rounding out numbers for dinner. Particularly at those occasions where the company is dreadfully mixed and one despairs of success. He possesses excellent address, wit, and a decent if not sizable fortune. Though he is often dry and given to sarcasm, he is never arrogant. That is a trait I find too deplorably common these days in the legions of men-about-town."

"A pattern card of virtue!"

Lady Meriton laughed, laying down her quill. "Hardly. He is far too languid for perfection. If it were not for his wit, the man would be a dry stick. No doubt that will be his old age fate. But why all this sudden interest in Sir Branstoke?"

She shrugged. "Curiosity," she said lightly.

Restlessly, Cecilia crossed to the small sofa and sat down. She fumbled in her work basket on the floor, drawing out a needle-point seat cover with a developing brick and gold Etruscan key design. She was not a dab hand at artistic needlework, needle-point being her singular accomplishment. For her it was a sooth-ing accomplishment, something for when her mind ran steadily and relentlessly on like one of those new steam engines. The seat cover was one of four destined for the chairs around the card table in the drawing room.

"I saw him last night at the opera," Cecilia said, her needle plunging rapidly back and forth through the canvas, keeping pace with her thoughts.

"Who?" her aunt asked absently as she dipped her quill in ink.

"Jessamine! Sir Branstoke, of course, who else have we been discussing?"

"I'm sorry, I didn't realize we were still discussing him."

Looking up from her needlework, Cecilia threw Jessamine a disgusted look, drawing an answering smile from her aunt.

"I found the gentleman's behavior quite odd," Cecilia ex-plained, "particularly for a man who is reputed to be so som-nambulant."

"Cecilia, my love, have your wits gone a-begging? This is Sir James Branstoke we're speaking of. What could he possibly have done to rouse your suspicions? Sir James Branstoke is one of the most polite and courteous men of this generation."

"I don't say he isn't. But that is precisely the point. Don't you see? He is *too* perfect. It's—it's unnatural, that's what it is."

"Cecilia, I'm surprised at you," chastised Lady Meriton.

Her niece fidgeted. "I suspect he is merely acting in order to cover something else."

"And what would that be?"

"I don't know," she admitted. She pursed her lips, sliding a glance at her aunt. "But I am beginning to suspect some involvement on his part in Mr. Waddley's death."

"Sir Branstoke!" Lady Meriton swiftly rose from her seat by the desk and crossed to her niece's side, laying a cool hand on her brow. "You do not feel feverish. Odd. I was certain you must be to suggest such a thing."

Cecilia captured her aunt's wrist. "Jessamine. There has to be some logical explanation to the gentleman's attentions. Heaven knows I've worked hard enough to present an image of undesirability with a coterie of illnesses. There is no reason for a man of Sir Branstoke's ilk to pay the slightest attention to me." Her grip on her aunt's arm loosened, then fell away.

Surreptitiously, Lady Meriton began massaging that maltreated member. "I'll own it is odd. But he has always been a unique man, a style unto himself."

"Well, I hope he doesn't intend to adopt me as his latest flirt. It could be difficult then to make acquaintances in Randolph's crowd. From my observation, they operate in different orbs."

"Very true! Though the odd thing about Sir Branstoke is that he is readily accepted everywhere—and by every group and type of people. Around politicos, those interested in furthering the arts and letters, those who are science minded—even the evangelicals! Why, on the list of prospective guests for mama's upcoming house party, he was among the first names she wrote!"

"What house party?"

Lady Meriton sighed. "I knew you were not attending me at breakfast this morning. I told you that last night I received a long letter from mother. The long and short of it is, instead of coming to London this season, they wish London to come to them. She and father are planning a three-day house party culminating in a large ball to which the world, it appears, is to be invited."

"At Oastley Hall?"

"Where else? There are to be at least thirty to forty people for the first two nights, and I would fain not guess at the numbers for the ball."

"Gracious!"

"Most of the invitations went out yesterday. Mama left a few gaps in her invitation list that she wishes me to fill based on who is new and interesting this season. A harder request I've never had."

"May I see the list?"

"Good gracious, yes. And if you can offer any suggestions, I'll certainly be appreciative. It appears the list is short on younger single men. I don't believe the young women on this list would appreciate the aged roués who number as father's friends."

Cecilia studied the list in silence for a moment, then a broad grin showed small pearl-white teeth. "This is a perfect opportunity for us to do a little more investigation."

"I don't trust that look in your eyes, Cecilia. What deviltry are you planning?"

"No deviltry, just an opportunity to bring together a group of possible suspects and do a little eavesdropping and snooping. Oh, don't look at me like that, Jessamine. Last evening I realized I need to become better acquainted with Randolph's cronies. But how can I do so under normal social circumstances? A house party where we are all thrown together is perfect! We shall round out Grandmama's list with friends of Randolph's."

"Do you think they'd come?"

"Naturally. If not for the company—though the Duke of Houghton still carries a certain cachet—then at least for the opportunity to drink endless amounts of Oastley ale."

"I don't believe it was ever mama's intention to invite Randolph's friends. She thinks they're all as ramshackle as Randolph and therefore bad influences upon him."

"They are. But if there are people she doesn't want invited, she should tell you, or do the entire list herself."

Lady Meriton looked doubtful. Cecilia took one of her hands in both of hers. "Look, I've realized that until this week I never actually saw any hope of discovering my husband's murderer. All my talk over the last few months has been merely a means of aiding my recovery from the shock of Mr. Waddley's death. I know that. Now, to suddenly be confronted with a possible avenue for investigation is a miracle! I can't let it go to waste, can I? Besides, what harm can it do to invite Randolph's friends? It would be far more volatile to invite my father!"

Lady Meriton smiled. "Though the Baron Haukstrom has mellowed with age, the Duke of Houghton has not."

"What the baron has mellowed with is dropsy," Cecilia said drily. "But to return to the invitation list, I must tell you Jessamine, that I am as suspicious of Sir Branstoke as I am of Randolph, and Branstoke is already on the invitation list. What harm can it be to assemble the rest of the possible suspects together?"

"If they are suspects, which I very much doubt," Lady Meriton said repressively, though there was a thoughtful, considering expression on her face.

Cecilia shrugged and smiled. "Then allow this to be an opportunity for me to learn that," she said winningly.

Her aunt sighed, her lips compressed in a thin line as she considered Cecilia. She was silent a moment, then nodded shortly. "All right. I will have invitations sent out to Randolph's friends. Do you have any particular names in mind?" she asked, rising to cross to her desk.

"A few. I was hoping you could suggest others."

"I don't make any promises, but I'll see what we can do."

Cecilia smiled and it reached her eyes.

Lady Meriton was amazed at the brilliance reflected in her niece's eyes. She decided whatever happened, it was worth it just to bring that light into Cecilia's expressive eyes.

In the end, they winnowed down the list of Randolph's cohorts to three names: The Honorable Reginald Rippy and Sir Harry Elsdon, both of whom were with Randolph after the opera; and Lord Havelock whose family's estate had burned to the ground some years past. There were, perhaps, one or two others of his cronies that he spent as much (if not more) time with; however, in correlating their lists, those three names were the only ones of his immediate circle who were in attendance at Lady Amblethorp's musicale. They were also, interestingly enough, the only ones that they agreed were likely to possess the moral turpitude for murder.

Afterward, Lady Meriton professed herself amazed at the numbers of gentlemen she considered capable of cold-blooded murder. It made her shiver just to consider it. In high dudgeon she wrote a letter to her husband relating that fact. In agitated tones she found herself importuning Lord Meriton to return to England at his earliest convenience. It was the most crossed and recrossed letter she'd ever written to her globe-trotting spouse, and one she nearly did not send. In the end, Loudon saw it conveyed to the mails and Lady Meriton heaved a sigh of relief. She'd finally told another of her niece's madcap schemes and therefore felt absolved of ultimate responsibility. Happily she returned to her paper and scissors, taking care to order from the stationers adequate supplies for her journey south to Oastley Hall.

As Cecilia anticipated, Randolph's friends were quick to respond positively to the invitation. Randolph himself nearly cried off, but his invited friends shamed him into attending. He grumbled and argued that Oastley was "a dashed dull dog of a place," but no one listened to him; after all, it was the home of the infamous Franklin Cheney, one time rumored highwayman and smuggler, now fourth Duke of Houghton.

Soon talk of the proposed house party dominated salon conversation throughout Mayfair, and Lady Iantha Cheney, the Duchess of Houghton, was moved to write an agitated letter to her daughter demanding to know what stories were being circulated about the proposed gathering. It seemed she was suddenly besieged with letters from people proclaiming long lost friendship and saying wouldn't it be nice to visit together. It was keeping her secretary busy devising imaginative delays. The duke, on the other hand, replied to any who had the effrontery to write him in a similar vein with the words, *"No, and be damned!"* As it was a response totally in keeping with this eccentric peer's personality, no offense was taken in any quarter.

Ultimately, the house party guests who would attend numbered some thirty-eight, well within the bounds of the capabilities of the Cheney staff, some of whom were old enough to remember the wild orgies held by the duke in his bachelor days. Those parties saw well over one hundred young bucks and doxies in attendance. Of course, with that crowd private accommodations were not always necessary, nor private beds a requirement.

But those days were long past and the thirty-eight guests invited to this party would fill the guests rooms nicely. On the night of the ball, the mansion would be filled to the rafters. As a consequence of the enormity of the party, Cecilia and Lady Meriton journeyed to Oastley three full days before the invited guests in order to help oversee the final arrangements. They took with them Lady Meriton's dresser and Sarah, a young housemaid with aspirations to be a lady's maid.

Cecilia entered into the preparations with a verve that raised her grandmother's thin, aristocratic eyebrows and caused her grandfather to pound her on the back and bluffly proclaim he knew her various and sundry illnesses stemmed solely from inactivity. It was unfortunate his action coincided with her swallowing a small sip of sherry. It set her coughing and sputtering dreadfully, for which he glared at her and stumped away.

Nonetheless, it was with a feverish excitement that Cecilia met the first guests as their carriages pulled up before the estate. Anticipation sizzled through her veins. With her color high and a decided sparkle in her eyes, never had she looked prettier. The gown she wore was new for the occasion—ordered so by her grandmother—and designed to compliment her fair coloring. It featured twining spring flowers printed on a white ground and trimmed with rose-colored silk ribbons. Her shawl was of a deeper rose shade and edged with long tassels. In lieu of a lace cap, by order of her grandmother, Cecilia's silver-blond locks were dressed high on her head, adding inches to her petite stature. A spray of artificial flowers, cunningly wrought to resemble the arrangement printed on her gown, was pinned among the pale curls. The overall effect of her attire was refreshingly springlike and elegant. Banished were the lavenders and grays of lingering mourning.

Cecilia was pleased and touched by the wardrobe her grandmother bestowed on her. She was also amused for she realized the house party was the duchess's way of matchmaking and so she whispered to Jessamine in a lull between arrivals.

"You mean you have just fallen to mama's machinations? Fie on you, Cecilia," her aunt jested. "I realized that when I read mama's letter requesting I complete her invitation list. As if I pay any attention to single young men about London! That's why I knew mama would not be happy with filling the guest list with Randolph's cronies."

"Why didn't you tell me?"

"What, and have you cry off or go into one of your spells? Hardly. It was better to see you excited about the party. Besides, no matter what mama thinks she is arranging, if you are not ready to remarry, no man will be able to catch your attention."

Cecilia smiled ruefully. "That is true enough. . . . Isn't that virulent green and gold the Cresswell livery?" she asked, pointing to a cumbersome traveling coach mounted with servants in the distinctive livery that was pulling around the great drive.

"Unfortunately, it is. And before you get hipped at mama's

matchmaking inclinations, let me remind you that if she were dead set on securing you a husband, she would not have invited Miss Cresswell to number one of the guests."

"Society's latest rose shall have the bees buzzing around her for sure. I think you're correct. With competition like that, I stand in little fear of being swamped," she conceded. "Come, let's go greet London's sensation. It will probably be the only time we have the opportunity."

"Lucky us," murmured Lady Meriton drily.

Cecilia laughed and wrapped her shawl more closely about her shoulders as they went outside to wait on the broad stone steps.

Miss Philomel Cresswell, the reigning queen of the London season, was the first to descend the steps of the large traveling coach. She paused on the step to look up at Oastley Hall, a curious, satisfied expression on her face. She turned to laugh gaily at something said by her traveling companions, then stepped lightly down into the drive.

It was easy to see why she was society's darling. She was beautiful. Her hair was a glossy dark brown and dressed in masses of ringlets atop which perched a small tricornered hat of cherry red trimmed with dyed black pheasant feathers. Her curvacious figure was displayed to perfection in a well-fitted traveling dress of cherry red trimmed with black silk scallops and braid. Amazingly, her full, pouting lips echoed the cherry red of her outfit while her brown eyes sparkled with teasing invitation.

Cecilia pursed her lips and risked a side glance at her aunt. Lady Meriton caught her glance and raised an amused eyebrow. Together they watched the duke and duchess greet Philomel and Mrs. Cresswell, who descended the steps after her daughter. Behind Mrs. Cresswell came Sir James Branstoke.

Chapter Five

CECILIA'S EYES met Branstoke's for a fleeting moment as he descended the steps; then his attention was claimed by Miss Cresswell. The exchange of glances was so swift, so casual, it might not even have existed. Yet in its wake, Cecilia's chest hurt, as if metal bands were wound about her constricting her breathing. A sudden spring chill in the air sent reflexive shivers radiating through her body. She pulled at her shawl and threw one end across her chest to drape over her other shoulder. Her chin rose and she pulled every ounce of her short stature up in an illusion of height. Cool elegance touched her features while the breeze tugged at the confining pins anchoring her silver-blond hair high on her head. The wind was winning. Gossamer wisps of spun silver twisted free in the wind, blowing across still features that might have been carved in stone.

Sir James Branstoke exchanged greetings with the Duke and Duchess of Houghton and gave Miss Cresswell and her mother an arm to lead them toward the elegant Elizabethan mansion and the two women standing in front of its heavy, carved oak door. His sleepy gaze missed no detail of Mrs. Waddley's still form. A slight smile—that had nothing to do with greetings—pulled the corners of his finely chiseled lips upward.

Mrs. Waddley, he surmised with masculine satisfaction, was aware of him in more ways than that of guest or male acquaintance. It was evident in the arrogant little tilt to her head and the studied neutral defiance underlying her calm, set features. That awareness pleased him, first as a man and second as an explanation for her recent behavior.

Since the evening of the Italian Opera, he'd noted a determined effort on her part to stay out of his orb. When she failed and they did meet to exchange pleasantries, her voice was abnormally high, her manner a trifle arch. She was quick to include others in their conversations then beg out owing to the incipient onset of some illness or another. Then she would scurry away to virtually hide behind Lady Meriton's skirts, leaving that poor woman to make her excuses.

Mrs. Waddley's machinations amused him, and until now he'd been content to allow escape for he realized his observation concerning dragons upset her badly. When he made the statement he drew bow at a chance. His aim was true. The comment caused her eyes to flare wide, revealing midnight, nightmares, and fear in their fathomless blue depths. She was neither ready nor able to trust him. From her haunted look, he guessed she found trust difficult under the best of circumstances. Before his eyes, she'd withdrawn physically and emotionally to become a mere husk. Mechanically she'd bid him goodnight and fled into the house.

The memory of her besieged expression was etched in his mind. Since that evening, he'd endeavored to foster his own set of false impressions, to shore up his image as an innocuous, phlegmatic gentleman of pleasant company. For reasons as yet unclear even to himself, he wanted her to grant him her trust. He possessed an unusual, quixotic desire to play knight errant to her damsel in distress and rescue her from the dragons that plagued her. Setting Hewitt to investigate Thornbridge hardened his determination. Romley's recent report from Hewitt stated Thornbridge was making discrete inquiries into Randolph Haukstrom's finances. The reason or object of the inquiries was as yet unknown, but Branstoke would wager it was at Mrs. Waddley's direction. What was her purpose?

He anticipated discovering answers at this house party. She could not as assiduously avoid him in company here as she did in London. However, he would neither startle her with his attentions, nor allow her to ignore his presence. It was really a stroke of genius that led him to accompany the Cresswells to the Houghton estate. He knew it allayed Mrs. Waddley's fears, yet he hoped it also piqued her. His wry smile broadened as he approached her. He found himself wondering which way his absurd little rabbit would jump.

Cecilia knew she had to get herself in hand. Her breathing was much too fast and the beating of her heart sounded abnormally loud in her ears. There was no logical explanation or reason for the heightened physical manifestations she experienced around Sir Branstoke. She couldn't help it. It was like he looked into the depths of her soul every time their eyes met. That frightened her. She didn't—no, *couldn't* allow anyone to get that close.

Branstoke also bothered her because she was certain he knew things he wasn't willing to share, and that he derived a secret amusement at her expense. He was an obnoxious gentleman, a society gadder, a parasite whose existence thrived on the idiosyncrasies of others! One best left in the hands of the likes of Philomel Cresswell, she decided decisively as he and that woman and Mrs. Cresswell approached. Unfortunately, her mental harangue did not ease the fluttering feeling in a hollow stomach.

She tossed her head and pulled a tight, bright smile upon her face.

"Mrs. Cresswell, Miss Cresswell, so delighted to see you," she cooed in a voice oddly shrill. "Coming to the country is such a nice break from the pressures of the season, don't you agree? Please, won't you come this way?" she babbled, not giving them time for response. She hooked her arm in Mrs. Cresswell's and drew her before the others, all the while steadfastly ignoring Sir Branstoke. "So beneficial to one's health, too—coming to the country, that is. I swear I have not suffered half so much as I do in the city. All that coal smoke, most likely, and that rackety noise from the streets at all hours. It makes my head ache just to think of it!"

Lady Meriton pursed her lips in disapproval then turned to smile at Miss Cresswell and Branstoke. She murmured polite words of greeting as she ushered them through the door. Behind her came the Duke and Duchess escorting Lord Soothcoor, a dour middle-aged gentleman whose plain carriage contrasted sharply with that of the flashy Cresswells.

"—Depend upon it, we shall have a comfortable time of it," they heard Cecilia say as they entered the mansion.

"A comfortable time of what, Mrs. Waddley?" Sir Branstoke drawled, deeming it time she formally recognize his presence.

She glanced at him, then away, then back. "Oh! Ah, the company, the informality." She coughed, a slender white hand raising a lace-edged, monogrammed handkerchief to her lips. "I beg your pardon. A touch of congestion, the cold air—" she suggested, trailing off while smiling wanly, anxious to divert Branstoke.

"Nonsense!" boomed out the duke's voice. "I'll have none of that missish twaddle from you, gal."

Cecilia winced and fought a rising tide of color. She'd forgotten her grandfather's attitude toward illness. He didn't believe in it—that was unless *he* was ill. "Just a temporary problem," she said blithely. She was taken by surprise at a true huskiness in her voice. She cleared her throat and smiled again. "Ah—here is Mrs. Pomfret, the housekeeper. Mrs. Cresswell, Miss Cresswell, she'll show you to your rooms."

"When you've changed and rested from your journey, we shall all meet in the salon," the duchess interceded smoothly. "Lord Soothcoor, Sir Branstoke, Stephen will show you to your rooms," she said, indicating a nearby footman.

Cecilia felt the tightness in her chest ease as she watched Branstoke mount the stairs. Somehow it felt more comfortable to see him walk away than toward her. She relaxed and turned toward her grandparents.

The duke was scowling at her. "Cecilia!" he demanded, his overly loud voice reverberating in the open entrance hall. "Been right as rain for days. What's the matter, company got you spooked?"

Color rose in her face again. Instinctively she looked up the grand staircase to see if Branstoke could have heard. He had. He looked down over the banister, a hand lightly resting on one of the carved oak allegorical animals surmounting a newel post. When he saw her flushed face glance upward, his thin lips kicked up in a wry smile and vague salute; then he turned and continued up the stairs after the footman and Lord Soothcoor. Exasperation thinned Cecilia's lips as she stared after him. She would not let him irritate her further. She was stronger than that, of this she was resolved.

"There you are, Cecilia. I was beginning to wonder if you were going to cry off this evening," Lady Meriton said crisply, an arch note in her tone.

Cecilia paused in the doorway to the salon, slight color staining her high cheek bones. She nibbled on her lower lip. "It was overplayed, wasn't it? I can't explain it; but something about maintaining polite chatter brings out the true ninnyhammer in me," she said breezily. Mentally she modified her statement, replacing *polite chatter* as the cause, with *Sir James Branstoke*. Cecilia had been shocked by the strength and suddenness of her reaction to the man. So shocked that she spent the intervening hours since his arrival determinedly honing her ability to control those wayward feelings he roused.

She crossed to her aunt's side, sitting on the red brocade sofa next to her. She sighed dramatically and dimpled roguishly at her aunt. "I shall have to depend upon you to protect me from the error of my ways."

"La! I'll have none of your cozening ways, baggage!" Lady Meriton scolded. Cecilia could tell Jessamine's heart was not in her reprimand and laughed gaily

"Ahem—I trust I am not intruding, ladies?" Sir Harry Elsdon asked from the open doorway. A frown creased his lightly freckled brow and the light in his brown eyes dimmed. "We were told to meet in the salon, were we not? I mean, this is where we are gathering before dinner?"

At the sight of one of her quarries, Cecilia Waddley rose gracefully from her seat next to Jessamine and glided toward him. "Yes, yes it is. We three seem to be early, that's all. I expect the room will fill swiftly. But please, won't you sit down?" She guided him to a vacant sofa set at a right angle to the first.

"Nothing but sit and sit and eat and eat!" he declared dramatically. Then he grinned at her. "Petruchio, one of my favorite characters."

Lady Meriton laughed at her niece's obvious confusion. "You will soon discover, Cecilia, that Sir Elsdon is a devotee of the stage. Lines and allusions constantly fall from his ready tongue."

She clapped her hands together, looking at him wide-eyed. "La, sir, you fascinate me! Lamentably I am not well versed in plays, my husband preferring opera. I would like to learn. Please, before company arrives, tell me of your favorite plays, roles, and lines."

Scarcely were the words out of her mouth when noisy chatter was heard in the hall and the door opened to admit a large group. She made a moue of disappointment spawning indulgent laughter from Sir Elsdon. Reluctantly she made her excuses and went to greet the guests. Mentally she reminded herself to contrive more time with him at a latter date.

She was all smiles and charming affability as she greeted the guests. Not even Miss Cresswell's appearance as it neared the dinner hour ruffled her unduly—even though Philomel Cresswell did enter draped on Sir Branstoke's arm. Cecilia knew her nervousness and trembling of hours before were safely buried. That knowledge eased an unaccountable tightness in her muscles that she hadn't been aware existed.

Relaxed, Cecilia Waddley moved fluidly through the growing crowd of guests, stopping to chat briefly with this person or that. A gentle touch, a brief empathy, she had them all smiling like bemused idiots. Sir Branstoke watched, his brown eyes alert behind heavy lids, as she manipulated this person then that, leaving in her wake a growing trail of laughter and goodwill. This child-sized woman, a fragile willow wand, moved among the company like an evangelical did among an avid flock. Though she clutched one of her ever-present handkerchiefs in her hand, she did not utilize it to reinforce any of her illnesses. A lace end fluttered and swayed before her, exaggerating rapid hand motions as she talked.

Branstoke eased himself away from the growing circle of gentlemen surrounding Miss Cresswell and set an interception course for Mrs. Waddley. It was his desire to put her at ease and work further toward acceptance and trust. Under her current demeanor, he foresaw an opportunity for success.

"Mrs. Waddley—" he began formally.

Cecilia turned swiftly, startled at his approach. For a heartbeat she gauged her reactions. When her pulse remained relatively stable she knew instant relief. She smiled questioningly up at him, her royal blue eyes catching the light of the brilliant cut crystal chandeliers and reflecting it back.

Branstoke paused, thunderstruck, then he raised a dark brown eyebrow while his eyelids drooped lower and his mouth quirked upward at the corners. "May I be permitted to say, madame, that it appears the country air agrees with you."

Cecilia's smile broadened and her eyes twinkled.

"More'n likely it's being among her own kind that agrees with her," declared the duke, coming up behind them. His loud voice caused several nearby heads to turn in their direction.

"Grandfather!" protested Cecilia, torn between laughter and exasperation.

The old duke patted her shoulder though he addressed Branstoke. "Glad to see her easy in company. Was a time, you know, she had some damned silly notion of inequality. Had it since she was a child and Haukstrom blew his wad. Veritable court card my daughter married. I won't have him here, you know. Not after he married Ceci here off to that damned merchant fellow."

Cecilia's sense of humor vanished. A cold arrogance chilled her eyes to blue ice. "Grandfather," she said slowly, "I'll not allow you to say one word against Mr. Waddley. Because of him, I do not have to live my life as some parasitic charity case grateful for whatever crumbs are thrown my way!" Her voice was low yet quavered with painfully suppressed emotion.

"Listen to her, like a she-wolf protecting her cub," Lord Cheney said indulgently. Around them, a growing number of people stopped talking to unabashedly eavesdrop.

A rare anger flared in Cecilia, shaking her to the core. She stamped her foot. "Mr. Waddley was good to me," she insisted.

"Aye, I'll grant the man was a good enough sort, but not good enough for a Cheney."

She threw her head back and glared challengingly up at him. "Then it's fortunate that I am a Haukstrom and not a Cheney!" she declared frostily.

The room was as unnaturally still as the air before a storm. The duke's bushy brown and gray brows clamped down over his eyes.

"Mrs. Waddley, I have been curious about these wall hangings," Branstoke said placidly, as if totally unaware of the palpable anger coalescing in black clouds above Cecilia and her grandfather, threatening to explode in lightning fury. He hooked his arm in hers and turned her toward the closest wall hanging. "Are they Mortlake tapestries?" he asked, raising his quizzing glass to study the elegant weavings. Behind them, the seething duke stumped away.

Mrs. Waddley's chest rose and fell rapidly in the wake of the anger coursing through her. Branstoke allowed her time to recover, pretending an absorption in the detail work of the tapestry.

"Yes—yes, they are Mortlake tapestries," she managed. She tossed her head to clear it of lingering anger and took a deep breath, letting it out slowly. "Grandmother had this room redecorated some years back to display them to better advantage." She touched her handkerchief to her lips, a delicate shudder rippling through her body.

Branstoke looked at her closely, then noncommittally steered her toward the next tapestry hanging on the walls.

"This room was originally known as the Great Parlor. Of recent years it's been called the Tapestry Parlor, or identified by the modern term—the salon," she continued neutrally as they circumnavigated the room. "As a child I spent many hours staring at these tapestries, making up stories to complement each scene." Finally, she dared look at Sir Branstoke, her breath coming out on a long sigh, a gentle, wistful expression on her face. "Thank you," she murmured.

He smiled. It was a pleasant, non-threatening smile. "Occasionally fribbles such as myself have their uses," he said dispassionately. He casually swung his quizzing glass by its riband. "Actually, I believe we may be the best sorts for routing dragons. So unexpected, you see."

Cecilia froze at the word "dragon."

Branstoke looked at her pointedly, waiting for her reaction. He could see her battling inwardly with some emotion. Color came and went on her face leaving dark blue eyes blazing out of a pinched countenance. She blinked rapidly and her face cleared. She simpered and clutched her handkerchief to her chest.

"Would you mind if I left you to your perusal of the tapestries by yourself, Sir Branstoke?" she said weakly. "I must sit down a moment. I feel one of my dreadful headaches coming on. So unfortunate for I have been much better here. It is my nerves. I know it is just that, but la! little good does knowing do me," she prattled on and laughed shrilly, edging toward a vacant chair.

Branstoke allowed her to escape while maintaining a phlegmatic expression on his face and perfunctory words of consolation on his lips. Mrs. Waddley needed to come to terms with his intuition and to learn he was not a threat. He would not pursue her further, merely allow her time to assimilate this knowledge. It was a chancy game he played; nevertheless, he'd wager an intelligent woman hid behind that social ninnyhammer.

Dragons! What could he know of dragons? She sat down weakly and delicately moped her brow with a shaking hand.

Coward! The accusation rang in her head, yet the part of her that instinctively reacted to Sir James Branstoke was clamoring loudly. No longer could she continue to confine the jangling nerves and hollow flutterings. They exploded free, leaving her limbs trembling.

Why did he have to look at her like that? That sleepy, bored expression he habitually wore concealing a keen discernment in those brown-gold eyes. Why did he have to turn that discernment in her direction and look at her more intently that anyone ever did, including her own family? For years she'd been safe within herself, no one bothering to delve into her thoughts or feelings other than on a superficial level. She was able to keep herself inviolate and private from others and therefore safe and in control of her life. Sir James Branstoke had an uncanny ability to blast open those hidden doors and pull her out into the light. She didn't like that. It knocked her out of control. Worse, it forced her to acknowledge a burgeoning attraction for this enigmatic peer. Ruthlessly she forced those feelings aside.

That attraction, she decided, probably grew from some insidious weakness or desire within herself to turn her problems over to another to solve. She would not allow herself to fall back into such weakness. She could and would manage her own life. She would discover Mr. Waddley's murderer and display before society the seamy underbelly of its glittering, superficial existence. Then she would hire as companion a woman who did not desire to spend her life as a charity case at her relatives' beck and call, sell her holdings in London, and retire to the country.

Her decisive thoughts did much to ease the jangling nerves. Carefully she tucked away the last of the besetting emotions. A small smile curled up the corners of her mouth. It was certainly comical that she feigned irritation of the nerves, yet when actually afflicted, she worked hard to dispel the complaint. She did not understand why anyone would actually submit to wild emotions. It left one so out of control and vulnerable. So inelegant, too.

She counted herself fortunate to have escaped the emotional, nerve-wracking feelings until her present age. The maturity of age allowed her to dispassionately examine the sensations and place them in their proper perspective. She did wonder, why was she now experiencing these emotions? Why was she spared until her five and twentieth year? And there was not only her reaction to Branstoke to consider; there was also her unnatural burst of anger with her grandfather.

All in all, she supposed she should own to a modicum of gratitude that she was finally experiencing emotional upheavals. It gave her an understanding of the concept of crimes of passion.

She wondered to what extent Mr. Waddley's death was due to his murderer being in the grips of some uncontrolled emotion. Truthfully, she hoped his death stemmed from a spontaneous, emotional rage versus a planned, cold-blooded murder. Somehow, it wouldn't seem so hideous then.

She looked up to search out Sir Branstoke, to see if he was still watching her. He wasn't. He was back, comfortably ensconced amongst Miss Cresswell's coterie. Loud laughter from the vicinity of the door drew her attention in that direction. It was Randolph, late as always, entering with the Honorable Mr. Rippy and Lord Havelock.

She rose gracefully, switched her skirts into place, then moved to the doorway to greet her brother and his friends.

"Randolph, I fear I'd despaired of your ever coming down before dinner," she said, gliding up to his side and laying a hand on his arm.

"Dash it all, Cecilia, a man needs time to set himself to rights. Especially after traveling on horseback to get here. Don't know why I let Rippy here talk me into bearing him company instead of traveling by coach."

"But Randy, old fellow, said yourself this was great riding country," protested Mr. Rippy.

"So it is, but ain't good riding *to,*" Randolph stubbornly complained.

"I fear the close confines of a carriage over that abominable road would have been worse," drawled Lord Havelock, closing his eyes. Boredom with a topic that had obviously been discussed before was evident in his tone. Slowly he opened his eyes and looked down his nose at Cecilia. "Randolph, as you love me, please introduce me to this fair creature who stands before us."

"Oh, right! Right at that. Yes, ah—Cecilia, this is Charles Dernly, Marquis Havelock. Havelock, this is my sister, Cecilia—Mrs. Waddley, you know."

The marquis bowed punctiliously over her hand, granting it a chaste salute. "I would not have dreamed my friend Randolph could have sprung from among angels," he said smoothly, keeping hold of her hand a moment longer than was seemly.

Deliberately, Cecilia withdrew her hand, though her expression remained friendly. She was not deceived by Lord Havelock's unctuous behavior. The degree of his bow and the feather light perfunctory nature of his kiss on her hand told another tale. The marquis possessed an elevated opinion of himself. He contrived to make certain others knew his lofty elevation and respected it. Though he might rub elbows with the riffraff of life at a prize fight or in a tavern, he was certain to control the degree of interaction and throughout maintain his separateness. Cecilia was willing to wager even his mistresses were allowed only a limited degree of intimacy.

"Please, I beg of you, Lord Havelock, spare my blushes," Cecilia said coyly.

"E'gad, is that spider-shanks butler come to announce dinner already?" whined Randolph. "I've not had a moment's rest."

Cecilia laughed softly. "Well, come have a hearty dinner and become so redolent you fall asleep."

Randolph's friends laughed along with her; but he pouted and glared at his sister.

"There is sometimes a lack of delicacy in you, Cecilia, that I find deplorable. No *ton* at all."

"Yes, well, consider I missed that somewhere in my education process," she said lightly.

Lord Havelock and Mr. Rippy smirked at the implied slur on Randolph, but as Cecilia expected, her comment sailed over her brother's head, her deeper meaning lost to him.

"Mrs. Waddley, may I have the honor of escorting you to dinner?" Lord Havelock asked, full of appreciation for her unexpected wit.

"Certainly, sir." Cecilia gracefully laid her arm on his and allowed him to lead her out into the hall and up the stairs to the Great Chamber where dinner awaited them. She remonstrated herself for falling out of her simpering character. But not too severely. She had to own a certain pride at getting a part of her own back. After all, she was proud of the machinations that achieved her purpose of claiming Lord Havelock's attention. A smug little smile tilted up the corners of her bow-shaped lips.

From across the room Sir Branstoke saw that smile and his lips turned downward to a corresponding degree.

Chapter Six

THE DEW BLANKETING the pale green blades of spring grass glinted and shone like heirloom silver in the scraggly morning sun. The air was cold, yet still, and in the dips and valleys fog clung to the land.

Cecilia Waddley softly closed the heavy oak door and paused on the wide stone steps of the servants' entrance to stare out at the silent landscape. She breathed in deeply, savoring the smell of damp earth and vegetation. She pulled the large, serviceable blue wool shawl she wore over her head and shoulders, one hand clasping it under her chin while in her other she carried a bonnet-shaped willow basket. Stepping off the stone steps, she made her way toward the old herb garden laid out at the end of the east wing and banded by tall, precision-cut yews. Dew sprayed up as she walked through the thick grass, soaking the sturdy brown leather boots and the hem of her plain gown. At the entrance to the garden was a black iron gate. As she lifted the latch and pulled it open, it protested, creaking and groaning loudly in the still morning air. Cecilia bit her lip at the horrid, strident sound and glanced up at the row of windows for the state apartments that looked out over the tiny garden. They were small bedchambers, designed over two hundred years ago for royalty's retinue, should any visit. As far as Cecilia knew, none had. Now they were the rooms assigned to the single gentleman guests of the house party.

She screened her eyes against the pale morning sun. Not a curtain moved nor a hand or face appeared at any window. Apparently they were all sleeping late. She had it from one of the footmen that most of the gentlemen stayed up until night lost its inky darkness playing cards and billiards and drinking deeply of Oastley ale or the special stock found in the wine cellars. Stock that Cecilia knew never entered the country by legal routes. None of the gentlemen were yet awake to see her; nonetheless, she dared not risk closing the gate lest the repeat sound succeed where the first failed. She needed this time alone to sort out her wayward thoughts and to plan without emotional pressures or reactions. She walked down the moss-covered stone pathways inspecting the beds as she passed. The garden had been a favored haunt for the child suddenly uprooted from a decaying manor and endlessly abjured to be a lady. It was as if by being ladylike she could somehow make amends for her father's and brother's profligate existence. No one wanted to know how she felt. It was more important what others thought of her. The garden had been a place she ran to when she was confused and hurt. There she worked to tend the plants alongside Great Aunt Martha, an elderly spinster sister of her grandmother's. Under Great Aunt Martha's guidance, the garden was a lush, fragrant oasis. But the old woman didn't limit her herb gathering to the garden. She trudged far and wide across the countryside for plants. A worn copy of *Culpeper's Complete Herbal and English Physician* was her treasured possession. From Great Aunt Martha Cecilia learned the lore of herbs and their medicinal uses. It was a knowledge that curiously aided her now in her sickly acts. She missed Great Aunt Martha. She passed away quietly in her sleep shortly after Cecilia married Mr. Waddley. Cecilia doubted the garden had been tended since then, save for the small cook's patch and the roses for bouquets. Two days ago she set the gardener to cleaning out the dead and overgrown plants. In the few days she was at Oastley Hall, she would thin and transplant the surviving plants. Slips from some she would take back to London to plant in Jessamine's tiny back garden.

She shook her head dismally at the sight of the thin and scraggly chamomile border. To return it to the thick and lush condition of her memory, it would need additional pruning and some division of the thicker clumps. It looked like the comfrey, sweet woodruff, and other plants would need a similar treatment. Sighing, Cecilia wandered on down the stone paths, her object this morning to cut slips for rooting in Great Aunt Martha's potting boxes that were yet kept in the stillroom.

Great Aunt Martha. It was odd, but she had not thought of that dear lady in years. Cecilia had been the closest to her of any of her relations for there was a gentle, non-intrusive understanding in her sweet smile. She never expected Cecilia to be any different from herself. She accepted Cecilia's stubbornness, her fears and lack of trust, yet by her actions alone, Great Aunt Martha built trust. She was the only member of the family not to harangue Cecilia to be a lady, nor fault her retiring demeanor, for she knew it did not stem from a shy personality. It grew out of Baron Haukstrom's impatience with his daughter's existence coupled with the sour knowledge that her dowry was untouchable.

Cecilia sighed at the memories. So many reminded her of the necessity to live without encumbrances. If it weren't for the necessity of investigation, she would already be living a retiring life in the country where she would not be a burden to anyone—not to her grandparents, her aunt, her father and brother, or to Waddley Spice and Tea.

But now she had a responsibility to George Waddley. It took precedence over her own heart's desires.

She stooped to clip a wormwood plant and place the stem on the damp cloth that lined her basket.

At dinner last evening she sat between Lord Havelock and the Reverend Septimus Whilber. It was not quite the auspicious positioning she'd hoped. The effusive gallantry Lord Havelock displayed before dinner did not extend to the table. Once they were seated, his conversation became directed to the young matron who sat on his right. To Cecilia's curious, half-listening ear, he beguiled the woman with the same flattery he'd bestowed on her. He was like a library with one book. Cecilia wondered caustically if he intended to read from the same volume to all the women in the company.

She went over in her mind what she knew of the gentleman. Lord Havelock was a well-known figure in London society. A man of exquisite taste, he was arrogant and self-indulgent in personality tempered by an exacting politeness and elegance of manner. He was reputed to have a more than easy competence, yet occasionally speculation rose as to why he declined to have Havelock Manor rebuilt after a fire six years ago destroyed the beautiful mansion. He chose instead to live in rooms in London, though it was seen that he purchased a prodigiously handsome townhouse in Bath for his mother and sister. He intrigued Cecilia for the apparent dichotomy in his personality. On the other hand, as a person she could not think well of the man. To be fair, she supposed that his overwhelming self-indulgence smacked too closely of the attributes characterized by her father and brother, and that was what disgusted her, not the man himself. Nonetheless, she was thankful she did not have to listen too long to his elegant bouncers! They put her to the blush more than she cared to admit. But, she wondered, could he not, perhaps, be leading society astray as to the thickness of his wallet? Could Lord Havelock's elegant bouncers be designed to hide greater lies?

Then there was the Honorable Reginald Rippy to consider. He was one of Randolph's constant shadows. With his bony build and protruding Adam's apple, he was an exaggerated dandy. But shadows don't make suggestions such as he did as to his desire to ride to Oastley. Nor do they persuade men of Randolph's ilk, let alone that of Lord Havelock, to dispense with their comforts to accompany him! How did he do it? He was seated across from her last evening and appeared decidedly uncomfortable throughout the dinner, though he had a favored place next to Miss Cresswell. On his other side was Jessamine, and despite her best conversational efforts, he did not return more than a few monosyllables, and those were in agreement to her comments rather than venturing anything of his own.

Sir Harry Elsdon, when he wasn't dramatizing, was the most at ease and natural of Randolph's confederates. His taste in dress was simple, yet elegant. His manner was open and friendly. He was a generally well-liked gentleman. He seemed to always have something to smile about and encouraged those around him to smile too. On him, with his carrot-colored hair and light dusting of freckles on his pale skin, his smiles reminded one of country folks' tales of mischievous elves and fairies. At dinner he appeared to adroitly entertain old Mrs. Martcombe and Miss Amblethorp, for there was much laughter coming from their end of the table.

Following dinner, when the men finally rejoined the ladies in the parlor, there was little occasion for private conversation. Three of the young ladies (who possessed marriage-minded mamas) were pushed to show off their skills at singing and playing the pianoforte or harp. After this forced entertainment (which Cecilia was thankful being a widow allowed her escape), the gentlemen retired to the billiard room before more could be offered, leaving the ladies with no recourse but to continue gossiping among themselves or to seek their own beds. Cecilia, envying the gentlemen their retirement to the billiard room, opted for the latter choice.

The company would be at Oastley for two and a half more

days. In that time she must discover ways to ingratiate herself with Randolph and his friends and learn more about them. Once everyone returned to London, her task would be more difficult. Her first endeavor, she decided, should be to search Randolph's room, then perhaps those rooms assigned to the other gentlemen. She hoped to find something within Randolph's chambers, for the idea of entering a single man's chambers was somehow embarrassing, not to mention the ramifications should she be caught. But she would not be caught. She would be very careful of that.

She clipped a couple stems of pennyroyal and placed them in her basket, then crossed to the back of the garden to see how the new marigold and heliotrope shoots were faring. She crouched down to thin the beds to encourage stronger growth.

Behind her Cecilia heard brisk, light footsteps. She turned around, instinctively crouching lower. She watched motionless as Miss Amblethorp ran down one of the stone paths. Seeing the stone bench at the end of the path, she flung herself down on it and hunched over, her face in her hands.

Rising, Cecilia stripped off her work gloves and dropped them into the basket slung over her arm. The young woman was obviously in great distress and probably came to the herb garden to be alone. Cecilia understood the need to be alone. She'd come to the garden for the same purpose. Unfortunately, there was no way Cecilia could leave without Miss Amblethorp seeing her. It would likely embarrass the poor child. The only recourse was to brazenly offer help and sympathy.

Cecilia walked slowly toward the distressed young woman, uncertain how to make her appearance known without unduly startling her. She worried her lip a moment, then sighed and bent closer.

"Excuse me, Miss Amblethorp? Is there some way that I may be of assistance?"

Miss Amblethorp's head flew up, bright color flowing over her rather common features.

"I'm sorry, I did not mean to intrude, only I was already here when you entered," Cecilia offered apologetically.

"Oh! I did not see you!"

"That is hardly surprising. I was crouched down, tending some plants. May I?" she asked, indicating the stone bench with a sweep of her hand.

"Yes, of course." Miss Amblethorp slid down to make room all the while staring at the willow basket and its contents. "You like to garden?" she asked slowly, surprise rippling through her voice.

Cecilia laughed. "It brings back fond memories," she said, startled by her own truthfulness. "But really, Miss Amblethorp, is there some way in which I may help?"

"Please call me Janine. I've never been comfortable with Miss Amblethorp. That's what my elder sisters were called, never me. But to answer your kind question, there is no way you can help unless you can convince my mother to allow me to retire to our home. I just do not seem to have the constitution for London." She wilted visibly. "I find I cannot get excited about balls, gossip, or the ultimate purpose of a Season—husband hunting."

"Don't you wish to marry?"

"Oh, yes, indeed. However, I have yet to meet a gentleman who feels as I do about the social whirl."

Cecilia nodded and laid an understanding hand on Janine's arm. "And if they exist—which I assure you they do—you would not find them in London. They avoid it like the very plague."

"You see my problem," Janine said drily, some of the frightened doe image receding. "And I do know they exist, or rather have existed before being twisted and jaded in the social milieu. I hold the example I know of in my heart in hopes of meeting another more immune to society's siren call as a panacea for unhappiness," she confessed, bitterness gnawing at her words.

"Gracious, my dear, don't tell me that you have suffered a disappointment in love!"

"If it was a disappointment, it was a disappointment in calf love for I was a child of twelve. No, the gentleman I knew has been changed these seven long years and while he lived, I was merely a neighbor's granddaughter upon whom he bestowed a few kindnesses. But I always thought I should want to marry a man like he was then."

"I have never considered myself a prodigiously inquisitive person, but you have me intrigued."

Janine laughed mirthlessly. "It is difficult even for me to fathom, but I carry around within me an infatuation for the former Viscount Dernley, a personage who no longer exists."

"The Marquis of Havelock? Lord Havelock?"

"Knowing him now, it does seem incredulous. But he was not always so arrogant and self-absorbed. At one time he was extremely personable and charming. My eldest sister, Sophia, had set her cap for him and was confident she could bring him up to scratch."

"Ah-h—"

"Though she did intend to change his mind about London's delights," Janine added wryly. "It used to make me angry to hear her prattle on about changing him, molding him to be the man *she* wanted him to be. Now look at him."

Cecilia shook her head. She couldn't imagine Lord Havelock being the man Janine described. Oh, for the innocent eyes of youth! "What happened?" she asked softly.

Janine's mouth twisted bitterly. "Havelock Manor burned, the conflagration claiming the life of his father and younger brother. In a fit of pain and sorrow, his mother blamed him for he was away that night, attending a lecture on modern agricultural techniques. Grandmother told me she made his life an unending misery for weeks. Finally he left, disappearing for over a year. He returned the man we now know."

"Does anyone know where he went?" Cecilia asked.

"He claims he was in the Mediterranean, enjoying the climate while assiduously avoiding Napoleon. Sophia would have it he went off in search of some insignificant relative who disappeared. She was quite put out. I think because Dorothea Rustian was considered quite a beauty. She tried to convince herself, and anyone else who would listen, that the little red-headed hussy seduced him away from her."

"Did she?"

"Sophia never had him to begin with. Her catty words were a mere sop to her pride. Anyway, no one knows what happened to Miss Rustian. Havelock swore he did not run away with her. And by the time he returned Sophia was married to Wentworth Aldrich."

"And no doubt just as loudly decried where formally she praised," Cecilia hazarded, smiling.

"Precisely. And there were other, juicier scandals for the gossips to enjoy. I'll admit I've never been reconciled to how he is now. He was in the breakfast parlor when I descended this morning. My headlong flight from the house to the isolation of these gardens was to avoid speaking to him. I know if I am forced to make private conversation with him I will be reminded of how he used to be and undoubtedly embarrass myself by tears. And then what a hubble-bubble should I be in! I would be questioned and plagued unendingly. But what can I do? It would be catastrophic for anyone to discover the extent of my dreams. It would lead, I assure you, to enduring merciless teasing and jibes from my family. Especially from Sophia."

Cecilia laughed. "Am I to understand there is no love lost between you and Sophia?"

"Not in any overt manner. We have always been two different people. Truthfully, my attitudes are constantly at odds with my family's—for all the good it does me. Mama never listens to me. She'd rather listen to herself carp; that way she can be assured she is doing her duty and so tell anyone else who will listen."

"You seem to have a ready understanding of people."

Janine cocked her head. "If I do, I suppose it's because I'd rather be an observer than a participant."

"Tell me, what do you make of my brother Randolph and his friends?"

She wrinkled her nose. "I doubt you'd want to know."

"No, seriously, I do," she assured her, leaning forward and resting her hands on her knees.

Janine looked around absently for a moment as she gathered her thoughts. "The only one who seems real to me is Lord Havelock."

"Havelock! Oh, you mean because you've known him for so long."

"Partly. Also I've spent considerable energy studying the changes in him. At any rate, I see him, quite clearly, as totally wrapped up in himself, and sadly, entirely consistent in that manner. The Viscount Dernley I knew is dead. Mr. Haukstrom—" she paused, looking guiltily at Cecilia.

"Go on, please. Nothing you could say about my brother will upset me in any way."

Janine nodded and plowed on. "Mr. Haukstrom is all flash and no substance, the Honorable Mr. Rippy likes to play the fool, and Sir Elsdon is just too happy and carefree for my tastes. And truthfully, I am not familiar with half the plays he is forever quoting—let alone do I understand them!"

Cecilia laughed. "That is a succinct, yet I'll own brilliant conclusion. What do you make of Sir Branstoke?"

Janine smiled. "I like him. If you stripped away his enjoyment of London's frivolities, he would be a great deal like the Viscount Dernley that I knew."

Cecilia pulled back, shock and puzzlement reflected in her wide blue eyes. "Oh, Janine, surely not. Havelock could never have been that languid."

"No-o, but those are only manners, not the measure of the man."

"You don't think manners are the measure of a man?"

"Certainly not! Manners are like clothing, worn for effect in society. To know a man's true measure, one would have to view him away from society, away from the need to be anything other than himself."

"If we accept your statement, then the corollary of it must be that in society, no one is as they seem."

Janine laughed. "Yes, I suppose that would be true. All of us actors and actresses upon a stage. Didn't Mr. Shakespeare write something to that effect?"

"Very likely," Cecilia said absently, her thoughts running swiftly down another road. "The question then becomes," she mused slowly, "what does one look for to know the true measure of a person?"

"I beg your pardon?"

Cecilia looked up and smiled brightly, self-consciously. "Oh, nothing, merely some conclusions for myself." She hooked her arm with Janine's. "What do you say we return to the house and partake of a little breakfast. There are bound to be others up now. Neither of us shall be forced to converse with those we dislike." An odd feeling rippled down her spine. Instinctively she looked up at the row of windows. The clear panes winked emptily in the morning sun.

She turned back toward Janine, enveloping herself once again in her mantle of signs and symptoms. "Besides, if I stay much longer in this cool air, no doubt my plaguey cough will return. So disagreeable, you know. Just as one is about to speak to someone, lo, what happens? A coughing fit wracks one's body leaving one too weak to stand, let alone continue in conversation," she prattled while guiding Janine toward the gate.

Janine looked at her askance, her expression quizzical and hurt. Cecilia saw it and knew she was questioning her odd behavior. And remembering their conversation, wondering what was odd and what was real. It smote Cecilia to realize how, in maintaining her persona, she might hurt others in return. Were her machinations any better than the rest of society's just because she believed her motives were sincere? Who was she to doubt anyone else? She should be tarred with the same brush.

No matter, she thought wearily, she would continue as she began. She had no choice.

A figure stood by a window in one of the state apartments, cloaked in shadows as the morning sun streamed past him. He stood, unmoving, watching Miss Amblethorp and Mrs. Waddley in the garden below. Keenly his eyes followed Mrs. Waddley, noting first her sympathy, humor, then serious demeanor. Finally he saw her relax and fade back into the Mrs. Waddley everyone knew. He watched them until they rounded the corner of the mansion and disappeared from sight. A slight smile curled up one side of his lips while his eyes grew thoughtful and considering. The grounds were empty again. He turned and headed nonchalantly toward the door.

Cecilia led Janine through the back entrance so both would be spared questions regarding their early morning ramble with subsequent sodden shoes and skirts. The servants hall, just off that entrance, was a flurry of activity. Something was being planned. Cecilia shooed Janine on up the stairs and followed in her wake, determined to change quickly in order to discover what was transpiring.

When she descended the stairs to enter the drawing room off the salon that was designated for the house party's informal meals, it was to discover a riding expedition planned to the edge of Romney Marsh. No doubt the duke had been cajoled to lead his guests on a tour of some of the more infamous haunts of his highwayman and smuggler days. His exploits were almost forty years old, but to hear him tell it, they occurred only yesterday. Cecilia smiled, shook her head in amusement and declined an invitation to join the large party. Such an excursion would be far too damaging to her fragile health.

She served herself a small wedge of ham and a dollop of potatoes from the sideboard and sat down to listen to the conversations around her as she ate small, bird-like bites of breakfast.

"Is Miss Cresswell coming, do you know?" asked the Honorable Mr. Rippy, his Adam's apple bobbing as he sipped his ale.

"Do you think she'd miss an opportunity to show herself to advantage? Especially if Sir Branstoke were to be in attendance? Don't be a blockhead," drawled Lord Havelock, his lip curling in a faint sneer.

"They've started placing wagers at White's, y'know," said Sir Harry. *"Oh, how many torments lie in the small circle of a wedding ring!* Colley Cibber, *The Double Gallant,"* he explained to no one in particular.

"He ain't been caught yet, for all he moves so slow. Stab me if I understand what all the gels see in him. Fa! but it's a dull dog!" complained Randolph.

"It's more'n money or looks," assured the Earl of Soothcoor, setting his mug on the table and raising his napkin to his lips. He rose from the table.

"What's more than money or looks?" inquired Lady Bramcroft, sailing into the room wearing an imperious air and an outmoded blue riding dress.

"Sir Branstoke's attraction with the ladies," supplied Sir Harry. Several pairs of male eyes glared at him for including a woman in their masculine conversation. He shrugged and smiled congenially. All, it seemed, had forgotten Cecilia's presence.

"Soothcoor is quite correct," said Lady Bramcroft. Laying a pair of blue kid gloves on the table, she took a cup of coffee from an impassive footman. "And you gentleman could do no worse than to study Sir Branstoke's methods."

That brought a guffaw of laughter from the gentlemen.

"And what would you have us do? All walk as slow as a snail and fall asleep on our feet?" asked Sir Harry. "Or, do you believe: *He is the very pineapple of politeness?"*

Lady Bramcroft's thin gray brows rose and a dismissive sigh flared her pinched nostrils for she recognized Sheridan's Mrs. Malaprop in Elsdon's quote. "You gentlemen are without your senses if that is your opinion. Sir Branstoke is the epitome of the word *gentleman,* isn't that correct Mrs. Waddley?"

Cecilia's head flew up followed by a tide of red. It was not her intention to be singled out and certainly not to voice her opinions of Sir Branstoke! Her mouth opened and closed, then she cleared her throat. "I—I really don't believe I am in a position to say."

"Oh, come, come, Mrs. Waddley. I've seen you several times in Sir Branstoke's company. Do not be coy. Tell these gentlemen what makes him amenable to us ladies."

"Well, I think it is his address, and the way he has of listening to one as if whatever you say is of great import."

"Exactly. Very good, Mrs. Waddley," approved Lady Bramcroft, much in the manner of the headmistress of the girls' academy Cecilia once attended.

"Ha! Anyone who could stomach Cecilia's long list of complaints and illnesses would find favor in my addle-pated pretty little sister's eyes. Probably came from being married to that damned merchant," jibed Randolph.

Sir Harry winced and Lord Havelock studied the plaster and wood ceiling.

Lady Bramcroft drew herself up and glared at him. "And it is even far easier to discern why you find favor with so few!" She set down her coffee cup, picked up her gloves, and sailed out of the room, the very rustle of her heavy skirts loudly proclaiming her disfavor.

Prudently, Cecilia found it incumbent to follow in her wake while behind her Sir Harry was advising her brother, amid fulsome theatrical quotes, that once again his actions with regards to his sister were bad ton. The Earl of Soothcoor emphatically seconded that sentiment. Cecilia didn't hear her brother's response.

Cecilia retired with her work basket to the salon and settled on one of the white and gilt painted sofas upholstered in red damask. It faced wide double doors left open onto the entrance hall and vestibule. From her vantage point she could see everyone as they entered or left the mansion. For nearly an hour her quick needle plunged in and out of the canvas, filling in the red-brick-colored background around the golden keys. She saw nearly the entire house party leave. From comments dropped, she gathered some of the older ladies were gathered in her grandmother's private drawing room and that a few of the elder gentlemen had retired to the library for a morning nap.

When the house had been still for some time, Cecilia packed up her workbasket. She headed first for the stillroom to check on her slips to see that they were still damp and would come to no harm until she could plant them. But her journey to the stillroom served another purpose. It brought her past the large servant's hall. She peeked in. As she hoped, several of the valets were at their leisure. Her brother's man held a deck of cards in his hand and was soliciting players. Like master like man, mused Cecilia. It should keep him well engaged.

She climbed the stairs to the long gallery that gave access to the state apartments. She paced the gallery twice, listening for the sounds of others in the wing and deliberately creating noise to draw out the curious. No one came. Satisfied, she crossed to the door to the small blue withdrawing room that gave access to the room Randolph used. She eased open the door and slipped inside, crossing the blue and white patterned carpet quickly. At Randolph's door she paused and looked toward the other two rooms that gave off the withdrawing room. They were silent and closed. She opened Randolph's door.

It was not a neat room. Disgust for the habits of Randolph's man curled her lip upward. She shook her head dismally, wondering where to start looking. More so, what should she be looking for? She'd only had some vague idea before of searching Randolph's room, never forming any clear idea of what she should be looking for. She stepped farther into the room. Anything of import would most likely not be among his clothes and toiletries, for they were scattered about the room. It would be put away, in a drawer, a trunk, somewhere. She started to pull open drawers, carefully sifting contents. She checked the wardroom, his portmanteau, under his pillow—nothing. No journal like Mr. Waddley kept, no books, no scraps of paper of any sort. There were gloves, stockings, and cravats in abundance along with several fobs, snuff boxes, and a signet ring he must have had designed for himself for its emblem was unknown to her. She sighed as she closed the last small drawer in a French Boulle writing desk. There was no help here.

Quietly she left the room and moved swiftly toward another of the rooms. Suddenly her nose began to tickle. Frantically she withdrew the clean handkerchief from her sleeve and held it tightly to her nose, praying it would stop the threatening sneeze. Swiftly she ran back to the entrance door and slipped out into the gallery, relief flooding her that she'd made it back safely to the public part of the house. She sighed and lifted her head up, her hand and handkerchief falling to rest on her chest. She gasped and blinked. Standing not twenty feet away with his back to her, staring out tall mullioned windows was Sir James Branstoke!

He was supposed to be out riding! What was he doing h-h-here—?

Aachoo!

ᴄ᷂᷉ Chapter Seven

Sɪʀ Jᴀᴍᴇs Bʀᴀɴsᴛᴏᴋᴇ ᴛʜᴏᴜɢʜᴛ ʜɪᴍsᴇʟғ ᴀʟᴏɴᴇ. He came upstairs to think, to pace the long gallery, and to stare out the windows that gave onto the courtyard between the wings in expectation of seeing Mrs. Waddley. He knew she did not attend the riding party. A subtle question to her maid produced the information that she was not in her chamber. A cursory inspection of the public rooms also failed to produce the woman.

He was curious as to her whereabouts and activities, for he didn't believe she was at Oastley Hall merely for frivolity. He noticed her eyes restlessly tracked the movements of Randolph and his friends. That crowd did not strike him as the types to catch Mrs. Waddley's romantic fancy. Nor was her expression one of avid expectation, as most women were wont to wear when they desire to be noticed by a man. Quite the opposite. Watching her, he received the impression that she would prefer blending with the furnishings and it was obvious that she heartily resented the duke's and duchess's efforts to bring her into society's fold.

He wondered where Mrs. Waddley could be. For all her laments and protests, he doubted she was sitting idly somewhere. That was the reason he was in the gallery. Earlier in the day he discovered the gallery was an ideal vantage point for watching the comings and goings around the hall. Already he'd noted a small party returning from the expedition betimes; and following them, one figure who, with his tan greatcoat collar turned up and his curly-brimmed beaver hat pulled down low, Branstoke judged reluctant for his return to be public knowledge. Sir James Branstoke had been studying the unknown man, puzzling his identity, when he heard the sneeze behind him. He assumed it was one of the servants. He turned at the sound, amused for it was curiously more like a mouse's squeak than the muffled, dainty little sneeze it was.

"Mrs. Waddley!" Surprise at discovering his quarry so near at hand quickly gave way to concern and suspicion.

In a few strides he was by her side, urging her into one of the Chippendale chairs lining the linen-fold paneling of the gallery.

"I did not hear you approach. A thousand apologies, madame. If I'd heard you, I would not have been so rude as to keep my back to you."

"No, please, it is nothing," protested Cecilia. Her hands fluttered, echoing her words. "Really. It is equally rude to sneak up on someone. Such was never my intention, I assure you, Sir Branstoke. But I was certain—I—I mean I thought you would be with the riding party."

"That had been my ambition, however, on further reflection I realized I had no taste for spending a chilly morning jockeying for a position near the object of every male member's gallantry. I and my horse would stand in constant danger of being nipped, kicked, or left with dust swirling up our noses. No, no, a most disheartening proposition," he congenially explained, sitting down in a chair near her.

Cecilia relaxed and laughed. "Is that a suitor's expectations around Miss Cresswell?"

"Oh, decidedly, Mrs. Waddley. It is all part of the game. However, since I am not—how shall I state this?—not an ardent suitor, the entire proposition struck me as entirely flat. A sad waste of energy."

"Or perhaps shrewd politics," she offered archly.

He raised a brow, then a smile transformed his features. "You are referring, are you not, to the possibility that I may claim Miss Cresswell's attention later in the day as recompense for my lack now?"

Cecilia pursed her lips to repress a smile though her royal blue eyes twinkled with humor. "It strikes me that is a viable option."

"One does not win battles by charging willy-nilly into the fray."

He was delighted at her bantering humor. Perhaps at last she was becoming comfortable around him. Or was she striving to prevent unwanted questions, such as why was she in the room that led, he knew, only to gentlemen's quarters? That door had been shut when he entered the gallery. It was now cracked open.

"I understand bets are being placed in White's as to Miss Cresswell's success," Cecilia was saying.

He smiled at her, leaning back in his chair, crossing one leg over the other, his hands clasped about his knee. "It never ceases to amaze me how history repeats itself and lessons are never learned. Those who have learned shall reap the rewards, the others shall visit the gull gropers. However, *I* have learned it is not politic to place bets where a woman is concerned."

"Oh! And how am I to take this? Do you mean to suggest women are fickle?"

"No—though that may be an aspect for some—it is that they take it amiss," he said, shaking his head. "They consider it an affront to their virtue. A very apropos summation, I will admit." He looked at her pointedly, his sleepy-eyed gaze steady. "In a group, a man's viler instincts thrive."

"Ah—that I have had occasion to witness."

Branstoke's brow rose. "You surprise me, Mrs. Waddley—unless you are referring to Nutley's behavior at the opera. That was alcohol speaking, not the result of the herding tendency of men."

"No, I know the difference. I am not, sir, a woman that men recognize as existing. I blend into the furnishings. Therefore, sometimes comments are made in my hearing which should not be," she admitted roguishly.

Sir Branstoke laughed. "Mrs. Waddley, you amaze me. I find that inconceivable." Privately he considered that more her design than the actuality.

"Fudge, Sir James. You know as well as I that a woman with a propensity for illness is not well received. I am the butt of jokes. I know it. I assure you, I do not repine. I cannot change what is, I can only strive to do the best with my limited capacity."

He smiled slightly, noting the casual use of his name, but refrained from commenting. "Mrs. Waddley, I am not such a gudgeon as to swallow that. *I* know your health is not an issue with you. I would that you would allow me that simple knowledge, too."

Her expression stilled until a haunted look invaded her blue eyes, darkening them to purple. "I'm afraid I do not understand your meaning." She uneasily patted a stray lock of hair back into place, her eyes shifting under his regard. "I'm sorry if I disturbed your ruminations. Please excuse me. I have just recalled I have yet to plant my slips." Cecilia rose from the chair, her handkerchief falling to the floor unnoticed.

Sir Branstoke raised an eyebrow and watched her retreat down the gallery, scurrying like a frightened rabbit; he smiled.

Sunlight was high in the windows, poised before its descent into long shadows as a lone figure walked the gallery. He spied a scrap of white beside a chair near the door to the blue withdrawing room. Curious, he picked it up. His long fingers traced the monogram embroidered in one corner. A dark frown momentarily twisted his countenance into a mere semblance of its social norm. He looked at the closed door to the withdrawing room, a contemplative expression on his face. Pocketing the little square of linen and lace, he opened the door and went quietly inside.

"Jessamine! Jessamine! Oh, there you are. What are you doing kneeling on the floor? Get up before you soil that dress!"

"Cecilia, come help me. I've lost my littlest pair of scissors somewhere around here, I think. Leastways, I was seated in that chair the last time I used them."

"When was that?" Cecilia asked, obediently falling to her knees to look under chairs and tables.

"This morning after breakfast. I was doing a silhouette of Miss Cresswell in her riding regalia. I swear that woman would have me do one of her for every outfit she owns! She acts like I'm her personal silhouettist."

"If you feel that way, why don't you just say no?" Cecilia said over her shoulder as she crawled awkwardly in her long skirts. Disgusted, she rolled back on her heels, gathering her skirts in her hands.

"I would if there wasn't someone always around to say what a lovely picture she would make and won't I please cut it. La, it's enough to make me wish Princess Elizabeth had never introduced me to silhouette cutting."

Cecilia laughed. "Don't try to gammon me, Jessamine. You have a natural talent for the art along with a memory that allows you to finish a picture even if your subjects move. You're in great demand at functions just for your little clippings. Your talent will see you invited to all manner of social events even when you're old and gray."

"What a dismal thought," Jessamine said, casting her niece a sour glance.

"But true. Ah—I think I see them, over there under that couch."

"How could they get way over there? I wasn't over there."

"Perhaps someone kicked them by accident." Cecilia bent down to retrieve them. "I don't know why your husband hasn't figured out that you could be a great asset to him on his diplomatic missions," she went on as she handed them to her aunt.

"Thank you. I will admit I've often thought so myself, and truthfully, it has crossed Joseph's mind, but we wish to wait until Franklin is of age. Meriton has no living family on his side, and I certainly would not care to leave my son to father's less-than-tender mercies while I'm out of the country."

"True. But what about to my tender mercies? I realize it was not fitting while Mr. Waddley was alive to have anything to do with me owing to his class, but now it would be all right, wouldn't it?"

"Oh, Cecilia, how could we have all treated you so cruelly?" Anguish throbbed in Lady Meriton's voice.

Cecilia laughed and patted her aunt's hand. "Nonsense, Jessamine. It is the natural order of things in society. I do not repine or bear grudges—except toward those responsible for Mr. Waddley's death."

"Have you discovered anything useful, dear?"

"No, and I'll admit the more I talk to Randolph's friends the more I feel that either they're all culpable and capable, or none are! I will say, however, none of them are quite as coarse as my own brother. I had not realized how vulgar he'd become. It quite embarrasses me to call him brother. *Him* I can understand being involved in any sort of slimy doings."

"What are you going to do now?"

"I don't know. My best recourse will be to continue the acquaintance of Randolph and his friends, though I belive after what happened this morning my hopes of continually being talked around as if I don't exist have been quite dashed."

"Why, what happened?"

"Randolph made some vulgar comments about me in my hearing for which he was snubbed quite brutally by Lady Bramcroft. His friends did not bear him sympathy, either. Odds are, however, that now he will be very cognizant of my presence."

"Oh dear. But he shall recover, for Lady Bramcroft—though a tartar—is not a scion of the ton. She and Lord Bramcroft live fairly retired. Moreover, I'm surprised they came to Oastley Hall."

A knock on the parlor door interrupted them. "Excuse me, ma'am," the footman said, addressing Cecilia.

"Yes Stephen?"

"The duchess is asking for you. She's in the Chinese room, ma'am."

"Thank you, Stephen, I'll go to her at once." The footman bowed and left. "And you, Jessamine, why don't you lay down before dinner? You look quite done in. You know you'll need your energies this evening in order to be able to do Miss Cresswell's latest ensemble," she teased.

"Bah, don't remind me," grumbled Jessamine good-naturedly. "But I'll own that is a good idea. I'll do that before mother gets the notion she needs my services as well."

"I say, Haukstrom, hadn't realized until we came here what a devilishly fine filly your little sister is when tricked out properly," declared Lord Havelock later that day as he watched Haukstrom rack up the balls for billiards.

Randolph straightened and cast Lord Havelock a long look. "Cecilia? Well enough, I suppose, but e'gad, who'd want to be legshackled to a walking apothecary?"

Sir James Branstoke, seated in a nearby chair reading the newspaper, raised his head to listen.

"Don't seem too afflicted to me," said the Honorable Mr. Rippy, chalking his cue stick.

Randolph snorted. "I've done the pretty by her the past few months—escorted her to some dashed dull affairs, too; just as you suggested, Harry, to raise my esteem in society. Which it has, I'll own. But let me tell you, this is one of her good spells. No, no gentleman. Only consider who she's been married to!"

"Ecod Randolph, don't be such a snob. It isn't as if she smells of the shop, not being brought up that way and all," protested Sir Harry. *"If you were men, as men you are in show, You would not use a gentle lady so."*

"It is my understanding that it was a marriage you and your father arranged to see you through some, shall we say, rough seas?" offered Branstoke raising from his seat and sauntering toward the group. What an ill-assorted group, too. He wondered what drew them all together. Deep play?

"Well, what of it? That's all in the past. I'm Nye's heir now, though I don't get the titles, dashed unfair that is. And Waddley's dead."

"Precisely," Branstoke said blandly. "So I ask, why the prejudice against your own sister?"

"I ain't prejudice against Cecilia. At least not directly. I don't like how that Waddley fellow changed her. Nor all the strings he placed on the ready when I was not so plump in the pocket." He picked up his mug of ale from the sideboard.

"Changed her?"

Randolph grunted and wiped his mouth with the back of his hand. "Before she married him, she always was a quiet, biddable little thing. Looked at you with big blue eyes, all innocent-like."

"Perhaps she just grew up," suggested Branstoke.

"That wouldn't make her harp about her confounded health, or try to cut a wheedle when you talk to her about Waddley or of that confounded business of his."

"But as you said, that Waddley fellow's dead. *Nothing in his life became him like the leaving it . . .* Now it's your sister as has all his money. Be a good chap," cajoled Sir Harry, buffeting him on the arm. "Consider your friends. We don't have any rich relations giving us health allowances. Let us have a chance at her."

"Eh, what? Yes. Let the best man win and all that!" agreed Mr. Rippy.

Randolph pulled at the tip of his nose. "Does seem a damned shame to let all that money rest in her hands. She'd probably just spend it on one quack physician after another."

"It might answer," murmured Lord Havelock looking at the ceiling, his lips pursed in thought.

"Am I to understand you gentlemen are going to take up the pursuit of Mrs. Waddley?" Branstoke idly asked, pulling out his snuff box and flicking it open with his thumb.

"Yes, just so. Care to place a wager, Branstoke, on the chances of any of us succeeding?" Sir Harry asked, the light of play in his eyes.

Branstoke smiled enigmatically. "No, gentlemen. That bet I will not take. Not because I believe any of you will succeed. More because I know you won't," he said softly. Smiling casually, he made his farewells and quietly left the room.

"Dashed queer fish," muttered Randolph. He turned back to

his friends, "So, Reggie, think you can beat me, eh? Show me the color of your money and we'll just see. . . ."

Never before had Cecilia felt suffocated in a press of people. Seated next to her on the sofa was Sir Elsdon. Standing behind her, breathing down her bare shoulder with wine-soured breath, was the Honorable Mr. Reginald Rippy. Seated in a chair drawn up too close for propriety was Lord Havelock. To close this circle was her brother, blithely and enthusiastically enumerating each gentleman's sterling characteristics. She was ready to scream. What was this, feast or famine? Though she wanted to get to know each gentleman better, this was impossible! Undeniably a climate in which Miss Amblethorp would say society manners completely obscured a gentleman's true measure.

None of her normal ruses was working. When she complained of the heat, one of them took her fan and obligingly fanned her. When she swore her heart was pounding in her chest till she was nigh on swooning, they produced vinaigrettes, asafetida drops, and feathers which they offered to burn. In passing, she actually considered staging a fainting spell, but rejected the idea for fear that one of them—or all!—would conceive the plan of carrying her upstairs. The thought of any of them holding her in an intimate manner was repugnant. Why couldn't grandmother have planned dancing for this evening in addition to the ball tomorrow evening?

She perfunctorily accepted a lavender-water drenched handkerchief from Sir Elsdon, absently looking about the room as she held it to her brow. Unfortunately, her need for the lavender water was real, not imaginary. Her head ached. Lady Meriton was not helping matters. Seeing the little group, she proclaimed it a marvelous study and begged they all refrain from moving about while she cut the tableau.

Out of the corner of her eye, Cecilia saw Sir Branstoke in company with Miss Cresswell. There was a peevish set to that beauty's features and her full red lips were turned down in a decided pout. With the defection of Randolph and his cronies, her court was diminished, and she did not like that at all. She glared at Cecilia and whispered nasty little asides to Sir Branstoke; but he did not respond with the shared humor she hoped to garner. So she sat, simmering, glowering, and throwing dagger glances Cecilia's way. Cecilia wished her new entourage would return to worshipping at the Cresswell altar. From there she could pick them off—like ripe fruit—one at a time for questioning.

Sir Branstoke might have been asleep as he sat there with his tortoise shell eyes gleaming gold highlights from under dark lashes. A wisp of a smile pulled at his finely chiseled lips. Cecilia looked to him, a request for succor fleeting across her pale, expressive face. In response, his smile pulled his lips tighter revealing straight white teeth. He inclined his head slightly in understanding and promptly turned his attention to Miss Cresswell.

Cecilia clenched her teeth, damning herself for the momentary weakness that let her expect rescue from Sir Branstoke. She spied Janine sitting off to the side under one of the more grisly scenes depicted in the Mortlake tapestries collection. As her illnesses were strangely not affecting these gentlemen, she would try another venue: the older woman seeing that the shy young miss is not forgotten. She glanced at her aunt. It appeared Lady Meriton had nearly completed her cutting.

"I am overwhelmed at the kindness you gentlemen have bestowed upon me," she said in a tone heavily laced with treacle. "I'm sure it is quite unfair to the other ladies, especially when one considers how my miserable illnesses have aged me."

The gentlemen were quick to refute her comment, but she airily waved their words aside.

"No, no, not another word or I shall be forced to assume you are making a May-game of me. Or a wager?" she ventured, remembering Sir Branstoke's earlier words about men's viler instincts surfacing in a group.

A purple blush suffused her brother's dissipated countenance. "Dash it all, Cecilia! Here are my friends anxious to do the pretty and be nice to my poor widowed sister, and you display this sniveling suspicion. Ecod! Can't you have the grace to accept a few sincerely proffered compliments?" he grumbled and pouted, though she did note a sheen of sweat on his brow.

Cecilia's eyes sparked, then banked. Closing her eyes briefly, she pulled confusion and uncertainty into her expression. She simpered, her hands fluttering. "Compliments! Oh, my word, I haven't had compliments since I was a giddy young girl. Gentlemen, forgive me please, I had no idea. I mean, it's so unusual, and after this morning—Well, what was I to think?" she said guilelessly, opening her royal blue eyes wide and staring at each of them in turn.

"Mrs. Waddley, you are too intelligent for us," said Lord Havelock smoothly, taking her small hand between his long slender fingers. "But you are incorrect as to its genesis. The unfortunate occurrence this morning led us to see *beyond* what we may have casually observed." His tone was florid and designed to wheedle a woman into good humor. Cecilia knew that, but couldn't help responding positively to this overture. She wondered to what extent her reaction was caused by Miss Amblethorp's revelations.

"Yes," said the Honorable Mr. Rippy, his head bobbing nearly as sharply as his Adam's apple. "Stands to reason. Always knew Randolph was a gudgeon."

"That's doing it too brown. You're just knocked acock because I beat you at billiards!" declared Randolph.

"Easy, lads," said Sir Elsdon, laughing. "We've all been a pack of blind sapskulls, Mrs. Waddley. Make no mistake about that. We're just trying to amend matters in our clumsy fashion."

"Thank you, Sir Elsdon, your truthfulness does you honor," said Cecilia.

"Honor, bah! I'd like to soak your head," grumbled Randolph.

"At least, Randolph, I may depend upon the regularity of your opinion, of little value though I may deem it," retorted Cecilia, affecting an exaggerated pout.

"Ho, she's got you there, Randy!" crowed Mr. Rippy, slapping him heartily on the back.

"I realize," she continued coolly, watching Mr. Rippy's reaction out of the corner of her eye, "it can't be helped—considering the company you keep."

"Huzzah! She has you, too, Reggie!" said Sir Elsdon, thumping his friend in turn. "*A crew of patches, rude mechanicals.* That's how we appear, no doubt."

Randolph grumbled under his breath but refrained from further comment.

During the momentary discomfort suffered by the group, Cecilia made her excuses and left to join Miss Amblethorp.

"I depend upon you, Miss Amblethorp, to be my salvation," she said *sotto voce* as she slid into a chair next to the young woman.

"Well, you may have it only if you will refrain from addressing me as Miss Amblethorp. I am fagged to death of Miss Amblethorp," returned her friend with no little asperity.

Cecilia grinned and relaxed. "I knew I could depend upon you to relieve the stale air. I tell you *truthfully,* my head aches, yet not for a moment would that group grant me reprieve! I really don't know what has occasioned their solicitude. Nothing, I assure you, that I have done! It is most disquieting."

"It is you who are most disquieting," returned Janine sharply. Then she blushed furiously at her rudeness and looked down to where her hands were grasping and twisting her fan tightly. The delicate sticks snapped under the pressure. "Oh-h-h, no," moaned Janine dismally, loosening her grip on the maltreated fan to survey the damage. "Your behavior is so changeable—I don't understand it."

There was a moment of silence between the two women. Cecilia covered Janine's shaking hand with her own as the young woman unconsciously traced the break in the sticks.

"All I can say," Cecilia began slowly, her eyes intent on Janine's flushed face, "is that there are reasons for my behavior, no matter how good or bad they are. All I can ask is that you trust me."

Trust me. The phrase echoed in her head, mocking her. Trust was something she did not grant easily. When one granted trust, one placed an emotional burden on the other person. Those burdens were too heavy. Such burdens should be personal, not something to be willy-nilly handed over to another. Who was she to ask another to share the weight of her emotional burdens? Her fears and problems? She stared at the carved plaster and wood ceiling a moment and sighed heavily, for no answer would come.

"I think I should retire. I cannot seem to think clearly any longer." She absently patted Janine's hand and stood up slowly, moving like a person who'd long ago run his race. She bid the young woman good-night, then went to her aunt and grandmother, exchanging similar words. Smiling charmingly, vacantly, she wished the rest of the company good evening and headed for the door.

Sir James Branstoke was before her. He lounged against the door frame, absently studying the filigree snuffbox he held in one hand. "Still claiming to blend with the furnishings?" he murmured when she got to the door.

She turned her head to consider him, her lips pursed. There was laughter glinting out from under those heavy eyelids. She'd wager he knew the instigator for her new entourage. She would not be surprised to discover he had a hand in suggesting it in some macabre fashion. "What has happened?" she demanded bluntly.

His eyebrows rose and he looked at her with social credulity. "My dear Mrs. Waddley, isn't it obvious?"

"Do you take me for a flat, sir?"

His thin lips tightened in a ghost of a smile. It sent tingling rivulets down her back.

"Never that, Mrs. Waddley. Many other things, perhaps, such as a beautiful, willful woman—but never a flat."

She opened her mouth, then shut it, damming ill-considered words. She scowled at him, her temples throbbing. With a curt good-night and a swish of her skirts, she left the room.

Chapter Eight

"I THINK we may join our guests now," said the Duchess of Houghton the next evening on hearing ten chimes from the ornate Louis XIV clock. "Any stragglers after this hour don't deserve to be received properly."

"Bar the door, I say," grumbled the duke. He stretched and put a hand against the small of his back and groaned. Muttering oaths under his breath, he straightened and offered his wife and Cecilia an arm to lead them into the Great Hall. "I suppose you'll want to dance," the duke groused to his wife.

"Of course, my dear, and so will Cecilia."

The duke scowled sourly. Cecilia was quick to deny her grandmother's words.

"Nonsense, dear. This ball is as much for you as for our enjoyment. More so, actually. You never had the opportunity of a London season before you married. That has always been a great disappointment to me. Now, at least, we can see that you take your rightful place in the *ton,*" said the duchess, smiling and nodding regally to people they passed. "Houghton will be delighted to dance with you, won't you, dear?"

"Your grandmother has the right of it. We're agreed to seeing you well established again."

"But not among Randolph's sort!"

The duchess's words were sharp and edged with anger, though outwardly she continued smiling. Cecilia wondered how she did it. But that was just one of many things that dogged her mind so the thought was fleeting. *There is no peace, saith the Lord, unto the wicked,* she thought ruefully.

Last evening she stayed awake long into the night, staring into blackness. She had finally achieved her desire for friendship among Randolph's cronies, and what did she do? Ran like a startled rabbit. Oh, she argued long and hard with herself about the unnaturalness of their attentions; but truthfully, sincere or false should have made no matter if she was intent upon, and genuinely believed in, her goal.

Self-doubts and fears came crowding in upon her. What was she trying to accomplish? Solve a murder? Find a way to start living after the lethargy she fell into following Mr. Waddley's death? Or—perhaps just find a way to start living her own life. It was true Mr. Waddley had been a kind husband, a good man, and that he always insisted on the finest in everything for her. She was doing this honorable man's memory a great disservice to suggest he'd been anything less than an ideal husband. For all that, she felt he regarded her as more of a precious object to be kept locked in a glass case than a flesh-and-blood woman. The few times she tried to tell him how she felt he only laughed and chucked her under her chin. He declared that's exactly what she was, his most valuable possession.

Dear man, he meant well, he just never understood. Now the glass case was open. Unfortunately the doll that had been placed so long inside no longer knew what she wanted. If she did move to the country to live a retiring life, might she not be trading one glass case for another?

Perhaps that was why Branstoke so easily upset her. He sensed her dichotomy of commitment. He knew her uncertainties and played upon them.

But that didn't explain why she reacted strongly to him. Or why last evening she instinctively looked to him for help. She found him often in her thoughts. Memories of what he said or did, or sometimes just a look, or a smile would leap into her mind pushing everything else aside. It didn't make sense! She could not be attracted to him. She had to stay out of his presence. She couldn't think straight with him around. Worse, sometimes she didn't know if she wanted to.

There he was, standing just outside the circle of gentlemen surrounding Miss Cresswell. The crooked smile on his lips attested to his knowledge that he could walk into the circle and wrest Miss Cresswell's attention from her court at any time he chose. Cecilia hated and envied that knowledge.

His head turned, and she found herself trapped, drugged, by his somnambulant gaze. His eyebrows rose and he cocked his head in wry salute before he let her gaze free though he continued to observe her.

Cecilia hurriedly turned her head away and looked about the Great Hall. The room was packed with a glittering array of the cream of London society. The ball might as well have occurred in London for half of London was present. All day long carriages arrived at Oastley Hall discharging guests who would stay over the night for the ball. Many current guests were required to change rooms or double with another to make more rooms available. Cecilia heard the local inns were full and that anyone with a home within carriage distance found themselves visited by friends attending the ball.

She wondered how Miss Amblethorp was faring. She looked about the room for Janine, hoping to see her dancing. She should have known better. She was seated near the dowagers. Cecilia made her way through the press of people to her side.

"Come, Janine, take a turn about the room with me," she invited.

"It will serve no purpose," Janine said, rising from her chair.

Cecilia did not pretend to misunderstand her. "Oh, fustian. You don't know that. And consider it a way to assuage Lady Amblethorp."

Janine smiled reluctantly.

"Excellent! Now, what shall we discuss? Shall we be two cats and discuss those we do not like until their reputations are in shreds, or shall we—" She broke off, staring across the room.

Randolph Haukstrom, talking to someone near the carved wood screen at the end of the hall, angrily tugged a ring off his little finger and dropped it in his pocket. Taking the stairs up to the minstrels' gallery two at a time, he ducked out the narrow door at the top. It led, Cecilia knew, to the long gallery.

Quickly she followed him, weaving through the crowd like a willow wisp, unheeding of Janine's gasp. Branstoke could scarcely keep track of Cecilia as she made her way across the room. He had to pin his sights on the white-blond hair massed high on her head. He followed her, moving with fluid, unhurried grace.

"Do not be offended, Miss Amblethorp. It's just a bad habit," he said as he passed that young woman. He gave her hand a squeeze, but his eyes never left the top of Cecilia's head.

Holding her ivory net and silk skirts high, Cecilia scurried up the stairs after her brother. By the minstrels' door that led to the gallery, she paused, carefully opening it. The gallery was deserted. She quietly entered, straining to listen for any sounds. Long dark shadows cloaked the end of the gallery, and patches of blackness shadowed areas between glittering candelabra. She crept down the long carpeted expanse of gallery. Hearing a faint murmur of voices coming from the direction of the blue withdrawing room, she tiptoed to the door.

"It was an oversight!"

It was Randolph, but the answering voice was too indistinct for her to hear. When Randolph spoke again, his voice was softer and Cecilia couldn't make out his words distinctly. She edged closer to the door. Her toe caught the leg of one of the Chippendale chairs, knocking it gently against the paneling. It made a small, but distinct *click.* Panicked at the slight sound, she jumped away, colliding violently with a chair at the other side of the door. It clattered loudly against the wall.

"Hush, you fool! Someone's out there!"

Frantic, she backed from the door. Suddenly strong hands grasped her shoulders, propelling her ungently around, and a hard, masculine mouth came down on hers.

Branstoke!

Shock robbed her of strength. His sensuous kiss swirled her senses, prolonging her lassitude. She savored the heat that rose up within her, the musky masculine scent of the man, and the searing pressure of his lips on hers. Her arms drifted to his shoulders to entwine his neck.

"E'gad, Cecilia!"

Cecilia jumped, breaking the kiss. She spun away from Branstoke, her chest heaving. Her lips tingled and a delicate flush gave way to a crimson tide.

"Damn it, what the hell are you doing?" demanded Randolph, his fists planted on his hips and his face taking on a dangerously choleric hue.

"I would have thought that rather obvious," drawled Sir Branstoke, casually straightening his coat. "And if you will kindly turn around and go back into that room, I will continue in that most pleasurable occupation which you so rudely interrupted."

"The hell, you say! I've a mind to call you out, Branstoke."

"Oh, stop the theatrics, Randolph," snapped Cecilia, her arms crossed over her breasts, her delicate pointed chin leading. Her breathing was fast and her eyes glittered with an unnatural feverish intensity. She kept her eyes fixed on her brother, not daring to look in Sir Branstoke's direction. What had she been thinking? She returned his kiss! No, more than returned it. She welcomed it and drank from his lips like her thirst would never end!

She was so embarrassed. How could she speak, let alone look at Sir Branstoke again? His kiss had been a brilliant ruse to save her from a potentially more embarrassing, and perhaps even dangerous situation. Like some giddy, foolish schoolgirl she gave herself up to his kiss. What must he think of her? Her cheeks flamed anew at the thought.

"Dash it all, Cecilia," protested Randolph, shifting from one foot to the other, "you've no more feathers than a downy chick. Branstoke's got a reputation, y'know."

"If he has, I'd wager it's a dashed sight better than yours!"

Randolph went rigid and flushed, his lips protruding in an ugly pout. "I'm still your brother and I've an eye to your reputation!"

"If you were so concerned about my reputation, you would not have married me off to Mr. Waddley! Your concerns consisted of yourself and your pocketbook. Do not preach filial affection to me, dear brother, for it won't wash." Cecilia's slight frame trembled with years of suppressed anger. Her voice shook in a strident key, but she kept herself in hand, and it did not rise in volume.

"You ungrateful wretch. I saved your life!" her brother stormed.

Cecilia gasped. "What effrontery! But I know it to be merely another of your silly acts. I am five and twenty, Randolph, not some shy sixteen-year-old you can manipulate by declaring pauperism a fate worse than death. Legally I am my own woman with a fortune to command. I do not need you or anyone else in my life. There has been too much management of me for too many years and I'm tired of it. I won't have it, do you hear me?"

Standing a step behind her, Branstoke applauded. His instincts regarding the little widow were proving delightfully accurate.

Cecilia whirled around, aghast. She'd nearly forgotten his presence. Now he was gazing at her and smiling that enigmatic smile that never failed to send shivers through her. She felt warmth rise in her cheeks. Flustered, she turned to glare at her brother again. "Oh, leave it be, Randolph. I am getting another of my plaguey headaches," she said petulantly. She massaged a temple and irritably wondered how she could have been so lost to her surroundings and so caught up in her mystery that she failed to hear Branstoke approach. She knew she should be thankful to him, but remnants of the heat that coursed through her from his kiss reminded her of her own forward behavior.

"A glass of Madeira," suggested Branstoke.

"I beg your pardon?" she said.

"What you need at the moment is a soothing glass of Madeira." He looked at Randolph through the veil of his lashes. "Shall we see you downstairs, Haukstrom?"

"What? Oh, yes, in a bit."

"Until then," Branstoke said blandly. He offered Cecilia his arm.

She hesitated a moment, then gratefully accepted it. They turned to walk down the gallery, leaving Randolph to stare angrily after them.

"That headache of yours," Branstoke said conversationally as he held another door open at the end of the gallery. It led to the Great Chamber which was mercifully empty at the moment. "It is probably due to an irritation of nerves. I believe you did one time say you were particularly susceptible to that disorder? Rather that resorting to some medicinal draught prescribed for you by Dr. Thornbridge—mind, I am not impinging on the man's learned judgment—my suggested remedy is a little Madeira and a little dancing. I have a theory," he explained stolidly, "that such disorders are better cured by relaxation and frivolity. I would like the opportunity to test my hypothesis."

"Really, Sir Branstoke," laughingly protested Cecilia.

He stopped and turned her to face him. "The other day you addressed me as Sir James," he gently reminded her.

She stopped, her smile dimming, and a wariness haunted her eyes. "I did?" The words came out on a mere breath. The hammering of her heart was louder in her own ears. She looked up at him, trying to read the meaning of his words in his face, and half afraid to try.

Sir James looked at her calmly, a slight, encouraging smile on his lips. There was no sensual need or banked flames burning in his eyes. "I am no Borgia, my dear. You are troubled, I know, though I cannot begin to imagine what could bedevil your gentle soul. But as I think I've told you before, I am willing—nay, wanting to help you battle your dragons."

His quiet words brought a sheen of tears to Cecilia's eyes and an unaccountable lump to her throat. "I—I thank you for your concern, but it is best you stand away from me, sir, and do not get involved."

He seized on her words. "Then I am correct, there is something bothering you."

She sighed and looked about her, anywhere but at him. She stared for a moment at a painted cherub on the ceiling. "Yes," she admitted, and felt a great weight lift from her chest. "But that is all I will say. Please, don't plague me with questions."

"I'll agree, only under the condition you promise to call on me if you need help."

She smiled wanly at him, a flicker of her energies returning. "I promise. Now, I suggest we rejoin the ball. We have both been absent much too long and that is bound to cause talk. What will Miss Cresswell think?" she asked teasingly.

"Hang Miss Cresswell."

Cecilia was in mixed spirits when she returned to the ball. Her mind was so troubled she threw herself into the gaiety, searching for some numbing balm for the riotous emotions she felt.

She laughed and danced willingly, first with Sir Branstoke and then with her grandfather. After them, she whirled across the floor with every male who could claim a dance. So full was her dance card, not all could. She was gay with a feverish intensity that had some matrons looking at her askance. Dire mutterings behind gloved hands said she'd no doubt be confined to her bed on the morrow. Even Jessamine, who was well acquainted with her stratagems, felt it behooved her to drop a word in her ear.

"Fudge. My reputation is quite ruined anyway," Cecilia said breezily.

"What are you talking about?"

"Randolph caught Branstoke and me together in the Long Gallery and came up with the most amazing conclusions," she said, carefully omitting the substance of the encounter.

Lady Meriton dismissed her fears. "Randolph judges everyone by his own lamentable standard."

"True, but I should not have been alone with a gentlemen. In defense I shall say it was not deliberate."

"There is no need to tell me that! I well know your opinion of Sir Branstoke. Although when I consider it, it would do well for Randolph to spread his scandalous story, whatever it may be. You cannot be taken amiss for being in Branstoke's company as you could among any of those ramshackle court cards Randolph calls friends. It will actually do you credit."

"Credit?" asked Cecilia, remembering how she responded with searing intensity to his kiss. She pinked at the memory.

"Yes, for he is considered a gentleman of exquisite taste and manners." She cocked her head to study her niece. "You know, my dear, I do like the new way Sarah has of doing your hair. It will cut out beautifully. Will you sit for me now?"

"Jessamine, you must have hundreds of pictures done of me."

"Yes, but none in quite this style. Come, I've my own corner arranged with proper light and everything." She hooked Cecilia's arm in hers and guided her toward the corner she'd been using. "Besides, I think you need a respite. Your color is a trifle higher than I like."

"At least that won't appear in your picture."

Lady Meriton chuckled. "Most unfortunate. Here, now sit down and turn your head to the right. Lift it up a bit . . . perfect." She sat down in a nearby Hepplewhite chair and pulled her portable desk onto her lap. "I've noticed Randolph's friends have been as attentive this evening as they were last night. What have you done to encourage those connections?"

"Nothing! I swear, I did nothing, other than perhaps hope, pray, and scheme to claim their attention. Suddenly last night they were huddled around me like bees around honey. My suspicion is that Randolph has said something to remind them of my wealth, and they, being unscrupulous as to the source of my funds, have decided I am worth pursuing."

Lady Meriton clucked her tongue and paused in cutting to push her glasses up on her nose. Cecilia stared out over the throng of guests. She was surprised, yet gratified to see Sir James Branstoke dancing with Miss Janine Amblethorp. But she did not examine her gratification too closely for she didn't know if she was glad he was dancing with Janine or glad he wasn't dancing with Miss Cresswell.

She pursed her lips. What business was it of hers if he danced with Miss Cresswell or not? She pulled her eyes away from where the couple promenaded down the line.

"Cecilia, I wish you would relax your mouth. If I cut your profile in that manner you'd look like a fish."

Cecilia dutifully did as requested then wrinkled her nose when she saw one of Randolph's coterie headed determinedly in her direction.

"Cecilia, please. I am attempting a close profile which is much more demanding than a group portrait. You must refrain from contorting your features."

"I'm sorry, Jessamine. Please, take as long as you like. I'm in no hurry to quit your side."

Lady Meriton looked up from her paper, blinking owlishly. "What—?"

"Um—um, excuse me, Mrs. Waddley, ma'am?" The Honorable Reginald Rippy eased down next to her on the Egyptian-style fainting couch complete with crocodile feet.

"Not so close, please, Mr. Rippy, my aunt is engaged in cutting my silhouette."

"Oh! Right—sorry," he said, edging to a far corner.

"Now, how may I serve you, Mr. Rippy," Cecilia asked blandly.

"Serve me? Oh, dear me, no, ma'am," he assured her, mopping his brow with a large white handkerchief. "It is just—well, you see, as we'll all be returning to London tomorrow, I was wondering—that is, I hoped, that you would allow me—" he paused, mopping his brow again and running a finger under his tight stock. "What I mean, ma'am, is I hope you'll allow me to call on you in London," he finished rapidly.

"Certainly, Mr. Rippy. I believe that would be quite pleasant." She turned to her aunt. "Have you finished, Jessamine?"

"Yes, dear. I believe I am. Just allow me a moment to look it over carefully one last time. . . ."

"Thank you for your kind consideration, Mr. Rippy. I shall look forward to receiving you in London," Cecilia said, summarily dismissing him. He stuttered and stumbled a moment more, then made his leg and retired to the card room.

"You see, I told you being in Branstoke's company would stand you in good stead," said Lady Meriton.

Cecilia made a face, then groaned. "Now it is Lord Havelock coming this way. I fear, Jessamine, I may have unleashed a demon." *Or perhaps more aptly, a dragon,* she thought, remembering Sir Branstoke's willingness to battle the beasts.

Wearily she curved her lips in a pleasant smile and contrived to speak cordially to Lord Havelock, and in his turn, Sir Elsdon. All three gentlemen solicited permission to call on her, and to all three she granted permission. Now, perhaps, she could learn something to good purpose. She should have been pleased that events were falling so naturally into place.

Why then did a heaviness fill her chest? It couldn't have anything to do with Branstoke waltzing with Miss Cresswell—*could it?*

𝒞ℊ Chapter Nine

LIKE A SHIP in heavy seas, Cecilia's emotions rose and fell with seemingly unending repetition for the remainder of the ball and on into the next day with her return to London. And like that ship on a storm-tossed sea, all she could do was helplessly ride the waves of emotions as they swept through her.

There was one niggling thought that kept her anchored in the worst of the buffeting. It was the image of Randolph yanking a ring off his right hand and shoving it in his pocket. Why was that ring important? She was confident that's what Randolph was referring to when he told whomever was in the room with him that it was an oversight. But of what import could a ring be?

She wondered if it was the unfamiliar signet ring she saw in his room. If it was important, surely he would not have left it out in plain sight! Then again, he hardly would have expected anyone to go sneaking about in his room. And carelessness on Randolph's part was typical of him. It was also the reason she'd decided to look in his room.

She wanted to see that signet ring again. She thought she might recognize it if she saw it, though she could not form a clear image in her mind of the device carved on its flat surface.

She needed to see Mr. Thornbridge. If the ring was important, maybe he'd come across some mention of it in his investigation of Randolph's affairs. She sent a message ahead from Oastley advising of her return that day and requesting him to visit in the afternoon. A hurriedly scrawled note greeted her return, one that sent uneasy ripples through her being. She read it again, for the fifth time:

Mrs. Waddley,
   I beg you will hold me excused until tomorrow. I think I may have answers, though my thoughts are so heinous, I pray I am wrong.
   Tonight I go to discover the truth. I daren't say more.

My thoughts are unworthy.

David Thornbridge

It too closely echoed the last entry in Mr. Waddley's journal, the one he made the day he died. Her hand closed convulsively about the letter, crumbling it in her hand. She should never have asked Mr. Thornbridge for help. Now an unreasoning fear built within her as thoughts and fancies mushroomed in her head. She paced Lady Meriton's front parlor, consumed by a restless energy that would not let her be still. Something was about to happen. She knew it, but could not say what or how she knew. The feeling was like waiting for the actors to enter and the play to start. Anticipation shivered through her.

Lady Meriton was occupied with the cook and the ordering of staples. There was no help in that quarter for conversation and speculation that might ease her mind. Her pale brow furrowed and her eyes narrowed in thought. Outside the bright morning sun was giving way to a slate sky, and a rising wind clicked together branches covered with new, pale green leaves.

When the knocker fell twice, deliberately and heavily against the white, carved oak front door, Cecilia stilled. She stared at the closed double doors to the parlour until they opened slightly to admit Loudon.

"Excuse me, ma'am, but there's a gentleman below who would like to see you on a business matter."

A pale eyebrow rose. "Oh? Do I know him?"

"I would venture to say no, ma'am. Here is his card."

Hiram Peters, Solicitor, it read, with an address off of Fleet Street.

"A business matter, he said?"

"Yes, ma'am."

Cecilia pursed her lips a moment then nodded. "All right. Show him up."

"Shall I inform Lady Meriton?"

Cecilia laughed. "Loudon, I am not a young girl in need of a chaperone. No, do not bother her. I will see my guest alone."

After he bowed and left, Cecilia smoothed out the crumbled note then refolded it and tucked it into her bodice. She positioned herself on her aunt's rose-colored sofa in a semi-recumbent position, tossing a woolen shawl across her feet to complete the image. She sprinkled lavender water on her handkerchief from a vial resting on a nearby table. She lightly held it to her forehead, thankful this time she would not reek of the scent.

She watched the door, her alert eyes shielded by the hand raised to her brow.

Mr. Hiram Peters brushed Loudon aside and walked confidently into the parlor. He was a thin, scraggly-looking man attired in rusty black. His hair was a mop of lank gray still laced with strands of a darker, indeterminate hue. His eyebrows were grizzled and stood out, prominent above deep-set, black eyes. He walked with a self-confident strut with his shoulders so far back it was a wonder he didn't fall backward.

"Mrs. Waddley, so kind of you to see me on short notice. I do apologize, but you will understand when I explain *all,*" he said lugubriously, his eyebrows wriggling.

He extended his hand to take one of hers in his, but she pretended not to see it. Truthfully, she saw it only too well, and the black dirt under his nails did not speak well of the gentleman. His hand fell to his side with a small arrow of uncertainty piercing his confident air. Cecilia saw it and was pleased. She allowed her hand clutching the handkerchief to fall limply to the sofa. With the other she feebly waved him into a straight-backed chair.

"Loudon tells me you are here on a business matter, Mr. Peters," she said faintly.

"Yes, Mrs. Waddley, and my errand is such that it will bring you joy."

"Then please, proceed, Mr. Peters. I'll own I am so fatigued and threatened with incipient illness that I stand in great need of joy. You find me a most attentive audience," she said feebly. An image of Branstoke's amused reaction to her mien tickled her mind, but she brushed it aside.

"I am empowered to offer you a very generous contract for the purchase of all the London operations and holdings of Waddley Spice and Tea."

Cecilia's body went rigid. "I see. Who wants to buy the company?" she asked in a carefully neutral tone, though warning bells clanged and clamored in her mind.

"That I am not at liberty to say. And it is not the entire company my client wishes to purchase, only the London portion."

She dabbed her handkerchief to her head, stalling. "I—I

hardly know what to say! No, that's not true. I believe I know what Mr. Waddley's reaction would be to your proposition," she said.

"Yes?" Peters said with faint stirrings of unease. This interview was not proceeding with the dispatch he'd anticipated. She was not supposed to be a woman with the wherewithal to ask questions.

Her soft voice grew firmer, unsheathing the steel it hid. "You come to me, a stranger and agent for another, proposing to buy my late husband's company, yet you will not divulge the purchaser's identity. No, I am sorry, Mr. Peters. My late husband would not do business in that manner, and neither will I."

"Now see here, Mrs. Waddley. At least listen to the terms I am empowered to make. They are very generous. Nay! Too generous! But such are my instructions."

"I'm sorry, Mr. Peters, but there is no reason to prolong this conversation," she said distractedly. She knew she had to get rid of this pompous windbag before she could think clearly.

"Mrs. Waddley, you are acting in a highly irrational manner," declared Mr. Peters angrily. His tone was like that reserved for erring underlings and social inferiors.

Cecilia gasped. "If I am, you are most impertinent to say so. This interview is at an end." She reached toward the bell pull to summon Loudon.

Mr. Peters caught her hand in a cruel grip before she touched the rope. "Mrs. Waddley, my client is used to getting what he desires, and if he desires Waddley Spice and Tea, then he will get it, one way or another. At least this way he is offering you a profit. His subsequent methods may not prove as genteel," he threatened.

Cecilia glared at him and methodically pulled her hand free while her eyes, turned dark as lapis, held his in challenge. Her hand claimed the bell pull and gave it an imperious tug. "Get out!" she whispered. The venom that dripped from her soft tones accented her words like no loud, screaming order could.

A flicker of uncertainty crossed Mr. Peters' face and he backed away awkwardly. When the door opened to admit Loudon, he seemed to draw himself together.

"You'll regret this, Mrs. Waddley."

"Show Mr. Peters the door, Loudon. He will not be returning," she said meaningfully.

Mr. Peters scowled and hesitated, then flung himself toward the open door, a muttered oath on his lips, and strode out of Cecilia's sight.

A long shuddering breath passed her lips. She swung her legs to the floor and sat on the edge of the sofa, her arms wrapped about her stomach. She rocked slightly, her mind recalling every word of her conversation with Mr. Peters. She was angry—and a little frightened.

Ruthlessly she pushed the latter emotion aside. How dare he threaten her! An anonymous buyer, *bah!* She must be close to discovering something. Why else the offer to purchase the London operation? It was well known that trade through London had decreased in recent years in favor of other ports closer to the manufacturing centers, such as Bristol and Liverpool. Truthfully, Mr. Waddley made most of his money in London as an insurance investor and speculator. Cecilia really didn't know why he even maintained the London operation, though she suspected an emotional attachment on her husband's part to what had been started by his grandfather and grown substantially under his father. She had no particular attachment to the firm, and did hope to one day sell it—in its entirety. But she wouldn't sell it in a havey-cavey manner. Nor would she sell it until she solved the mystery of her husband's death or satisfied herself it was a cause well lost.

She surged to her feet and began pacing the room. The veneer of manners on Mr. Peters was like cheap gilding. What manner of person would hire a vulgar, dirty lout to make his business dealings? She ventured it could be no one interested in pound dealing. Or anyone with a regard for her intellect. And that worm wanted to kiss her hand? Her instincts were right when she ignored the gesture. *Ugh!* The thought of the greasy man with his supercilious air made her shudder. It also sharpened her anger.

"Excuse me, ma'am," ventured Loudon from the doorway.

"Yes, what is it?" snapped Cecilia, continuing to pace.

Loudon flinched. "Sir James Branstoke is below," he said half-apologetically.

"I am in no mood for further visitors, Loudon. Please inform him so," she said, not pausing in her frenetic pacing.

Regret, will I? she thought. She stopped and stared sightlessly out the window, her hands planted firmly on her slim hips. "In a pig's eye!"

"Lady Meriton's man warned you were not in spirits," drawled Sir Branstoke from the doorway.

Cecilia whirled around. "Who let you up here? I gave Loudon orders that I was not seeing anyone!"

He closed the doors behind him. "Yes, your sails are flying, aren't they? Who got your wind up?"

"That is none of your concern. Get out. I don't want to see anyone, particularly you!" she said, still smarting from his defection last evening back to Miss Cresswell's camp and her embarrassment at the shared kiss.

"Tsk, Tsk," he said mildly, advancing farther into the room.

"I am tired of people flagrantly doubting my intelligence."

"Never I."

"And attempting to manipulate me as if I were some feather-brained silly widgeon."

"I can't imagine anyone so rash."

"Imagine, the audacity of someone hiring a—a toad like Mr. Peters to try to buy Waddley's from me!"

"He should have his cork drawn."

"And then daring to—to threaten me when I refused! It is not to be borne."

Sir Branstoke paused in withdrawing his snuffbox from his waistcoat pocket. He looked at Cecilia as she stormed up and down the room, studying her high color and the martial light glittering in her blue eyes. *What the hell has been going on!*

He stuffed the box back into his pocket and strode over to her, grasping her by the shoulders. "Cecilia! What are you talking about? Who threatened you?"

"Peters, of course," she snapped, looking at him as if he were a simpleton. She pulled out of his grasp and continued her peroration. "Claims his anonymous client is being generous." She turned to pace in front of the fireplace.

"Who's client?" he demanded, following her.

"Hiram Peters'. Says all his so-called client wants is the London operation."

"Cecilia! You are speaking disjointedly. Slow down, tell me everything from the beginning."

"Said if I didn't agree to sell, his mysterious client has *other* methods of obtaining what he wants. *Ha!* We shall see about that!" she went on heatedly, ignoring his request.

"Confound it, woman," stormed Branstoke. He reached out, stopping her in mid-stride. A soft growl emanated from his throat as he yanked her toward him, his lips coming down on hers with a blazing intensity. There was fury, exasperation, and passion in his punishing kiss. The feelings it roused in Cecilia descended to her toes curled inside her satin slippers and ricocheted back up to the top of her head which tingled and threatened to float away.

Then the punishing pressure gave way to a sensuous investigation of her mouth and drifted up the side of her face to her temple. The kiss slowly ended with a faint, feather-light promise for the future. Cecilia mewed and sighed. He gently held her against him while he guided her to the sofa. She let him seat her with him beside her, before she came out of her sensuous haze. Her cheeks flushed pink. She bit her lip and looked away.

Long, tapered fingers reached out to cup her chin and turn her back to face him. A wry smile twisted his lips and the warmth of banked fires came from his rich golden brown eyes; but he was too much the gentleman to allow them to flame.

A shy nervousness overcame her. She glanced furtively at him then down to her hands in her lap where she was twisting her handkerchief tight. "I'm sorry, I was a bit overwrought, wasn't I?" she said tightly. "I must say, you do utilize unconventional methods, don't you?"

"Is that all it was, Cecilia?" he asked, his voice a whispered thread of sound that wound itself around her senses.

She laughed shrilly. "Of course. What else could it be? Your reputation is well known. You hunt but shun the kill."

"Perhaps I've only been waiting for the ultimate prey," he offered whimsically, his eyes echoing his smile.

"Yes, well, that may be the reason you haven't ended your hunt. But really, I—I don't think I could take to being merely an exercise," she said lamely, staring up at him with stricken, but determined, eyes.

He smiled gently at her. "You, my dear, are anything but an exercise."

Cecilia wasn't quite sure she understood his meaning. She fidgeted a moment, then rose to cross to the table at the other end of the sofa. She unstopped the bottle of lavender water and sprinkled more on her handkerchief. She was disconcerted to note a slight trembling in her hand. She touched the damp white muslin and lace to her forehead, cooling her fevered brow. Without looking toward Sir Branstoke, who was observing her carefully for all his sleepy, relaxed demeanor, she wandered slowly to the window and looked out onto the street below.

Shadows were lengthening. The bright promise of the spring morning had through the long day been devoured by thickening clouds and a freshening northern wind that reminded man winter was not far in the past. The barrow boys, milk women, and other denizens of the streets by day were wandering each to his home, be it hovel or house. Passing carriages clattered swiftly through the emptying streets, their lanterns rocking, their coachmen all muffered.

Why did it now resemble nothing so much as an alien landscape? Unfamiliar and frightening in aspect? Why was her own behavior more like a Billingsgate fishwife than that of someone suffering from various ills? Her chest rose and fell as she took deep breaths.

"I had not thought to be so shattered after my grandparent's house party. Now I find my thoughts fractured, my nerves sadly shaken." She turned to look back at Sir Branstoke and smiled wanly. "I cannot think your remedy for a person suffering from a nervous disorder to have been successful. If anything, it has left your patient in a sadder fashion."

"I don't believe that, Mrs. Waddley. And neither do you," he said softly.

"La! You don't know what a trial my fragile nerves are to me, how they set my heart beating in a frightening manner and make me feel faint all over," she said easily, her patter descending over her like a protective cloak.

"Cut line, Cecilia. That won't fadge," he said harshly.

She looked at him warily. He took a couple steps toward her, then stopped. "You may halt the silly, sickly female ploy. I know it is foreign to your nature. You may continue to maintain that image in front of others, if you like, but in front of me, I will have your true nature. Good day, Mrs. Waddley," he said softly, his face impassive as he made his bow.

Turning on his heel, he left her, never looking back, never seeing her hand come up beseechingly, asking for what her lips could not shape into words.

* * *

Lady Meriton found her later in a room gone dark with night and guttered candles. She was curled up in a corner of the rose-colored sofa, her satin slippers off, her feet curled under her. Her elbow rested on a sofa arm so her head might be cradled in her hand. She didn't look up when Jessamine entered, merely shifted her eyes and let out a deep sigh.

"Gracious! What has you suffering blue megrims?" Lady Meriton asked, bustling about with the tinderbox. "Oh, blast, I've never been a dab hand at this," she muttered, struggling to get a punk lit. When it flamed, she smiled, satisfied, and lit branches of candles. Soon the room was bathed in a warm, rosy glow. She blew out the punk, set it down in a tray, then crossed the room to sit at Cecilia's side.

"Well?" she asked.

"I beg your pardon, Jessamine, what did you say?"

"What has you so dismal?"

"I've been contemplating stupidity, foolishness, and rash decisions."

"The universal concepts or do you have specifics in mind?" her aunt asked wryly.

Cecilia shook her head, a melancholy smile on her lips. "My own, of course." She sighed. "I've finally deduced my motivations for searching out Mr. Waddley's murderer. They are not pretty."

"One could hardly expect them to be all sunlight and roses, my dear."

A thin laugh escaped passed Cecilia's lips. "No, I suppose not, for murder is never pretty. But it is not the murder, per se, which compels me. It is more a search for identity which bears the strongest consideration. I have begun to feel that my life with Mr. Waddley was—well, it was stultifying. I existed like a doll in a shop window, or perhaps more accurately, like one of the animals at the Exeter Exchange. And while I've begun to feel that way, I also feel guilty for those sentiments. Mr. Waddley was such a good man, Jessamine, it seems somehow—I don't know—evil perhaps, to even think that what I was fortunate enough to have was not enough." Cecilia gnawed on her lower lip, looking forlorn.

Lady Meriton smiled understandingly and wrapped her arm

about her niece's shoulder in comfort. "It's Sir James Branstoke, isn't it?" she asked gently.

"What?" Cecilia's head flew up. She looked at her aunt, horror and hope mirrored in her deep blue eyes.

Lady Meriton laughed and leaned back on the sofa. "And I'll wager my best diamond studs that it's mutual. Though I'll own it is not what I'd have envisioned for you, I dare swear it will admirably serve."

"Jessamine, now you are being even more nonsensical than I!"

"Gammon," said Lady Meriton, serenely. Then she sobered and sat straight on the sofa, taking Cecilia's hands in both of hers. "It is not disloyalty to Mr. Waddley for you to seek the chance for a better life. You were happy before because you did not know what you were missing. Except for shopping jaunts or opera expeditions, you might as well say you were living as cloistered as a nun. Now you are free of that stuffy convent; free to see more, to feel more, to experience more. Cecilia, you are free to fall in love. Don't be afraid of that, whether it be Sir Branstoke or someone else. Don't live in the past. It's not necessary nor wise, and you, my dear, have a store of innate wisdom. Follow it."

Cecilia's eyes blurred as she listened to her aunt. When she finished, Cecilia gave a watery chuckle. "All right, I hear you and I will try to take your words to heart. But how did you get to be so wise?" she teased, pulling a handkerchief out of her sleeve and dabbing her eyes with it.

"Age, my dear, merely age."

"Oh, pooh! I must tell you, however, that while I will admit to developing a warm regard for Sir Branstoke, I will not agree that his emotions are likewise engaged. He is a hunter interested only in the thrill of the chase. He is not in it for the kill—let alone its denouement."

Lady Meriton cocked her head to the side. "Um-m-m, we shall see," she said, smiling slightly. "Come upstairs with me and throw some cool water on your face, change your clothes and fix your hair and you'll feel much better. Then we'll have a quiet dinner and a comfortable gossip about all that happened at Oastley," she said, rising to her feet and pulling Cecilia up with her.

Cecilia came willingly, even laughingly. "All right, all right, I believe I have received your message. No moping allowed."

"Perfect. Come along," she said, tucking her arm in Cecilia's. She drew her close to her side. "Did you hear what the under-housemaid found in Lord Bourqoin's chamber . . ."

ᘓᕷ Chapter Ten

NOT SO MUCH as the creak of a stair nor the nay of a horse betrayed the intruder. He silently lifted the wooden latch to the groom's chamber and slithered inside, keeping well into the shadows until he knew the layout of the small room. Stealthily he crossed a moonlit swath to stand beside the snoring sleeper. He prodded the man with the cudgel held in his hand. His victim murmured and turned in his sleep. Disgusted, he prodded him harder. The man woke with a start, thrashing, and emitting a quickly muffled yelp.

"Snabble it!" hissed the intruder, his hand pressed hard against the man's mouth.

The man blinked, his eyes wide and white. He nodded as best he could against the unrelenting pressure of the hand on his mouth, his eyes watching the raised, threatening cudgel.

"Yer soft, Romley. Yer shouldn't be taken by surprise like that. Gots t'sleep with one eye cocked if yer want t'see yer old age," advised his visitor, removing his hand and lowering the raised club. He settled on the edge of the bed.

"What do you want, Hewitt?" growled Romley, embarrassment feeding belligerence.

"Why, t'see his nibs, o'course. The house is all shut tight, or else I'd a taken myself on in," he explained congenially, his grin looking like a death's head grimace in the waning moonlight. "As it is, I need yer fiz to get me past his people."

"At this hour?"

Hewitt grabbed Romley by the collar and hauled him up. He was a small wiry man with a sinewy strength belied by his stature. Romley was surprised at how easily he was lifted. His respect went up a notch and he bit back a particularly vulgar epithet.

"Now see here, laddie, I wouldn't be here if it worn't for this little job his nibs give me. Showing my fiz in these parts ain't too healthy. Get me in t'see him, *now.* And I don't care if he's beddin' a baker's dozen. I gots to see him."

"All right, all right. Jest let me get me clothes on," said Romley, fumbling with the bedcovers. He hurriedly dressed, his eyes darting to his visitor. Ugly enough in the light of day, in moonlight and shadows Dabney Hewitt was a ghoulish figure. He seemed perfectly at ease now, but Romley knew only something very important would have brought him here. That was one of the conditions he strongly stressed when Romley met him at the Pye-Eyed Cock.

He led him back down the narrow stairs and through the stables and the small back garden of the neat townhouse to a window on the ground floor. He rapped lightly on the glass. In a few moments a mob-capped figure with a wool shawl draped over her night rail appeared at the window. Hewitt made a thin, appreciative whistle. Romley turned to snarl at him causing Hewitt to grin cheekily.

The window opened slightly, squealing stridently in protest. "Georgie, what are you doin' here at this hour?" whispered the young woman, her eyes round as saucers.

"Come unlock the door, Sophy, we got to see his nibs!"

"But he's asleep!"

"I know that, but it's important."

"I could loose me position," she said doubtfully.

"If this here bloke's information is as important as I think, we'll both more'n likely git rewards. Come on, be a dearie and do as I ask," he wheedled.

"Al—all right," she whispered, "come to the back door, but be quiet. Cook's a light sleeper, y'know."

"Aye, I remember," Romley said, grinning at her.

The woman blushed and hurriedly shut the window.

The two men crept to the door and waited for the sound of the bolt sliding back. The door opened, letting wavering light from the one candle held in Sophy's hand spill out. They quickly entered the stone-floored kitchen.

Sophy gasped and began to shake at the sight of the stranger with George Romley. "I—Is that blood," she stammered, pointing to the dark stains streaked across his coat.

Hewitt glanced down at his coat. "Happens it is," he said blandly.

Sophy raised a hand to her lips and bit on a knuckle, whimpering softly.

"Here now, none of that," Romley chided, though he glared

at Hewitt. He grabbed up two candle holders from the side-board. "Be a good girl and light these. I'll take him on into the library while you fetch Sir Branstoke."

"Me?!"

"Yes, you," Romley said, giving her a gentle shove.

She went hesitantly before them, glancing over her shoulder several times as she went. She hurried on up the stairs when she heard the library door close behind them. Timidly she went down the thickly carpeted hall at the top of the stairs and paused before Branstoke's bed chamber. She knocked lightly on the door.

There was no response. She bit her knuckle again for a moment then tentatively reached out to knock again.

"Sir Branstoke, sir?" she called softly. If any of the other servants caught her she swore she'd die of mortification. She knocked a third time. "Sir Branstoke?"

The door swung swiftly open. She fell back a step, shaking.

Branstoke finished knotting the sash to his long dressing gown and ran a hand through his disheveled hair. "Yes, what is it," he asked gently, for the little maid was obviously frightened.

"It—It's George, sir, George Romley. He and another gentleman are here to see you, sir. They say it's right important!"

"Where are they now?"

"In the library, sir," she answered briskly, feeling calmer now that Sir Branstoke was here and seemingly not put out by the late-night intrusion.

"Good. You've done well. Let me light a candle from yours, then I suggest you return to your bed."

"Yes, sir, thank you, sir," she said, bobbing a curtsy.

Branstoke descended the stairs and paused outside the library double doors, wondering what could possibly bring Hewitt at this hour, for he knew the second gentlemen could be no other than that ferret-faced former trooper. His expression grew grave, for his presence boded ill. He pushed open the door. Sprawled at his leisure before the desk sat Hewitt, a glass of his best brandy in hand. Romley knelt on the floor before the fire-place stoking glowing embers to life.

"I see you gentlemen have made yourselves at home," he drawled. His eyes paused infinitesimally on the stains on Hewitt's waistcoat and coat, then went on to the man's cheekily smiling countenance.

"I knew ye'd insist, guv'ner," said Hewitt cheerfully.

"Yes," Branstoke ironically agreed. He crossed to the brandy cabinet and poured himself and Romley glasses as well. He carried them over to the desk along with the bottle and eased himself into his chair, his narrowly open eyes taking in every aspect of Hewitt's appearance. He shoved a glass in Romley's direction then leaned back, waiting.

Hewitt eyed him cagily for a moment then grinned. Sir Branstoke was too smart to leap into conversation. He was neatly reminding him of his position. Hewitt nodded, pulled on a scarred, half-ripped earlobe, then rubbed his chin.

"I ain't by nature of bein' no thief taker, nor I ever squeaked beef 'afore, it not bein' a healthy occupation for a man o' my parts yer might say." He pulled a worn pipe with a well-chewed stem out of his pocket. He tapped it out on a small tray on the desk then patted his pockets in search of his tobacco pouch. He pulled it out empty and made a disgusted sound. He looked up at Branstoke, his expression one of cultivated cherubic innocence. "Yer got any fogus, guv'ner, that you might tip me a gage?"

Romley growled in protest, but Branstoke held up his hand to calm his groom. He rose languidly and crossed to an inlaid burl cabinet. Opening it, he removed a painted porcelain canister and brought it over to the desk, offering its aromatic content to his unexpected guest.

Hewitt pinched a wad for his pipe, tamping it down with a stained and dirty finger. He lit a sliver of tinder at a branch of candles and held it to his pipe, sucking in deeply and blowing out contented clouds of smoke.

Branstoke watched the ritual, amused. "Please feel free to replenish your tobacco pouch as well."

Hewitt took him up on his offer with alacrity. "Now that' right kindly of yer, guv'ner. Always wor a gentlemanly sort, fer a flash cove."

"Now that we have observed the amenities of drink and tobacco, I assume you have news of some import that it necessitates a personal visit at this hour? Or are you—as I believe they say—cadging the lay?"

Hewitt feigned shock and offense. "I couldn't do that, yer saved me life. Not many flash coves would do the same fer the likes o' me."

"I shall refrain from commenting," drawled Branstoke, leaning back in his chair. "What exactly brings you here, Hewitt?"

Hewitt puffed on his pipe a moment. "This Thornbridge yer set me to foller, he's a reg'lar bob cull, peery and not cow'hearted. Pluck up to the backbone, he is. Still, no 'countin' for why he's been in places he don't belong, if yer catch my drift. But, I figures that's why yer arsked me to foller the cull."

"Such contingencies had occurred to me," murmured Branstoke.

Hewitt nodded and rubbed his nose with the back of his hand. "First few days he jest made the rounds o' the City, like I reported to Romley here."

"To the various banking and legal establishments, asking questions about Randolph Haukstrom?"

"Aye. Couldn't figure his interest in that cove. Bad cess. Then it's wot starts gettin' interest'n like. He dons an old mish and topper," he said, grabbing his coat lapels in example, "and visits gull gropers and abbesses. All manner of 'em. He finally comes out of one house, his fiz white and all queer-like. After he went home t'bed, I nipped back there reet quick."

"And?"

"He worn't arsk'n about Haukstrom. He wor arsk'n questions 'bout missin' gels. He learnt from one bawd of a parlor boarder wot wor sold fer a fiver to a flash cove. Purty ginger-hackled thing she wor, and fresh from the country. No one's heard wot happened to her."

"Sounds a bad business. Any idea what caused him to ask those questions?"

"No, I'm sorry to say. Next night he gets all fancied dressed like some curst dandy and visits the fancy bawds. Afterwards, they worn't as forthcoming to yurs truly as I'd a liked, howsomever, he wor arsk'n the same sorta questions. After this, he begins to look'n real peaky. He spends long hours at his office, and wanders down on the wharf in deep thinkin', arsk'n more fool questions." Hewitt drained his brandy glass.

Branstoke leaned forward to refill it. "I somehow get the impression that we are approaching the reason behind this meeting. Proceed, Mr. Hewitt."

"Someone didn't like wot he's doin', that's fer sure. I've a mind to do some extry checkin' on my own. I don't like deep secretive rumbles of flash coves with lays in me district. T'ain't seemly. Nor coves settin' themselves up as badgers when it's plain as a pikestaff they ain't.'"

Branstoke straightened, his eyes narrowing even more as he studied Mr. Hewitt.

That man relit his pipe and sucked in deeply. "The bob cull was bit, sar, and would be cockin' his toes now if it worn't fer yurs truly."

"Thornbridge was attacked?"

"Attacked? Lor' guv'ner, worn't no simple thievery they had in mind. They wanted to hush the cull, and that's a fact. He's a game cock, though. Looked to advantage. But there wor too many of 'em and I seed he wor tirin', so I squeaked beef and laid club law on 'em. That set the snivelling lot running. The bob cull took a chive in his side. Claret flowed purty freely 'afore I could get him to a bone setter."

"He's still alive?"

"Aye, and likely to stay that way if he rests. Kept ramblin' on, though, bout Mrs. Waddley." He shook his head. "Wouldn't a taken him as one to give a feller horns."

Branstoke smiled grimly. "I assure you, he did not. It's Mrs. Waddley who requested he investigate certain matters for her. Haukstrom's her brother."

Hewitt whistled softly.

"Exactly. But what I want to know is what does Haukstrom have to do with missing prostitutes? Was Haukstrom the one who bought the girl?"

"No, I already checked that, guv'ner. The descriptions don't match."

Branstoke was silent a moment, his lips pursed in thought. He looked at Hewitt. "I know your debt to be cleared by your saving Mr. Thornbridge's life, and I thank you. However, I have further need of your assistance."

A slow grin pulled Hewitt's thin face tight. "I was hopin' yer might, guv'ner. Of course, this bein' a business-like arrangement . . ."

"Yes, Mr. Hewitt, you will be well paid for your time. I want you to see if you can discover what the connection is, and where Thornbridge's line of questioning was leading him. Since you no longer have to watch over Mr. Thornbridge, that should free you considerably."

"Aye, that it will."

"Now my concern becomes for Mrs. Waddley. I shudder to imagine what she shall attempt once she learns of Thornbridge's misfortune. George, we need to see that no harm comes to her. I want her followed and her house watched. Arrange for it. I don't trust her not to do something foolish, like attempt a midnight foray to the wharf."

"Plucky wench," observed Mr. Hewitt.

Branstoke grinned. "How right you are, Mr. Hewitt. How right you are."

"Excuse me, my lady, there is another gentleman here to see Mrs. Waddley," said Loudon.

By his tone and abject expression it was clear this third caller no more met with his approval than the previous two had. Cecilia laid her needlework in her lap and exchanged long suffering sighs with her Aunt Jessamine.

"Who is it?" Lady Meriton asked, resigned.

He rocked back on his heels, every inch the superior butler. "He identifies himself as the Honorable Mr. Reginald Rippy," he said, his eyes cast toward the ceiling, his hands behind his back.

Cecilia suppressed a giggle. "Do you doubt him, Loudon?"

"No, madame. Though, if I may be so bold, I will say it would serve the gentleman properly if I did. He has come without cards," he pronounced in dire accents.

"Manners are not what they once were, Loudon," said Lady Meriton, her lips twisted against laughter.

"No, my lady, indeed they are not."

"Well, we can't allow our manners to lack merely because another's have. Show him up. This time we shall dispense with the cakes. I could not touch another morsel."

Loudon bowed, as satisfied an expression on his face as his hang-dog countenance would allow.

"Poor Loudon, he is unused to climbing stairs this often," mused Lady Meriton.

"He could allow one of the footmen."

Lady Meriton laughed. "I don't think he would. I believe to him it would be another breach of etiquette. He fears all society to be on the brink of destruction. It is the Fall of Rome again. Nonetheless, he will see to it that he does his small part to forestall the inevitable."

Cecilia laughed and picked up her needlepoint canvas. She'd been attempting to finish the chair cover that day; however, the endless stream of visitors had rendered a quick completion doubtful.

She made a lovely picture, seated on the rose sofa bathed in bright light. Sunlight sparkled in her pale hair and her almost translucent skin was luminous. There was an ethereal quality about her. Mr. Rippy, following behind Loudon, was stunned.

"That I could write verse like that fellow Byron, I would pen one to you," he said gravely, pausing just inside the door. He was resplendent in yellow pantaloons, shaded lavender waistcoat and bottle-green coat.

"What a very pretty thing to say, Mr. Rippy," said Cecilia.

Mr. Rippy blushed, scuffed his feet on the carpet and murmured his thanks. "Always wanted to say something like that," he confided ingeniously. "Never saw the opportunity until I saw you sitting there in the sunlight."

She laughed and Lady Meriton, striving to appear busy with her embroidery, pursed her lips against a smile.

"Whatever the reason, please come in. You are the first to get me to laugh today and I do so enjoy laughter. It makes one forget—if only for a time—all of one's problems, big and small."

Mr. Rippy brightened at her words and came over in his curiously rolling gait to sit by her on the sofa. "Yes, well, to do that is important, right?"

"I think so."

"Good, good. Mrs. Waddley, may I escort you to the Waymond's ball tomorrow night?"

"I'm sorry, Mr. Rippy, but Sir Elsdon has been before you and claimed that privilege."

Mr. Rippy laughed. "Trust Harry not to be behind hand, as it were! Devilish sort, he is. Merry as a grig. I won't be outdone, however. Would you consider accompanying me in a turn about Hyde Park?"

She looked apologetic though laughter threatened. "Lord Havelock has claimed that honor."

"Dash it! How's a fellow to stand in good stead if his friends keep cuttin' him out?" He frowned and fidgeted a moment. "Mrs. Waddley, may I speak privately with you?"

Cecilia's eyebrows rose in surprise, her lips curved upward

in humor. "I believe Lady Meriton may be persuaded to give us a moment."

"What? Oh, you desire private conversation? Just as well. I must get on with my framing and matting," Lady Meriton said, hurriedly rolling her embroidery into a ball and shoving it into her workbasket. "I may trust you alone with Cecilia? Oh yes, silly me. It's not like she's new on the town, is it? I'll just retire to my studio," she said, pushing her glasses up on her nose and rising from the chair. "Now don't tarry overlong," she warned good-naturedly before scurrying out the door.

Mr. Rippy grabbed Cecilia's hand in a vise grip. Startled, she attempted to pull it free, only to give it up after observing the earnest expression on his young face.

"Mrs. Waddley, I am not polished with words like my friends, nor given to quoting plays or poetry. I'm just not quick to turn a phrase—nor, it would seem, to take advantage of your time to further my heart's desire." He slid off the sofa onto one knee on the floor. "But, Mrs. Waddley, before another may anticipate me, would you do me the honor of being my wife?"

His voice may have cracked a trifle on the last three words, nonetheless, his expression was sincere. Despite her suspicions of collusion and wagers, she was touched.

"Thank you, Mr. Rippy, for your kind invitation. I will not prevaricate. It has taken me quite by surprise. I hardly know what to say." She looked down to where his hand covered hers. "Marriage is not an institution I'd thought to enter again. I would that you would give me time to consider your kind offer."

Mr. Rippy, cringing ever so slightly in expectation of an immediate rebuff, was surprised and gratified. He perked up. "But of course! Wouldn't think to rush you. Not done at all, you know. Just hope I'm not yet cut out."

"No, no, Mr. Rippy. I assure you, you are not. I shall seriously consider your kind offer," she said, pulling her hand free.

He beamed. "Excellent! Well then, perhaps I could escort you to another function?"

She smiled. "I think that to be a splendid idea."

"Good, excellent. I'll look forward to that," he said, his head bobbing in confirmation. "I guess I'd best be going. Thank you for having me. Oh, and give my best to Lady Meriton. Fine lady, your aunt. Very understanding."

"I will," Cecilia said, her lips compressed against a laugh.

"Yes, well, best be going then," he said, rising jerkily from his seat. "You will save me a dance tomorrow evening, won't you?"

"Of course, Mr. Rippy. I shall be honored."

His cheeks pinked with pleasure. "Yes, then until tomorrow, Mrs. Waddley."

"Good-bye Mr. Rippy," she said smoothly, watching him back out the double doors. It was a wonder he didn't tumble down the stairs.

After he left, Cecilia leaned back against the mound of pillows at the head of the daybed. The day had been profitable. She was engaged to socialize with her three suspects. With time, one of them was bound to utter a mischance word or phrase that would lead her to a solution to the crime of Mr. Waddley's death. She merely needed to continue cultivating their acquaintance. Patience and perseverance. That was what was wanted.

The only circumstance to mar the tranquility of her mind was the continued absence of Mr. Thornbridge. That did not bode well. She picked up her needlework to resume filling the red-brick background, her eyes traveling occasionally to the clock on the mantel.

"Where is he?" stormed Cecilia later that afternoon as she came striding angrily into the little room near the top of the house used by Lady Meriton as a studio.

Her aunt looked up from the picture she was carefully framing. It was the silhouette she had cut of Cecilia at the ball. "Where is who, dear? We seem to have had a parade of male visitors today. By the by, what did Mr. Rippy want that necessitated private discourse?"

Cecilia made a moue of distaste. "What do you think? Marriage, naturally."

"Gracious!"

"I fobbed him off nicely. Though I do not wish to wed him, I do see him as a source of information I'm not fool enough to throw that away. But it is Mr. Thornbridge I have been expecting today, and he is the only gentleman who's failed to appear!"

"Besides Sir James Branstoke, you mean."

"I am not expecting him. Not after my lamentable behavior yesterday. But I could not help it. He asks for more than I am able to give."

"What does he ask for? I warn you, if you say your virtue, I shall know you for a liar."

Cecilia laughed, albeit weakly, and threw herself down on the narrow green upholstered bench against the wall. "Worse," she intoned. "He demands trust."

"Trust?"

"Yes. He knows I am plagued in some manner. He wishes me to unburden myself to him and *tell all.*"

"Why don't you?"

"Jessamine, how could I? First, I have only foul suspicions that Mr. Waddley was murdered—and you know how I was ignored when I made that suggestion at the time of his death. My suggestion was deemed hysterics by a grieving widow."

"But you don't know that Branstoke won't believe you . . . All right, don't look at me in that blighting fashion. I retract my comment. But you said that was your first reason. Do you have others?"

"Yes," she admitted slowly. "To me, trust is a very personal gift. Its giving carries great weight and forges bindings. I—I do not want those bindings for they hold both ways. Granting trust would likewise mean accepting trust. I don't want to do that."

"Interesting," Lady Meriton murmured. She was silent a moment, then a mischievous little smile lit her pale blue eyes. "Do you know what you are describing?"

"What do you mean?"

"My dear, you are describing *love,* in its ultimate expression."

"Oh." Cecilia fidgeted on the bench. "Then I would say love is something I do not want."

"Nonsense, Cecilia. The problem you have, my dear, is that you see the exchange as imprisoning rather than liberating— which I assure you it can be."

"I don't see how."

Lady Meriton laughed. "Don't worry. You shall eventually, and I dare say Sir Branstoke will show you, too."

"Nonsense," Cecilia retorted. "And I do wish you would stop linking me with Sir Branstoke at every breath. I am merely a curiosity to him for he senses some mystery. He is a much more awake gentleman than you, or anyone else, seems to give him credit for being."

"So you've said."

"Excuse me, my lady," said a young footman from the open doorway.

"Yes, Harry, what is it?"

"A letter just come for Mrs. Waddley," he said, handing it to her.

Cecilia grabbed for it, anxiously breaking the seal.

"Thank you, Harry," Lady Meriton said for her remiss niece. She dismissed the footman with a wave of her hand. He closed the door after himself.

"Dear Lord," murmured Cecilia.

"What is it? Bad news?"

"Yes. Though I gather it could easily have been much worse."

"I beg your pardon?"

Cecilia roused herself. "It's from a Dr. Heighton. He is writing at the urgent behest of his new patient, Mr. David Thornbridge. Mr. Thornbridge was attacked last night and stabbed."

"No!"

Cecilia reddened and bit her lip, her brow furrowing as she fought the wave of guilt and panic that assailed her. "He is weak and has lost a great deal of blood, but he will live. He writes that Mr. Thornbridge would not rest comfortably until he appraised me of his situation. He says as soon as he is well enough, he will allow him to travel to the country and recuperate there."

Cecilia lowered the letter, her face wet with tears. She swiped at them with a crumpled handkerchief. "Oh, Jessamine, it is all my fault! When he wrote yesterday I feared something horrible was about to happen. I should never have asked him to help me. I granted him a form of trust, and look at the horrible burden it placed on him. It nearly got him killed!" Her body trembled and guilt etched gray furrows in her blanched complexion.

"Cecilia! Stop it. Stop it at once! Mr. Thornbridge is not a stupid man. He knew the risks he was taking. I doubt you could have forestalled him if you tried."

"I don't know. Oh, I don't know," wailed Cecilia faintly, rocking back and forth on the bench.

"Cecilia, self-flagellation will not help Mr. Thornbridge now. What's done is done. Perhaps you now realize the gravity of the situation and will desist in your endeavors to learn the truth. It is not worth another life—Mr. Thornbridge's or yours, which might be next if you persist in this manner."

Cecilia looked up at her aunt, the tracks of her tears drying on her cheeks. She shook her head. "But Jessamine, don't you understand? I can't stop now! It would be unfair to Mr. Waddley *and* Mr. Thornbridge. As things are, I hope I know better than to involve others in my quest—and I certainly shall not say anything to Sir Branstoke! Lud, it would be scandalous at this point. He thinks Mr. Thornbridge to be my physician. To try to explain otherwise would necessitate unraveling all the skeins, and I am not willing to do that yet!"

A soft knock on the door drew their attention. It was Loudon. "Excuse me, my lady, but Sir James Branstoke is below. He asks to speak with Mrs. Waddley."

Cecilia decisively shook her head. "I do not wish to see him. Tell him I am plagued with a dreadful headache—which is nigh to being true at this juncture."

"Begging your pardon, ma'am. Sir Branstoke felt certain you would say something to that effect. He asked that I tell you he has just come from a Dr. Heighton's and has seen Mr. Thornbridge."

"*What? How?* Are you sure he said *Mister* Thornbridge?"

"Yes, ma'am, he did, and very distinct he was about it, too."

"Oh, dear, it appears to me you may not have any recourse but to confide in him," Lady Meriton said, suppressed laughter coloring her voice.

Cecilia chewed on her lower lip a moment. "Blast the man! There, see? How can I trust him? I tell him to stay out of my concerns and he ignores my words. Where is the trust in me?"

"Cecilia, you are hardly being fair. You don't know how he came about to see Mr. Thornbridge and know him not to be a medical man."

"All right, all right. I stand corrected. I shall not leap willy-nilly to conclusions. I suppose I'd best see him, to at least learn what he does know. Loudon, show him into the rose parlor. I'll be down directly." She turned toward her aunt, her handkerchief rubbing her cheeks. "How do I look? Is my complexion blotchy?"

"No, merely dewy. But straighten your fichu . . . there, you'll do; however, I do wish you'd smile. You look like some sacrificial victim."

Cecilia grimaced as she stood and shook out her skirt. "At the moment I feel that description to be very apt," she said wryly. Taking a deep breath, she walked toward the door. Behind her, Lady Meriton shook her head and smiled.

Chapter Eleven

CECILIA CLOSED the parlor door softly. She leaned back against its carved oak panels, her hands behind her back still clutching the door latch as if she were half-afraid to stay, to commit herself to talking with Branstoke.

"You wanted to see me?" she asked levelly, pleased at the light note she'd infused into her tone.

Branstoke stood in the middle of the room, regarding her dispassionately through hooded eyes. He waited.

Cecilia shifted uneasily, finally she straightened, releasing her death's grasp of the door latch. She took a few steps toward him, careful to keep her distance. She didn't trust being close to Sir Branstoke, but whether that was due to him or herself, she refused to examine.

"Is Lady Meriton to join us?" he asked, casually removing his snuffbox from his pocket and flicking the latch open with his thumb.

"No, she is occupied at present," Cecilia said, red surging up to stain her cheeks. She plucked her handkerchief from where she had tucked it at the end of her long sleeve and began wringing it with both hands. "You forget, sir, I am mistress of my own affairs and stand in no need of a chaperone. The idea is quite ludicrous at my age," she said with a tight laugh.

One dark eyebrow rose and it appeared his attention shifted to her full red lips. Noting the direction of his fixed gaze, Cecilia's discomfort increased for suddenly she remembered two occasions with him where a chaperone would have been wise.

She clasped her hands before her, tension evident in the tendons of her hand. "You mentioned Thornbridge to Loudon," she said formally. "How is it you know of his accident? I have just received a note from Dr. Heighton myself."

"Yes, Dr. Heighton informed me he sent around a reassuring missive." He took a pinch of snuff, snapped the tiny box shut and returned it to his pocket.

"Reassuring? Are his injuries graver than he intimated?"

"No. Though they well could have been. Cecilia, it is past time that we speak without prevarication or omission."

"I'm afraid I don't know what you mean," she said stiffly, her head flung up in silent challenge.

Branstoke crossed his arms over his chest, his head canted as he considered her. "I have observed a very interesting phenomena during the short time we have been acquainted," he drawled. "Did you know your eyes darken and a tiny pulse throbs in your neck when you lie to me? No, I don't suppose you do," he said with a thin smile as he watched color blazing into her cheeks again. "I assure you it is true. Now, shall we begin again? I am not a flat."

A tiny, reluctant smile creased Cecilia's lips. "Is that in conjunction with not being a Borgia?" she couldn't resist asking.

Branstoke's eyes glowed in appreciation of her humor. "Yes, along with being a man with a surprisingly limited fount of patience where you are concerned," he warned darkly, stepping closer to her.

Cecilia moved gracefully to the right to put a table between them.

He stopped and impassively studied the obstruction. "I see," he murmured. He turned and sauntered toward the fireplace. He stood with his back to her, staring up at the portrait of Lady Meriton with her son Franklin as a young child. "But I believe we were discussing *Mister* Thornbridge, the youngest manager at Waddley Spice and Tea," he said urbanely, turning to look at her over his shoulder.

Cecilia placed her fingertips on the table in front of her. "I admit, Sir Branstoke, you have the advantage of me. How am I to take that?"

"Honestly, I beg of you."

She sighed and compressed her lips. "All right, I admit I lied about his position as my physician."

"Why?"

She shrugged slightly. "It just seemed easier. And truthfully, society expects me to receive numerous visits from a physician."

"To add credence to your various illnesses?"

"More to reinforce those illnesses," she said drily.

"All of which are imaginary."

She had the grace to blush. "Except for some of the headaches," she qualified ruefully. "Of late those have been more real than I care." She came around the table and sat dispiritedly on the sofa.

"What was Mr. Thornbridge doing for you that nearly caused his death?"

She winced. "Was it that obvious?"

"To me it was, once I discovered his true occupation."

She looked away from him, thinking, and chewed her lower lip. "I wonder if anyone else has connected him with me? As of yet, I doubt it. If they had, I do not believe someone of Mr. Peters' ilk would have been sent to do business with me," she murmured.

"Cecilia, what maggot have you in that devious little brain of yours?" Branstoke demanded. He did not like her considering expression nor the slight smile that went with it. He crossed to her side and sat down next to her.

She turned her head to look at him. "I beg your pardon?" she asked loftily.

"Cut line, Cecilia. That pose will not work on me any better than your ill-health pose has. I did not cut my eyeteeth yesterday. What are you and Thornbridge involved with?"

"That is none of your concern. And who gave you leave to address me by my Christian name?"

"I did. I refuse to continue calling you Mrs. Waddley; it reminds me of a duck."

"How dare you!" she exclaimed, her eyes flaring.

Branstoke leaned back on the sofa and nonchalantly crossed his legs. "Oh, I dare a great deal where you are concerned. Lucky for Mr. Thornbridge that I do."

"What is that supposed to mean?"

"Otherwise Mr. Thornbridge would be dead and you would be carrying a load of guilt that I doubt you'd ever recover from."

Cecilia blanched at the reminder of how close Mr. Thornbridge came to dying. "Tell me about it, please. The accident, I mean."

"It wasn't an accident."

"I didn't think so. Did—did someone attack him?"

"More than one someone. Thornbridge would be dead if my man hadn't stepped forward to lend a hand. Hewitt informs me young Thornbridge displayed himself to advantage; unfortunately the numbers were not in his favor. Mr. Hewitt—believing rightly that I would wish him to—obligingly stepped forward to help. They routed the ruffians, but not before Thornbridge was stabbed. It caught him in his side. According to Dr. Heighton, it missed any vital organs by virtue of a rib."

Cecilia paled, her eyes wide. She stood up suddenly and began to pace before the sofa. "It was lucky your man—Hewitt you said?—was near."

Branstoke rose as she did, a wry smile on his lips. "Luck, my dear, had nothing to do with it."

She stopped. "What do you mean?"

"I mean exactly what I said. Mr. Hewitt was not coincidentally in the area. Prowling the wharfs near Waddley Spice and Tea is not his idea of a pleasant way to spend an evening."

"It did happen near the wharf?"

"Yes."

"Most likely in the same area Mr. Waddley was murdered," she mused.

Branstoke stilled. *What was she involved with?* He ran through his mind for what he knew of Mr. Waddley's death. Not much, for it was not a subject that unduly interested him. He did seem to remember someone commenting on his death in conjunction with the high crime along the river. He passed it off as an unfortunate run-in with that criminal element. But if Mr. Thornbridge was attacked in the same area and, according to Hewitt, by men lying in wait just for him, then might not that have been also true for Mr. Waddley?

He stepped forward, grabbing her by the shoulders and forcing her to look at him. "Cecilia, what was Thornbridge doing down by the wharfs at night?"

She shook her head. "I don't know," she said slowly.

His hands fell from her shoulders. He growled his disgust, "Stop it. Don't lie to me, Cecilia."

She glared at him. "You're the one who said you could tell when I was lying. Then you should know that I'm not lying now. I don't know what he was doing there. The last time I talked to him was the day you were here, before the Oastley house party. He was merely going to look into Randolph's financial affairs."

He ran a hand distractedly through his immaculate hair. "Which he did. And he learned something from all those bankers and lawyers that led his investigation on to a different line of questioning."

"What do you mean?"

"He began frequenting low resorts and asking questions about missing women."

"Prostitutes?"

Branstoke glanced at her out of the corner of his eye. "Yes."

"It doesn't make any sense. Maybe they're not related. No—they have to be," she murmured. She compressed her lips and began pacing again, her eyes darting about. What could be the connection with Randolph? Or with Mr. Waddley, for that matter? If Thornbridge did investigate Randolph as—"Wait a moment." She stopped pacing and slowly turned to face Branstoke. "How do you know Mr. Thornbridge visited bankers and lawyers? And how do you know he was asking about prostitutes? You had him followed, didn't you?" she declared with rising anger. "Of course you did. That's why luck had nothing to do with your Mr. Hewitt being available. How dare you? How dare you have the effrontery to meddle in my affairs? What gave you the right?" she demanded wrathfully, her voice low-pitched, but nonetheless throbbing with the force of her anger.

"Concern," he said simply in a deceptively bland tone. The rich gold-brown of his eyes was well-hooded; yet he watched her keenly with a cat's studied disinterest.

"Concern? Ha! More like arrogant curiosity stemming from boredom. No wonder you look out at the world like you're half asleep! You are! For some reason I managed to pique your interest and wake you up. A novelty, I'm sure. So with the arrogance of your breed you casually decide to meddle in my affairs for entertainment. Have you had your share of laughs at my expense? Has the entertainment value been worth your time and effort? So what would you have me do for the second act? Prostrate myself before you in supplication? Vow undying gratitude for your interest in my affairs? Ha! I promise you, Sir James Branstoke, it will be a cold day in hell."

Branstoke's eyes narrowed and his jaw went rigid during her tirade. "Are you quite finished? For if you are not, please feel free to continue. I shall wait upon you."

"See? See what I mean? That attitude is a demonstration of precisely what I've been saying. You are an arrogant, self-interested bastard!"

"I shall take that to mean you are finished. I have just one question to ask."

"What?" she said ungraciously, her chest heaving. She glared up at his impassive visage.

"Would you rather Mr. Thornbridge had been murdered?"

The hand seemed to rise of its own volition, but the slap across his face had the strength of her entire body behind it. The crack resounded in the quiet room.

Cecilia stared, horror stricken, at the glowing red hand imprint on his cheek. She covered her mouth with a trembling hand and backed away a step. "I'm so sorry, Sir James. That was uncalled for. Please forgive me. I do know you meant well, really I do. And I am grateful Mr. Thornbridge is alive. I don't know what got into me. That was a terribly foolish thing to do," she babbled.

His eyes glittered behind their heavy lids and through the veil of his dark lashes. His hands clenched, the knuckles white, then relaxed. Carefully he straightened out each finger, easing the tension. "Come here, Cecilia," he said, his voice frighteningly void of expression.

"No—" she said, backing farther away.

"I said, come here," he commanded, his eyes locked with hers.

She inched forward a step, fighting the command yet knowing herself to be at fault. He was well within rights to extract some punishment. She was thankful someone watched out for Mr. Thornbridge. If she had ever imagined the danger his inquiries would lead him to, she would never have asked for his help. She'd been a fool and Branstoke had saved her from a lifetime of guilt. In actuality, she held no anger toward Branstoke for having someone follow Mr. Thornbridge or even being interested in what she was doing. The galling truth eating at her was the attraction she felt toward the man; an attraction she wanted to deny and swore she didn't want. His proximity in a room set her pulse racing. That's why she slapped him. It was an abortive attempt to deny those insidious feelings within her. And she knew it.

"Come here, Cecilia," he repeated for the third time. He would not repeat it again, would not give her another chance to come forward on her own.

She came closer, her hand coming up tentatively to gently trace the pattern it had recently left. A twitch in his cheek muscle revealed his wariness. A single tear trailed out the corner of her eye. She ignored it. "I'm sorry," she whispered, her heart in her throat.

He settled his hands around her back drawing her closer. With what seemed an exaggerated slowness, his head bent closer to hers, telegraphing his actions. Cecilia emitted a soft cry of part fear, part desire, and infinitesimally raised her head to meet his kiss.

His lips came down on hers hard and demanding, full of checked anger and passion. Commandingly he drank her soul from her lips until she weakened, certain her knees would give way beneath her. Then the kiss changed, deepened, softened, and seemed to return more than it had ever taken. Filled with an intense longing to melt into him, to be one with him, she clung weakly to his shoulders and let the sensations ripple through her.

When finally he lifted his head to stare down into her twilight-darkened eyes, she didn't know what to say or do. Confusion ran riot through her. She returned his kiss with an honesty that told more of her secrets than she'd ever privileged anyone to know. That frightened her; yet curiously gave her peace. That dichotomy provoked her to nervously retreat before him.

He stared at her a long moment in silence. "I will be waiting until you realize you both want and need me," he said rawly. "Give my regards to Lady Meriton." He bowed formally and left, flinging open the parlor door with an uncommon force.

Lady Jessamine Meriton, coming down from her studio, paused on the last stair, her hand resting on the newel post. She looked up to see Sir James Branstoke striding toward her with unnatural haste. She opened her mouth to greet him amiably; but the words died on her lips. A set mask of black anger contorted his features until he little resembled the suave, urbane gentleman of her acquaintance.

He slowed as he came even with her, his features twisting into a semblance of a polite smile. He nodded curtly.

Pleased to see he was not completely lost to all niceties of manner, she was nonetheless quick to attribute his startling lack of legendary phlegm to her niece. It was odd—and rather delightfully comical—how Cecilia and Branstoke were suddenly prone to unusual and uncommon behavior. She wondered if either knew how serious was the malady—or if either had yet to properly name it.

As he would pass her, she put out a slender hand to detain him. "Will you not stay for refreshments?"

"No, thank you, Lady Meriton. I fear if I did they would end on my head," he said, glancing toward the closed parlor door.

"You mustn't mind Cecilia when she's in a temper. She gets that way when she feels—well, out of control, I suppose one would say. She prefers to have the management of all things."

"So I am to gather," he drawled.

"I think she feels safer that way," she went on ruminatively, glancing at him out of the corner of her eye. "So much of her life has been mismanaged by others, you know. When anyone does anything the least bit managing, she flies into a pelter. It is a reflexive action, I suspect."

Branstoke looked at her keenly, dark emotion settling out of his features. "I believe I begin to understand," he said slowly, a slight smile forming on his lips in quite his old manner. "Thank you, Lady Meriton."

She smiled. "You're welcome. And please come again, Sir Branstoke. You are a much more entertaining caller than the others who paraded through this morning and who, it appears, we shall be seeing more of."

He laughed shortly. "Haukstrom's cronies?"

"Dear me, yes. And all anxious to put it to the touch, it would seem. Mr. Rippy fired the first salvo this morning."

"And her response?"

"Can you not guess? No, of course. But she continues to encourage him to call. Truly, it is a comedy of manners to see those gentleman vie for her attention. Of course, they are only after her money; but watching provides sport. My only fear is that in a welter of guilt she will accept one of them. Particularly now, with this Thornbridge matter." She shivered slightly, then pinned Branstoke with a stern eye. "Is Mr. Thornbridge truly to recover?"

"Yes, he will, which is better than perhaps he deserves considering the foolish path he's tread."

"I only pray Cecilia does not stoop to pick up the dropped gauntlet."

"You think she would?"

"Unfortunately, yes."

"So do I," he agreed heavily.

They looked at each other steadily, a complete, shared understanding between them. "It is a stubborn, self-willed niece you have," Branstoke said, humor once again rippling his smooth voice. "Do not worry, I shall continue to watch out for her, despite her wishes to the contrary." He squeezed her hand in reassurance, then continued down the stairs with a light step.

Lady Meriton watched him leave, a satisfied smile hovering on her lips. When she heard the front door close after him, she roused and turned toward the parlor, wondering if it would prove as easy to lighten Cecilia's disposition. She opened the door quietly, peeking in to gauge her niece's attitude. Cecilia was standing by the window looking out into the street below.

"Yes, he finally left," she said wryly.

Cecilia turned toward Jessamine, her hand falling away from the drape. "He is, without any doubt, the most exasperating gentleman of my acquaintance."

"And you care for him."

"Jessamine! What a singularly erroneous idea! Don't tell me that is what *he* told *you?* The man is arrogant, opinionated, self-willed, conceited, and stubborn. And those are quite possibly his better traits!"

"Oh, dear, I see."

"Do you know what he did? He had someone follow Mr. Thornbridge about."

"Follow Mr. Thornbridge?"

"Yes. And while I owe him some thanks, for that is what prevented Mr. Thornbridge's murder, I still cannot like his motivation. He was curious. Can you fathom this: he assigned someone to follow and report on Thornbridge's movements merely to satisfy his curiosity about me and Mr. Thornbridge? What was he expecting to discover, do you suppose, that I am his secret mistress? I have never been so incensed!" She paused to draw breath, her slender body rigid with rage.

Lady Meriton crossed to a sidetable and poured her a glass of sherry. "Here, dear, this might help."

Cecilia took the small glass from her aunt and tossed off the contents. Lady Meriton clucked disapprovingly.

She set the glass down and resumed pacing. She shook her head, her pale brow furrowed and her full lips compressed in thought. "Jessamine, Sir Branstoke acts like he is playing an innocuous parlor game for amusement. To compound the ludicrousness of the entire situation, I believe he knows more than

I do. You should have heard him try to sidestep certain subjects. Oh! I swear my brain is beleaguered with ideas and suppositions. I would that I could talk with Thornbridge!"

"Perhaps you could visit him at this doctor's residence. What did you say his name was? Hilton?"

"No, Dr. Heighton. And you're right. That is probably what I should do first before I worry myself to flinders. Oh, but I don't even know if I could think straight to pen a coherent letter. My head is truly pounding."

"And you are promised to drive out with Lord Havelock to Hyde Park in a little over an hour."

"I completely forgot that engagement. I do not want to go. I can't go. My thoughts are swirling. I should be poor company and would most likely cause him to remain out of my company in the future which would not suit my purposes. No, I shall have to compose a note breaking our engagement."

"Perhaps you can suggest tomorrow afternoon as an alternate."

"Only if it is not too late and we are not out overlong. Remember, I am pledged to accept Sir Elsdon's escort to the Waymond's ball tomorrow evening."

"I remember. You know, of course, you'll have to grant similar privileges to Havelock and Rippy."

"Yes, I know. At least I may truthfully say I have one burden removed in the person of Sir James Branstoke."

Lady Meriton laughed. "Do not be so quick to cast him aside. I have noted a phenomena strangely suited to phlegmatic individuals such as your Branstoke."

"He is not *mine!*" Cecilia ground out, frustration and uncertainty authoring her manner.

Her aunt shrugged. "No matter whose he is, I wager he is tenacious. We have not seen the last of Sir James Branstoke, and you, my dear girl, are going to be extremely happy about that fact."

Cecilia glared at her. Lady Meriton smiled indulgently. "You'd best write that note to Lord Havelock if you wish to cancel your meeting, otherwise it will be too late and much too embarrassing."

Reluctantly Cecilia agreed and went off for paper and pen.

*   *   *

Late the next afternoon, pale gray woolly clouds were slowly converging when Cecilia accepted Lord Havelock's hand into his phaeton. She was grateful it was not a high perch model for in her continued preoccupied condition she'd likely have misstepped and tumbled back onto the pavement in an ungainly bundle of skirts and petticoats. Tooling about Hyde Park at five o'clock was not what she wished to be doing. Unfortunately, she knew no other recourse, for it would not be politic to break her engagement with the gentleman a second time. Consequently, she assented to accompany him and donned a new, colorful outfit of cornflower blue and yellow for the occasion. She looked lovely, and if her eyes did not sparkle or the roses bloom in her cheeks, it was not to be remarked upon. She was polite, pleasant, yet distant; for her mind remained bent upon considering Mr. Thornbridge and his activities.

She'd waited almost all day for a return note from Dr. Heighton. She waited in vain, for though Dr. Heighton did respond, it was not with the looked-for response. He disallowed her visit! She'd been shocked. He wrote with the greatest formality and deference, but he begged to inform her his address was not suitable for receiving visits by gentlewomen. Anyway, he continued, he was sending Mr. Thornbridge to the country to recuperate at his father's residence. Perhaps she could visit him there.

Visit him there! She didn't even know where his people came from! She supposed she could gain that information through Waddley's, but it would likely cause too many questions.

She felt confoundedly helpless. It was not a state she welcomed. She hated helplessness and all its attendant ramifications. She could not allow herself to float on the river like a punt without a pole. To be left to the mercy of wind, tide, and obstruction—natural or otherwise—was a fate to be abhorred. It was a fate to which too much of her life had already followed to dismal ends.

No! It was not fair to bundle her marriage with Mr. Waddley with dismal events. She smiled slightly. Maybe it would be best to say her life with Mr. Waddley had been a time floating on a particularly peaceful and slow-moving waterway.

"Ah! A smile," said Lord Havelock. "I was wondering if I was destined to spend the entire carriage ride with a statue—lovely though that statue might be."

"I beg your pardon, Lord Havelock. My mind is taken up

with other matters. Matters that I am sure you would consider ght, but in my existence carry much weight." She allowed her augh to titter self-consciously.

He appeared to consider her words. "I have experienced that ircumstance with my own mother and sister. I believe I may e trusted to understand and forgive."

Cecilia's eyebrows rose and she suppressed an urge to laugh. You relieve my mind," she managed in only a slightly strangled oice.

He nodded but did not look her way, his eyes on his leader. I understand Reggie has not been behindhand in soliciting your and in marriage."

"What would you know of the matter?" she asked carefully.

He allowed a slight smile to pull at the corners of his lips. From Reggie, of course. I also know you rejected him. Wisely one. He is a pleasant fribble, but easily cowed. Should you narry him, you two would no doubt flounder about. You need firmer and steadier hand."

"Oh? Do you have any suggestions? I ask merely for informa-onal purposes, that I may understand the drift of your mind."

"Of course. And may I say that is wise of you. Too many oung women would take offense at my words. I am pleased to ee you have the maturity to appreciate receiving wisdom and uidance from others."

"Thank you," she murmured pleasantly while her yellow kid-loved fingers curled into talons. How could this arrogant man ver have been the easy-mannered gentleman of Miss Amble-horp's memory? It did not seem possible.

"There are any number of gentlemen with the strength of haracter you need. There is myself, of course, and I would say ir Branstoke, though I understand he is not inclined toward aatrimony—"

"While you are?"

"Given the proper understanding from a woman and comple-aentary feelings, yes, I should say so."

"I see. Any one else? My curiosity, you understand. What bout Sir Elsdon?"

Havelock's eyes narrowed a moment. "Yes, I suppose he must e considered also, if he can be brought to forego his tendency oward levity. He can be a remarkably shrewd man. But I would ot recommend that any decisions be made with dispatch."

"I shall contrive not to."

"You think me too blunt perhaps?"

"No, not at all, Lord Havelock. Actually, I do not seriously consider remarriage. My health, you understand." She saw him nod solemnly and suppressed a smile. "By the by, have you seen my brother as of late? We had a slight family tiff while at Oastley, and I fear he is foresworn of my company. Silly really."

"Yes I have, and judging from his demeanor, I should say whatever transpired, you were the victor."

"Still pouting?"

"I'm afraid so. Tomorrow evening a group of us are gathering to rehearse a play—"

"Rehearse a play?"

He looked down at her, a wry smile pulling at his lips. "It is a short piece of Sir Elsdon's devising. We humor him. You and Lady Meriton shall have to come to the performance as my personal guests."

"We should be delighted," she cried, clasping her hands together.

"I believe Elsdon is sending out cards tomorrow. Until then it is to be a secret. I would appreciate it if you did not mention it to him until you receive your invitation. He can be tiresome if crossed."

She laughed. "You have my word."

"Anyway, as I was saying, tomorrow evening we rehearse for several hours then we adjourn to my quarters for cards. Randolph has promised to attend—and knowing his head, no doubt I shall be obliged to put him up for the entire night. While in my clutches, shall I contrive to hint to him that a reconciliation would be in order?"

"That would be most kind of you."

He nodded as if that were understood. Cecilia smiled again, and this time it lit her eyes, for the kernel of a plan was forming in her fertile mind. She kept up a lively conversation to atone for her earlier reticence, her hands fluttering about as she talked, until she happened to see Sir James Branstoke driving Miss Cresswell. Suddenly a heavy weight felt like it was pressing upon her chest. She turned to Lord Havelock and hinted that the clouds were becoming a worrisome dark gray and that the freshening wind threatened to chill her to the bone. They contrived to arrive back at Lady Meriton's house before the threatening fat raindrops began their steady fall. Snidely she found she hoped Miss Cresswell was not similarly fortunate.

"Plaguey weather, ain't it? A good night to stage *King Lear,* I should think, what with all its references to rain and wind," Sir Elsdon cheerfully observed as he settled across from Cecilia and Lady Meriton in the commodious carriage he'd borrowed for the evening from one of his many friends. He took his beaver hat from his head and brushed the raindrops from its flat brim before resettling it rakishly on his red-gold locks. "So what's that they say? About April showers and May flowers? Never could remember poetry. Anyway, shouldn't complain, I'll warrant."

Cecilia smiled slightly. "I'll grant you that; however, I find such weather to be deleterious to my health. Brings on colds and chills, you know, and sometimes the most putrid sore throats."

"Oh, please, Cecilia, don't go borrowing trouble," said Lady Meriton.

"No, I shall try not to, only I have felt so remarkably well the past few weeks, I cannot help but be wary."

"I would think there shouldn't be any harm in that. Makes you careful, that's all," offered Elsdon.

"Why, thank you, Sir Elsdon. That's kind of you to say and such is my thought as well."

"Stands to reason. I daresay you're like one of those hothouse flowers, the kind that take special handling. I understand the result to be well worth the effort."

Cecilia could not help but pink with pleasure, even though she was certain his words were contrived for just that effect. She believed Randolph's friends were making a play for her attentions, in all probability to satisfy a wager. Nonetheless, she was woman enough that she couldn't help but be pleased. Sir Elsdon was a genial gentleman with a quick wit and ready smile. Doubtlessly excellent traits for a gamester.

She tittered and coyly looked aside. "La, sir, I shall make certain I do not take your words seriously. They are too nicely done, by half."

"It is easy when the subject is worthy."

"I believe I shall count myself fortunate that we have arrived at our destination, and I do not need to respond to that," she said, laughing warmly.

"I am desolate. And here I thought to dazzle you with honeyed words. What is a courting gentleman to do?" he asked, swinging out of the carriage and turning to offer her, then Lady Meriton, his hand.

Cecilia chose not to respond to his outrageous sallies for fear he would cause more blushes to rise in her cheeks. Of all of Randolph's friends, he was the easiest to be with. That gave her a thought.

"Do you know if my brother plans to attend this party?"

"Don't believe he does. Spoke of having an intimate little supper with a friend."

"Ah, Miss Angel Swafford by any chance?"

His rusty-colored eyebrows rose. "Now how would you know that name?"

She laughed. "The evening of the opera a very inebriated young man mistook me for her rival and thought to steal me away from Randolph by informing me of Miss Swafford's existence."

"Nutley," he murmured, nodding. "And that's how you came to be in the company of Branstoke?"

"He, ah, relieved me of Mr. Nutley's presence," she explained, handing her cloak to a footman.

He frowned, thrusting out his lower lip. "Yes, well, you shouldn't have been left alone. I told Randy so, too. No malice in him, but sometimes quite a knuckleheaded fellow. Oh, excuse me, didn't mean to disparage your own brother like that. Not done. *Bad Ton,* y'know."

"Please, do not apologize. I well know my brother."

"Good, then for the nonce: *Illiterate him, I say, quite from your memory.*"

"Yes, Mrs. Malaprop," she said, laughing.

Still smiling, she went through the receiving line, greeting the Waymonds. Afterward, she found herself solicited for dances by numerous gentleman. Lord Havelock surprised her by asking for the waltz. Without knowing quite how it happened, she found herself enjoying the ball. That is until a twinge of uneasiness trickled down her spine. Instinctively she turned to find Sir Branstoke regarding her through his raised quizzing glass. Seeing he had her attention, he came forward.

Silently, Cecilia ground her teeth in vexation. Sir Branstoke was one gentleman she was not happy to see or speak with. He upset her equilibrium far too readily and made her feel the stuttering schoolgirl.

"Have you had an opportunity to speak with Mr. Thornbridge?" he asked.

"No, I have not. Though I suppose you have. No doubt you have discovered everything and are here to tease me with it."

He looked at her in surprise. "On the contrary. After your words of yesterday I made certain I did not interfere. I would have thought you would have gone immediately to Dr. Heighton's."

"I would have," she grudgingly conceded, "however, Dr. Heighton would not allow me to visit. He claims his residence is not a place for women. He suggested I visit Mr. Thornbridge in the country at his father's home."

Branstoke frowned. "Odd. I had not received that impression from Dr. Heighton. Well, are you?"

"Am I what?"

"Going to visit Mr. Thornbridge in the country?"

She flushed. "I would, but I must admit I do not know where his people come from."

"Ah—" said Branstoke, his face clearing and a slight smile turning up the corners of his lips.

Cecilia groaned. "Do not tell me. You know where he comes from."

He shrugged in apology.

"Excuse me, Sir Branstoke, but I feel another of my dreadful headaches coming on. Somehow, that seems common around you," she snapped. With disregard for appearances, she whirled around and left him, his laughter trailing behind her.

Cecilia made her way to the corner of the room were the dowagers and matrons sat gossiping. Carefully she pulled Lady Meriton aside. "Do you think we might leave?"

Her aunt breathed a rasping sigh of relief. "I would be most happy to. I fear I have succumbed to that malady you claimed this weather fosters. I feel awful. I have not been able to do a single cutting all evening for my hands are weak and my head too achy for plain sight."

"Jessamine! Why did you not tell me? Of course, we will go. Let me but inform Sir Elsdon." She settled her aunt on a chair in the corner then sent a servant in search of him.

Sir Elsdon was not to be found. Neither was Lord Havelock.

This was an interesting turn of events! Her eyes sparkled at the knowledge and she set off in her own investigation—or would have if she hadn't recalled her aunt. She bit her lower lip in frustration. She had to see to Jessamine's well-being.

She went down to the front hall to ask a footman to obtain a hackney for her and Lady Meriton.

"There is no need of that," said a languid voice coming out of the shadows. It was Branstoke. "I am on the point of leaving myself. My carriage has already been called. It will be here directly."

Cecilia compressed her lips at the thought of being beholden to this gentleman, but concern for her aunt stilled her too-ready tongue and would not let her reject his offer. "Thank you," she whispered. "I'll tell her we are ready to leave."

She hurried back up the stairs, refusing to consider how circumstance again had him managing her life. Tenderly she guided Lady Meriton down and saw her cloak wrapped warmly about her. She ignored Sir Branstoke as best she might. To her chagrin, he did not seem to notice. Then her argument with the man flew from her mind for her aunt was truly feverish.

A worried frown creased her fair brow. She settled next to Jessamine in the luxurious carriage, keeping close to her to help warm her. A silent Branstoke tucked fur throws about them both. At the Meriton townhouse he helped them to descend and by unspoken silent agreement he half-carried, half-led the weakening, feverish woman up the stairs and into the hands of her efficient dresser while Cecilia trailed helplessly behind.

In a shaky voice Cecilia offered her gratitude. "Truthfully, I am not much good with illness," she said apologetically.

A touch of his normal humor returned to his gold-flecked eyes. "Those who are rarely ill, seldom are."

She flushed, but refused to be drawn into another argument with him. "It is a wet, cold night. Would you care for a glass of port or something before you go back out into it?"

"Thank you, but no. As you say, it is a wet, cold night, and I do not care to leave my men and horses standing in it. Goodnight, Mrs. Waddley."

"Good-night," she murmured, watching him leave.

❦ Chapter Twelve

CECILIA PLUMPED the bed pillows behind Lady Meriton, then solicitously urged her aunt to lay back against them. Even after a night's rest, her aunt was no better, perhaps worse. She pulled up the counterpane, tucking it warmly about Jessamine while smoothing out the wrinkles.

"Isn't that more comfortable? Here, let me place this tray on your lap. I've prepared a special medicinal tea with honey from one of Great Aunt Martha's old recipes. It will help you breathe easier and soothe that raw throat," she said coaxingly.

"Thank you," rasped her aunt, carefully balancing the tray. Shaky hands grasped the cup and guided it to her mouth. She cautiously sipped the steaming drink. "It *is* good!" she exclaimed.

She quickly handed it back to Cecilia as a coughing spasm shook her frame. When she finished, her voice was husky, but clearer. "You shouldn't be here, my dear. I don't like to see you risking infection."

"Stuff and nonsense," returned Cecilia briskly, handing her back the cup. She watched as her aunt sipped more of the hot liquid. "You know as well as I that for all my counterfeiting, I don't have a sickly constitution."

"And I do? Illness is foreign to my nature, but ill I am." She set the cup down on the tray and absently plucked at her coverings. "It makes me terribly mawkish to be so low. And today I expect a load of Oastley ale to arrive. It needs to be locked away in the cellar lest it be consumed too readily by the servants. Can you see to it, Cecilia? My chatelaine is on that table," she said, pointing to a burlwood sideboard.

Cecilia crossed the room to pick up the keyring. "What is this key to?" she asked, singling out an especially large brass key.

Lady Meriton sneezed. "That's to Cheney House. Mother insists I have a key. It is her way of subtly reminding Randolph that though he lives there, Cheney House is not yet his."

"A wasted effort." Cecilia crossed back to her aunt's bedside.

"Randolph needs to be cracked over the head. Subtlety is useless."

Lady Meriton's laugh ended in another coughing spasm. She collapsed back against the pillows. "I am not good company for you, my dear. It would make me feel better to see you get out in the fresh air. Perhaps you could find me a new novel at Hatchard's or Bell's."

Cecilia laughed and sat down on the edge of the bed. "All right, I promise I shall leave you to the tender mercies of the servants this afternoon; but I shan't change my mind about attending Lady Orrick's gathering this evening."

"Cecilia, please go. I'm sure one of your callers would be only too happy to escort you."

"There you are mistaken, for it is my understanding they have plans for the evening."

"Plans? Is there a card party planned, or some debauchery?" Lady Meriton suggested with a laugh.

"Neither. I have it on the best authority that they gather to rehearse a play."

Lady Meriton groaned. "Do not tell me Sir Elsdon is organizing another of his amateur theatricals?"

"Yes, and I understand the play is one Sir Elsdon wrote himself!"

"Oh, no!" exclaimed Lady Meriton, torn between laughter and exasperation.

"I think you have the better of me and know something I don't. Has he written other plays before this?"

"Not exactly, but I do remember a ghastly rewrite he did of one two or three years ago. All who saw it were shocked, and a trifle angered. Fortunately we were all kept laughing too much for there to be lasting malice."

"I don't think I've heard this tale. Please, enlighten me. It may serve to prepare me for whatever he has in store for his audience. I'll have you know we have already received invitations—the first issued, I understand." She refilled her aunt's cup from the china pot then moved the tray onto a bedside table.

"It was a parody of sorts, though Sir Elsdon swore we were maligning him greatly to consider it such. He rewrote one of Shakespeare's plays."

"What did he do, make a comedy out of *Hamlet?*"

"No, nothing so broad as that. He rewrote *King Richard III,* making that beastly king seem saintly and divinely led."

"Gracious! A Herculean effort! How successful was his interpretation?"

Lady Meriton rolled her eyes. "It was a bit much to accept, though it was all done with verve. Some characters were pricelessly drawn. The two murderers were wonderful—but there, I'll admit he didn't alter the play drastically. Now that I consider it, I believe Randolph played one of them."

Talkers are no good doers.

The line echoed in the passageways of her mind. It was the line Mr. Waddley recorded in his journal. It was the line Randolph tossed off at Lady Amblethorp's musicale. It was a line from *King Richard III!*

"Cecilia, are you certain you are feeling well? You're looking terribly pale," worried Lady Meriton.

"What? No, I assure you, I'm fine. I'm afraid my mind was wandering, trying to recall what I could of the play. It will be interesting to see what Sir Elsdon has devised for his new theatrical. Were Mr. Rippy and Lord Havelock in that earlier production as well?"

Her aunt nodded. "Lord Havelock played Buckingham and Mr. Rippy, along with Randolph, bounded on and off stage in several different guises. It seemed to have a cast of thousands, and a very socially mixed lot it was, too. But that's common for any of the plays he decides to produce. This is an annual event with him, and has quite become a favorite with the *ton.*"

"I never knew any of this! I mean, we all are familiar with Sir Elsdon's penchant for spouting lines from plays, but I didn't realize he was so enamored with the stage."

"Oh yes, it has even been joked that he could out-Kean Mr. Kean. That is sheer nonsense of course. No one can match the great Mr. Edmund Kean! Nonetheless, that gives you an idea of the degree of seriousness with which he approaches acting."

"Yes, indeed. Well, you've talked long enough. It's not good for your throat to do so much talking. Why don't you try to rest now, and when you wake I'll have a new novel for you."

Lady Meriton reached out to squeeze Cecilia's hand. "You are such a comfort to me while Meriton is out of the country. I'm so glad I have you with me."

"I'm glad to be here, too," she assured her, smiling mistily.

She stood up and removed the cup from her aunt's hand, setting it on the tray. She pulled the blankets up farther on Jessamine's shoulder. "Now to sleep."

Lady Meriton nodded and turned on her side, her eyes already heavy.

Cecilia picked up the tray and carried it out of the room. Seeing Lady Meriton's dresser approaching her, she absently handed the tray to the woman. She restlessly tossed the chatelaine into the air two or three times, her mind analyzing possibilities and plots. She hurried down the stairs to the library and hopefully a collection of Shakespeare's works that included *King Richard III*.

The chilling rain of the previous night had blown through London leaving the air fresh and clean though unseasonably colder. Cecilia, dressed in a warm, lavender wool gown topped by a russet spenser, thrust her hands deeply into her fur muff when she set out for Bell's Gallery of Arts. In deference to her aunt, she was accompanied by Sarah, now officially raised to the status of lady's maid, and the two traveled via the Meriton carriage. Cecilia would have preferred walking briskly; but she knew that would not be in keeping with her public persona. She was beginning to chafe at the creation she made—and all its attendant limitations. Nonetheless, she had high hopes her quest was nearing its end and she could quietly retire from society and be the person she wanted to be. Not that she was too sure who that person was. She only knew it wasn't the flighty, silly widgeon of London repute. She was also beginning to think it wasn't the retiring country widow. What—or who—was left in the gulf between troubled her.

She looked out the window as the carriage clattered round a corner. Until recently, that was how she viewed life, through a carriage window. Protected from the elements and from her fellowman. She sighed. She'd been an onlooker at life for five and twenty years. That was not how she wished to spend the next five and twenty years. Her dreams of bringing Mr. Waddley's murderer to book served as a catalyst. Now she was uncertain as to the final result.

This business with the play troubled her. It hinted at an evil madness. While it was true that the real King Richard III had been partially vindicated by history of the crimes claimed by Sir

Thomas More and through him, Mr. Shakespeare, the fact that the play was used to perpetuate—and perhaps rationalize—crime, worried her. There was a sordidness to it. A joke gone awry, as Jessamine said Sir Elsdon's production had gone.

Did Sir Elsdon see himself as Richard? Did he possess that Machiavellian nature shown to such successful advantage in the play? Or was he yet another pawn?

She withdrew a kid-gloved hand from her muff and rubbed her throbbing temples. She'd not been prevaricating when she told Sir Branstoke that headaches plagued her. They were headaches of worry and uncertainty.

She closed her eyes, inhaling deeply, and letting her breath out slowly. She didn't open her eyes again until she felt the carriage stop and the footman jump down to open the door.

"Please, allow me." It was the measured deep tones of Lord Havelock. His tall frame stood at the door, a graceful white hand held out to her.

"Lord Havelock!"

"Mrs. Waddley," he returned with a bow.

"I mean, what a surprise meeting you here today! Such a coincidence and in my time of need."

He raised a dark eyebrow, his lips lifting slightly in unvoiced question. "Ah—then I take it you have not heard of the most recent scurrilous cartoons created at our dear regent's expense?"

"No, not at all."

"A sad business, but come and see," he said, leading her toward the press of people about the window.

Skillfully he threaded her through the crowd until she was in front of the window where several cartoons were displayed. They were lampoons against Prinny and showed Princess Caroline as the innocent victim.

"I swear, they are more comical against her for what she is not!" she blurted out, then hastily bit her lip. "Though I'm not certain I really understand them," she amended, looking up wide-eyed at Lord Havelock.

A puzzled expression flew across that gentleman's features.

"Do you think we might go in now? It is so dreadfully cold out here. So easy to take a chill. Lady Meriton has one, you know, a chill that is. She is feeling low, so I've promised to find her a new novel to read. Can you recommend one, my lord?" she prattled, looking up at him guilelessly.

He shrugged slightly. "Of course, madame. I believe there are one or two new ones, most likely written anonymously by *A Lady* or *A Gentleman.*"

"I do so love novels! Everyone in them is full of good health and wit. It fatigues me just to contemplate how anyone could devise novels! I cannot understand why they would wish anonymity."

"I understand that sometimes their characters are drawn from life and often not sympathetically. Their real-life models take offense."

"Oh. Is that why Sir Elsdon's version of *King Richard III* was not popular? Did he do that?"

"What do you know of that?"

She shrugged and frowned petulantly. "Nothing really. Only that he rewrote some of it and that his changes were not looked upon with favor. Aunt Jessamine told me about it when we were discussing Sir Elsdon's upcoming production." She clapped her hands together, lacing the fingers tight. "She said Randolph played one of the murderers of the princes. I should have loved to see that. I can't imagine Randolph as a murderer, can you? Oh, that's a silly question. Of course you can. You were in the play too, she said, as Buckingham."

"A traitor's traitor," said Randolph, coming up behind them.

"Oh, I'm so glad to see you, Randolph. I wanted to apologize for being so snappish at Oastley."

Lord Havelock bowed, leaving them to the private discourse he knew Cecilia desired. She smiled her appreciation.

"Eh?" Randolph looked at her in surprise. "What? Oh, that's quite all right, little sister. But you know, you could stand to listen to your brother now and again, especially as father is still off looking for cures for dropsy." He led her to an isolated bin of prints.

"Yes, I know, Randolph," she said humbly, her eyes downcast and her tongue set firmly between her teeth.

"You here without that dragon aunt of ours?"

Her eyes flashed upward then away as she recalled her supposed newfound humility. "She has been very nice to me. I don't like you talking of her so," she said, her gaze sliding to meet his. "Besides, she's sick, quite done up, poor thing. I know exactly how it is, too. I promised her I'd find her the latest novel to read."

"Someone sick besides you! Pon'rep if that ain't something! I was asked the other day—and dash it if I can recall by who— I was asked if you were sickly as a child. Had to think on that. Don't recall you ever so plagued."

Asked! She'd give a monkey to know by whom. "Not so much, no," she admitted carefully. "My health broke when Mr. Waddley died, you see. Both my spirit and my body crumbled. Dear, dear Mr. Waddley, such a gentle, God-fearing man," she murmured as she thumbed idly through a bin of prints.

Randolph gave a shout of laughter, drawing eyes from every corner of the establishment. "That's rich! What a naive little doll you are. That's what he referred to you as, y'know: his little doll."

"Randolph, what are you saying?" Cecilia demanded, dropping the simpering manner as if it were a hot coal.

"I'm sick of hearing you sing praises to Saint George Waddley. He was a nosy, prosy, hypocrite with—"

"Haukstrom!" snapped Lord Havelock, striding toward them. "We'd best be going. Elsdon's expecting us."

Cecilia watched, astounded, as Randolph virtually deflated before her eyes. She turned questioningly toward Lord Havelock.

He bowed, his lips set in a grim line. "I beg your pardon, Mrs. Waddley, I didn't mean to intrude, but we will be late. Elsdon is a tyrant about his productions and does not tolerate tardiness. You will excuse us?" he said rhetorically, taking Randolph by the elbow.

"I'm sorry, Cecilia. Best just forget what I said. My anger gets the best of me sometimes."

"Yes, yes of course," she said helplessly. At the moment, she could cheerfully throttle Lord Havelock. What did he not want Randolph to say? His interruption was blatantly well-timed, especially as she saw him out of the corner of her eye surreptitiously listening to their conversation. Lord Havelock definitely had something to hide.

Quickly she picked out a new book for Lady Meriton, paid for her purchase, and headed back for Meriton House, her mind busy.

"Any callers while I was gone, Loudon?" Cecilia asked as she handed her muff, gloves, and hat to a waiting footman.

"Yes, ma'am. Two. Sir James Branstoke—here is his card—

and the Honorable Mr. Rippy. He left this little nosegay of violets for you, ma'am," he said, handing her the delicate purple flowers. "Both gentlemen declined to leave a message and left quickly when appraised of Lady Meriton's continued ill health."

"Thank you, Loudon. I should like a tray with Lady Meriton this evening. I shall be staying in. As it will be a quiet night, I'm sure we can grant a few holidays among the servants."

"Yes, ma'am, and thank you, ma'am."

She laughed as she turned to mount the stairs. "Don't thank me, thank Lady Meriton. She has taught me well!"

"May I say, ma'am, there's not all that would agree with Lady Meriton."

"I know, but isn't there an old proverb which states the proof is in the pudding?"

"Just so, ma'am," Loudon said, but she was already up the stairs.

Cecilia peeked in on Jessamine, delighted to see she was sleeping peacefully, then tiptoed out and went on to her room. She had plans to make and things to do that would be best if there were fewer servants abroad to observe her actions. Quickly she changed and went out into the hall. As it was late in the day and most cleaning done, there were no housemaids above stairs. She crept down the hall to Franklin Meriton's empty room. Looking first up and down the hall, she went inside, wondering if she was to make a habit of surreptitiously entering men's rooms. Though away at school, Cecilia wagered her cousin hadn't taken all his clothes with him. She crossed to the wardrobe, pulling it open. It was nearly empty; however, her hunch proved correct. Aside from two outrageously colored waistcoats and a bright green jacket, there was a dark blue jacket and knee breeches along with a dove-colored waistcoat. Though she knew Franklin to be slight for his sixteen years, she wagered this suit was left behind as being too small. Eagerly she took it out and held it up to herself. It looked like it would fit well enough. Searching the drawers below, she came up with a shirt and several cravats. A search about the room failed to turn up a pair of shoes or boots—though she had her doubts of those fitting anyway. She was also disappointed not to discover a suitable hat, only a schoolboy's cap. It would have to do. Bundling her treasures together, she scurried back to her room.

* * *

It was not yet past eleven when the slim figure of a youth emerged from the Meriton townhouse, closing the door softly behind. It would not have been remarked upon if it weren't for the youth's furtive behavior. Closer examination revealed a woman's black kid boots on the youth's small feet. Then there was also the consideration that only the ladies or their guests used the front door, and that youth hadn't been seen going in.

The watcher from the shadows spit into the street then scratched his head, knocking his hat sideways. "Holy Mother and all the saints," he swore, "his nibs, he be a knowin' one al'right." Keeping to the shadows, he loped off after her in a curiously rolling, bandy-legged fashion. He hoped she weren't going far, and he wondered how he was going to get to tell his nibs about this hidey-ho.

Old Tim Ryan followed his quarry as closely as he dared through dark streets. Despite his concerns for his charge (for thus he readily took responsibility), he had to smile to himself when the slender youth avoided the Charlies, lights, inebriated gentlemen, and once a lady of uncertain charms. His grizzled brows rose when she turned onto the street where Branstoke lived, then his forehead furrowed deeply as the way led him past and around the corner. Finally his charge stopped before a large house on the next corner. The house was circled carefully. Tim knew note was taken of lights in the windows. The house was dark except for light from two windows on the ground floor near a side entrance. Satisfied servants weren't about, his charge walked boldly up to the front door, stuck a key in the lock, and entered.

Tim didn't know what to do. He scratched his chin and spat before he made up his mind. Branstoke's home was only a little over a block away. He turned and ran, rocking from side to side, running faster than he had in many a year.

The stable door banged open against the wall. "Romley! Romley! Wake up, man!"

A bang and a clatter greeted the call, followed by repeated thumps before a door opened above. A disheveled George Romley appeared at the top of the stairs, jumping on one booted foot while stuffing a bare foot in the other boot as he came. "What? Ryan! What are yer doing here? Yer aren't due ta be relieved yet."

"I'm doing what I's supposed to. Keepin' an eye on the mort. She piked, dressed like a grubby schoolboy."

"What?" George clattered down the stairs, bringing his braces up over his shoulders as he came.

"Aye. I followed her to a house in the next block. She had a key and nipped inside, nice as yer please—but very secretive, like she don't want to be seen. Go tell his nibs. I got to get back," Tim said, rocking toward the door.

"Wait! Yer aint told me which house!"

"The Dooks, that big one on the corner," he said before he disappeared back into the dark.

Romley grabbed a coat and hat from the peg and set out at a run for St. James, for he knew his employer—believing Mrs. Waddley to be spending the evening at home—was indulging in a quiet evening at his club.

The softly voiced words that erupted from Sir James Branstoke on being appraised of Mrs. Waddley's activities drew a reluctant smile from his groom. For all his society manners, he could still swear like a trooper. He'd also still be the man Romley'd like to have on his side of a fight. Hearing him, Romley didn't think he'd care to be in Mrs. Waddley's shoes when Sir Branstoke caught up with her. Didn't the fool woman know he was trying to protect her? As he kept pace with Branstoke, he couldn't help but remember all that blood on Hewitt's coat. Whatever was going on, it was serious business.

Tim came out of the shadows as the two men neared.

"Hasn't she come out yet, Tim?"

"Unless she did when I riled Romley, I don't think so, guv'ner. I seed a light flickerin' in a winder, right there," he said, pointing to a corner first floor window.

"Carriage comin'," warned Romley.

"I suggest, gentlemen, that we remove ourselves from sight," said Branstoke, though it was obvious his thoughts were not on the approaching carriage. The trio melted into the shadowed entryway of a house across the street.

The carriage drew up before Cheney House, disgorging three gentlemen: Haukstrom, the Honorable Mr. Rippy, and another man Branstoke didn't recognize. It was obvious that young Haukstrom was drunk and his two companions were nearly equally well lit. They talked loudly, singing catches of drinking songs, and hung onto each other for support. They slowly maneuvered up the short flight of steps to the door were Haukstrom then stood, weaving for several moments, before pulling a large brass key from his pocket. He was too drunk to fit it to the lock, so he kicked the door. He nearly fell forward on his face when it smoothly swung open.

Cecilia heard the raucous singing as she rummaged through the drawer of the small desk in the withdrawing room off Randolph's bedchamber. Hurriedly she stuffed handfuls of the miscellaneous papers it held into her pockets. Passing through the room into Randolph's bedchamber, she crossed to the tall window fronting the street. She looked out to see her worst fears. Randolph and his friends struggling up the steps.

Surely it was just midnight. What was he doing home this early? She was certain he'd be occupied until all hours of the morning, if not with the play, then with drinking and gambling afterward. It appeared the drinking took its toll early.

It was unfair! She'd hardly begun searching upstairs. She spent far too long uselessly examining the library. She should have known the library was not a room Randolph would frequent, even for his business purposes. Now she'd have to find a way to escape Cheney House without detection. It would probably be best to hide in one of the many uninhabited bedchambers and wait until the household resettled for the night.

She ran back to the withdrawing room, heading for the door when she heard voices on the stairs. Randolph's drunken revels had awakened a servant who was urging Randolph's friends to abandon him into his care. He'd see him put to bed immediately.

Cecilia chewed on her lower lip. She didn't dare come out of the room now for fear they'd see her crossing the upstairs landing to another bedchamber. She had two choices. She could hide somewhere within Randolph's room until hopefully he fell asleep, or she could go out a window.

She opted for the window.

She ran quietly back to Randolph's room. It was a large corner room with two windows facing the street and one on the side of the house. She went this time to the side window and slid it cautiously open. It opened with thankfully little sound. She stuck her head out and looked down. It was too far to jump, she'd need some form of rope. She ducked her head back into the room and frantically searched for something usable. Tearing the sheets off the bed would be too cumbersome. She fingered the thick drapes; so, too, would pulling these down. Cravats! She could tie cravats together! But would there be time? She started to turn toward his bureau when her hand slid down the drape encountering the satin rope swagging the drapery panel aside. Perfect! She unhooked it from the roundel at the edge of the window, pleased to see the looped rope ends were long, dangling to the floor. Still, one would not be long enough. She yanked its companion loose and hurriedly knotted them together. The roundel was firmly embedded in the wall so she looped one end tight around it.

Voices were getting louder. Her hands began to shake. With the window open and the rope dangling, they would know some-one had been in the room. She had to make it look like robbery. Quickly she grabbed up the black leather dressing case with the embossed coat of Cheney arms on the lid from the vanity table and ran back to the window. She stuffed the long, flat case into the waistband of her breeches, then lowered the rope out the window. She scraped her knuckles on the rough stone window ledge and the slick rope burned her delicate hands. Ignoring the pain, she lowered herself as quickly as she could. Suddenly she felt the two satin ropes slipping free of the knot that bound them. She was falling!

Chapter Thirteen

Oomph!

She landed abruptly against a man's broad chest, the dressing case pressing painfully against her ribs. Her breath whistled harshly out collapsing her lungs. His hands clamped tightly about her lithe form as her momentum tumbled them onto the ground in a tangle of arms and legs.

She gasped and struggled wildly to get up. To her surprise, her rescuer pushed her off his chest and surged to his feet. In the waning moonlight, his face was a harsh landscape of shadows; nonetheless, she recognized him as she would have recognized one of Jessamine's silhouettes. Her mouth gaped open in dumb surprise. Branstoke! Here, as he always seemed to be so fortuitously at hand. What tie, what silken binding as strong as steel tethered them that he should forever be her rescuer and she should take it as expected and frown if he did not appear, the avenging lord, at her side?

The one hand he maintained about her upper arm compelled her to rise as well. She pulled back, more from habit than with cause, and the dark blue cap she wore fell to the ground. Her hair tumbled down in a cloud of moonlight. He muttered an oath, fluidly bent down to scoop up the hat without breaking stride, and pulled her toward the street. He hustled her onward without a sound. His visage, revealed fleetingly in dim moon and lamplight, was sternly impassive yet bore a rigidity of the jaw that set Cecilia's butterflies in tumult.

They were at the corner when they heard the first shouts out the open window. Cecilia looked back, certain of seeing pursuers only steps away.

"They've spotted George and Tim. They'll lead them a merry chase, I'll warrant," Branstoke whispered, his breath warm and soft as down against her ear. A shiver ran through her. He placed his arm about her waist, hurrying her forward. "Come, my house is a step away. We'll go there until the first hue and cry has passed."

Mutely, she nodded, feeling strangely secure and trusting. The feelings rippled through her in wonder, to be measured against all her senses and come echoing back, replete.

To avoid standing on the street while he unlocked the door, he took her around to the back, letting them in by the servant's entrance. Keeping her firmly anchored to his side, like two wraiths they glided through the darkened house to his library. He led her to a chair by the fireplace then stoked the embers back to flames to take the chill out of the room and out of themselves. Though he doubted the warmth of a fire could warm the chill he felt in his heart when he saw her throw a leg over the window ledge and knew for certain her intentions.

When the flames leaped, casting light and warmth, he crossed to the windows to close the heavy drapes, to deny the outside knowledge that anyone was yet up and about. To deny the possibility that anyone should see a fragile silhouette in his window. He would protect her honor as well as her life though his body beat with an insistent tempo claiming—nay, demanding!—her honor as his own. His fingers curled into fists as he crossed back to the fire. He lit a punk and carried the flame to branches of candles on the mantel, taking his time, not looking at her as he sternly disciplined his body to follow his mind's set, if it could not its desire.

He knew she watched him. Wide-eyed. An innocent in spirit if not actuality. A nymph in a world of mortals. Her eyes would be their darkest blue shading into purple set in a face of smoothest alabaster. Her hair, loosed of the pins that normally confined it in its tight coronet and ringlets, would cloud about her delicate heart-shaped face. He remembered how it glistened like white gold in the moonlight and smelled of jasmine in its depths when he whispered in her ear.

How could she have been so foolish as to break into her brother's home? What was she looking for? Had she no idea of the risks she was taking? Did she love Waddley so that she could not let him rest until she discovered what or who killed him? And what did Haukstrom have to do with the mess? Damn it! Why couldn't she trust him?

He thrust a poker deep in the fire, stirring it higher. Rage burned like the flames before his eyes, running through his body following a fuse to his mind, burning, obliterating desire in its wake. Damn it, he would teach her to stop her silly games before a life was lost or another injured grievously. The next life to be forfeit might be her own. Didn't she care? And what about Lady Meriton? She could be bringing her into danger as well.

A muscle jumped spasmodically in a firm, set jaw while tortoise shell eyes gleamed with gold fire echoing hearth flames. Slowly he rose from his crouched position in front of the fire. Stubborn, willful, arrogant chit! He would not let her play ducks and drakes with her life, and she would learn that here and now!

He turned toward her with the speed of a striking snake, his face twisted in grim determination. "Cecilia," he snapped, goaded past endurance.

"Yes?" She looked up at him, the newfound trust she had to offer shining in her eyes.

The sight unmanned him. He sagged back against the side of the intricately carved marble mantelpiece, his breathing harsh. "Cecilia," he began again, bemused. He shook his head. "Why?" he finally asked, his eyes steadfastly looking at her as if he would read the answer in her soul.

"Why did I break into Randolph's house?"

"No. I mean yes, that too. But why do you offer me your trust now?"

She did not pretend to misunderstand him. She rose fluidly and took a step toward him. He lifted a hand as if to ward away her presence. She paused, smiling at it a moment, then walked straight into his arms, throwing her own about his neck. He held his head stiff a moment, regarding her warily through a veil of lashes. Her smile broadened in womanly wisdom as she pulled his head toward hers until their lips met.

At the touch of her lips, the invisible chains that seemed to hold him cobbled and fettered, fell away, and with a groan that came from the depth of his soul, he gathered her willingly to him, his lips searching out the contours of her face, memorizing each mound and valley, the shape of her ear, the sweep of her temple, the line of her pale brow, the hollows of her eyes, the curve of her chin, and the soft fullness of her lips. He traced the swan-like line of her neck to her delicate collarbone hidden behind an ill-swathed and tied cravat. Trembling fingers yanked the offending article away and parted the top of her shirt so his lips and tongue could trace the dips and hollows of soft fragrant skin there. She groaned against him, murmuring his name on little breaths of air as she sagged against him. His head came up to capture her lips again as he picked her up, cradling her against him like a child, and carried her to a sofa. He laid her down on the smooth satin, kneeling in supplication next to her. She smiled and looked dreamily into his eyes, one hand coming up to spear his silky, coffee-colored hair with trembling fingers.

"Why are you always there for me?" she murmured.

He caught her other hand, nibbling the soft pads of her fingertips. "I don't know," he said with stark, wondering honesty. "From the night of Lady Amblethorp's musicale, something has drawn me to you like you were my lodestar meant to guide me out of this world-weary abyss of habit and decadence. You've destroyed my ennui, altered my status quo, and cut up my peace. You've made me care for someone other than myself. Nay, more than care. Though how that may be, I cannot say for you have bedeviled, beleaguered, annoyed, inconvenienced, tried my patience, irked, and goaded me beyond measure, you little baggage. And well you know it! My mind is full of you, only you, until I'm not good company for any of my cronies. I find myself wondering what madcap lark you're up to when I should be exchanging amusing society anecdotes! I am a changed man—and only you can say for good or ill."

She sighed, drawing his head closer to hers that she might drink from his lips as she did at Oastley. "I thought I knew who I was and what I wanted. Now I can no longer answer that question or even imagine answers," she said whimsically while her hands lovingly traced the contours of his face. "I feel as if I've been let out of a cage, but don't know what to do with my freedom. There is a churning restlessness within me that haunts me. It only seems to quiet when you're around. Please, James—" she murmured.

His mouth claimed her joyously while his hands caressed her body through the rough wool of the ill-fitting suit she wore. Nimble fingers slipped the buttons of the waistcoat free and roamed heatedly over the cotton fabric of her shirt and the full mounds of her breasts. At his touch she arched against him, mewing sounds emanating from her throat. His lips slid from hers to trail featherlight caresses down her neck to her collarbone. Her breathing grew ragged and she murmured his name as a hand slid under her shirt to touch her hot skin with sensitive, trembling, cool fingertips.

"When George told me where you were, I didn't know

whether I wanted to beat you or kiss you senselessly," he muttered.

"I'm glad we were lucky enough to have your man near at hand, though I chafe to think I was seen. I was so careful," she said, her hands eagerly untying his cravat and pulling the ends to draw him closer.

"Would you bind me to you, witch?" he growled, nuzzling her neck while his hand found and closed over the mound of her breast.

She inhaled sharply. "Yes! But tell me while I am still able to think, what gave me away?"

He laughed and climbed on the sofa covering her slender body with his. "With you, my darling, I never leave anything to luck."

She stilled, her eyes slowly focusing on his face. "You've had me watched, haven't you?" she asked, her voice curiously empty.

He looked at her, a quizzical light in his eyes. "What is it? Of course, I had you followed. For your own safety. You wouldn't trust me with your dragons; I couldn't trust you not to do something foolish."

"Foolish!" She struggled to sit up, but he held her pinned to the sofa.

"What is this heat, my adorable minx?" The light of laughter was in his eyes.

His humor fueled her anger. "How dare you! Get off of me, you bull-brained oaf! Let me up! Let me up, I say!" She bucked and beat at him with her hands, a sheen of tears glistening in her eyes.

It was the last that caused him to release her. He sat up next to her. "Are you seriously implying that my watching out for your safety does not meet with your approval?"

"Yes!" she hissed, and scooted back on the sofa until she could swing her feet from in back of him to the floor. She blushed when she glanced down at the disarray to her clothes. She stood up, turning her back to him and with shaky fingers set herself to rights. "I have been managed and maneuvered all my life," she said over her shoulder. "I hate it! Do you hear me, I hate it!"

"I hear you, Cecilia, and I would not dream of managing or maneuvering you. Watching out for your safety is not controlling your life. It's protecting it so you can do what you like, be who you like," he said softly.

"But don't you see," she wailed, tears now falling down her cheeks, "I don't know who I am or how I want to be. I've never had the chance!"

"Hush, love, hush," he said, coming forward to comfort her.

She stepped away. "Don't touch me. Don't come any closer. I don't trust you."

"Is it me you don't trust—or yourself?"

"It makes no odds."

"But it does, my dear," he said, smiling at her. Abruptly he nodded, then bowed in her direction. "All right. We shall play this your way, for now."

"What do you mean by that?" she asked suspiciously.

"I shall not press you to admit your feelings for me—"

"Of which I have none!"

"—if you will tell me what you were looking for tonight and last week at Oastley."

"I can't."

"All right," he said, coming purposefully toward her.

"No, wait! Stop. I'll tell you as best I can, though I don't know everything. I suspect you actually know more than I. Can't we sit down?" she asked, edging toward a chair away from the sofa and its memories.

He nodded, then went to the cupboard where brandy and glasses were kept and poured her a small glass. He took it toward her. "Here, drink this, I believe you could use it."

"Thank you," she whispered. She took a swallow, grimacing at the strong flavor.

Branstoke laughed. "I see you are unused to brandy. Sip it. It will warm and calm you."

She looked hesitatingly at the remainder of the contents in her glass, but did as he suggested. It did seem to warm her, and calm—or was that numb—her jangling nerves. She relaxed against the chair, letting her head loll back. Branstoke watched her, satisfied, and went to stoke the fire again.

"As you may know, Mr. Waddley was killed one night near the docks at Waddley Spice and Tea. The official verdict was death by person or persons unknown with robbery as their motive. It was decided that he was an unfortunate man who was in the wrong place at the wrong time. I don't believe that. I believe—no, I *know*," she amended firmly, "Mr. Waddley was murdered deliberately. He was murdered because he discovered some occurrences at the docks that did not meet with his approval. Illegal occurrences."

Branstoke stood up, resting an elbow on the mantle, and crossed one foot casually over the other. "How do you know this?"

"From his attitude the day he died, the things he said, and from some of the references in his journal."

"What was it about his attitude?"

"He was unusually restless, grave even. He was muttering that his suspicions had best not be true, or there'd be hell to pay. And he kept staring at me with a fierce look in his eyes. It was frightening. Then, after dinner, he went upstairs to change and came back in a suit all in black. He said he was going out and not to wait on his return."

"Had he ever done anything like that before?"

"He had, on occasion, gone out late and not returned until the early morning hours, but never did he specifically change into all black clothing. Even his shirt and stock were black."

"Did he ever tell you where he went late at night, or where he was going that night?"

"No, Mr. Waddley was not communicative in that way. And before you suggest he went to seek other female company," she said with a blush rising in her cheeks, "I considered that myself. However, that wouldn't explain why, when he returned, his clothes were always dirty and bore that distinctive pungent smell."

He raised an eyebrow in mute inquiry.

"Fish, tar, and rotting timber," she said with a smile.

He nodded in wry understanding then uncrossed his foot and strode to the drink cabinet to pour a glass for himself. "What about this journal you mentioned?" he said over his shoulder. "It is that, I gather, which set you to investigating your own brother?"

"Yes. Though I still find it difficult to believe him capable of murder, I do believe he is involved. The journal mentions business meetings with someone he calls 'H'."

"Haukstrom."

"So I believe. Mr. Waddley also wrote down what he believed to be a code phrase of some kind. *Talkers are no good doers.*"

He looked at her quizzically. "Isn't that from a play?"

She nodded. *"King Richard III.* I confess I didn't tumble to it until today, when I learned Randolph played the part of one of the murderers who speaks that line in a production Sir Elsdon did a few years ago."

He crossed his arms over his chest as he considered her story. "On the basis of circumstantial evidence, it would appear your brother is involved. But I agree with you. I do not believe Haukstrom has the stomach for murder."

"What I can't understand is how Mr. Thornbridge went from investigating my brother to searching out information on disappearing prostitutes."

"I believe I do. There has also been a Select Committee of the House of Commons set up this year to investigate incidents of this nature, though I believe they center their interest on the growing number of flash houses. They do not—or will not—broaden their area of inquiry to instances of white slavery."

"White slavery?"

"Yes, the capture and exportation of young English women to appease foreign appetites."

"Oh," Cecilia said in a small voice.

"I understand their favored quarries are blonds and redheads. Most of them come from the lower classes. Some kidnapped, some purchased from their parents. For a particular wealthy client, they may procure children or kidnap the daughters of the middle and upper classes. A girl from a titled family is worth a king's ransom."

Cecilia blanched, her eyes wide. She took a large sip of brandy, coughing as it burned its way down her throat. Branstoke strode over to her chair and leaned over her, a hand clasping either chair arm, holding her in place. On his face was a mask of dark emotion.

"This is the nature of the dragon you so blithely chase! It is larger, fiercer, and uglier than you can imagine. Verily, it comes from the deepest, blackest, caverns of hell!" He reached up to finger a lock of her pale blond hair. "And you are his favorite meal," he finished softly.

She shivered and pulled her head back until her hair fell from his fingers. "And Randolph is involved with it?"

He didn't say anything, but looked at her steadily.

She took a deep breath and nodded, then closed her eyes as pain shot through her. When she opened them her eyes were glistening. "Please," she whispered, "take me home now."

He let out a long breath, like a deep sigh. He straightened, holding out his hand to her. She took it and rose to her feet, then stepped forward to wrap her arms about his waist and rest her head on his broad chest. Surprised at her impulsive action, he did not move. Then slowly, when he was certain she would not flee like a frightened bird, his arms wrapped about her in return and pulled her close. He rested his head on hers and together they stood in the flickering light giving and taking comfort in turn.

❧ Chapter Fourteen

IT WAS JUST BEFORE DAWN, that coldest and darkest hour before the rising sun, when Sir Branstoke escorted a subdued and melancholy Cecilia back to the Meriton townhouse. They didn't speak; too many words had already been spoken. There wasn't anything more to say that wouldn't lead to further distress and possible self-recrimination.

Though Cecilia and Jessamine joked about the skeletons in the family closet, never would they have imagined the depth of depravity to which Randolph had sunk. Cecilia felt unclean, as if by her relationship to Randolph she was somehow involved and responsible. She didn't know how to tell Jessamine—or if she even should. It was with a heavy heart she looked up at Branstoke to silently extend her thanks.

He looked at her face, so frail and pinched in appearance, and nodded in understanding, his own expression grim. He watched her safely enter the house before he turned to leave.

Cecilia threw the bolts home with relief and leaned back against the heavy entrance door. She looked about the hall with dim night vision and felt some of the ichor drain out of her. She was home. She was safe. Clutching the dressing case tightly to her chest, she made her weary way upstairs to her room.

Too tired to examine her small hoard from Cheney House, she opened a trunk in the corner of the room where many of her widow's clothes were stored. Lifting several tissue-wrapped bundles aside, she laid the dressing case in the trunk along with the papers she'd stuffed in her pockets. Then she hurriedly undressed and, shivering with cold, she laid Franklin's clothes in the trunk, carefully covering them with her widow's weeds.

She made her way to the bed and slipped the waiting nightdress over her head before collapsing on the big, wide bed. Pulling the heavy comforter over her shoulder, she sighed deeply, letting tense muscles find release. She was asleep, cradled in deep, exhausted slumber, in moments.

*　　　*　　　*

It was the rattling of china that woke her. She reluctantly opened her eyes. "Sarah, is that you?" she mumbled, struggling to raise herself on one elbow. "What time is it?"

"Yes, ma'am. It just wants ten o'clock. I'm sorry, I didn't mean to wake you, ma'am. I thought you'd be awake by now."

"That's all right, Sarah. I should have been. What have you got there? Breakfast? Bring it here."

"Yes, ma'am." She laid the tray on Cecilia's lap then arranged the bed pillows behind her. "Lady Meriton is still sick, but not quite so pulled by it now, I think. Leastwise she was in good spirits when I took her tray to her. She'd like you to visit when you're dressed."

"Of course. I don't mean to be confined to my bed."

"Lord knows, ma'am, you've seen enough of that!"

Cecilia's lips twitched with humor. At least it appeared her deception was still firm with the servants. "I agree." She raised her chocolate cup up in salute. "Here's to good health. Sarah, would you be a dear and lay out my blue floral?"

"Certainly, ma'am. And ma'am, I could fix your hair too, I could," she said eagerly. "Just like I did at Oastley."

Cecilia looked at her shrewdly. "I believe, Sarah, you've settled in nicely to being a lady's maid."

The young woman blushed.

She laughed. "Do not be embarrassed, my dear. I don't know what I would have done without you."

"Thank you, ma'am," she said and happily went to the wardrobe.

Cecilia watched her over the rim of her cup. It served her purposes well for Sarah to do for her. Lady Meriton's woman possessed an eagle's eye for worry or fatigue, and with the arrogance of long-standing family retainers, she asked too many questions.

Cecilia turned her head to stare at the trunk in the corner. She'd slept overlong. Its secrets would have to wait. Now she must see to her aunt's well-being and prepare for whatever visitors might come by to inquire of her health.

She made her visit to Jessamine as quickly as she could; but still it was past noon when she quit the room only to be informed Sir Elsdon was below. She found him standing in front of the parlor windows staring into the street.

"Sir Elsdon?"

"Ah—your pardon, Mrs. Waddley. I was wool-gathering, I'm afraid. Reviewing my play in my head, contemplating improvements."

"We received your kind invitation early this morning. Thank you. I didn't realize you were quite so talented. But surely you're not planning any changes now. Isn't the performance scheduled for this Sunday evening?" she asked while gesturing toward a chair. She sat on the sofa at a right angle to the chair.

"Yes," he said, flipping the tails of his coat up before he sat down. "But I do not let that consideration stand in my way. Rather it is an incentive! This is my first entirely original play."

"So I understand. What is it about?"

"Ah—now that I wish to be a surprise to all the *ton.* I've sworn my players to secret as well."

"With your interest in the theater, it is unfortunate you could not take to the boards professionally."

"Yes, the sad fact of my position at birth. I am convinced that had I been born a lesser man, I would have been a greater man," he said whimsically.

Cecilia laughed as she felt cued, yet nonetheless, she thought she detected a bitter ring of truth to his words.

"I understand Lady Meriton is still not feeling up to snuff?"

"That is true, though when I left her this morning she looked much improved. I quite had the feeling I no longer have to run from her in fear of infection," she said lightly.

"Yes, I understand you must guard your health preciously."

She looked down at her hands. "That has been the case until recently. I hope the good health I have enjoyed as of late remains."

"As do I, Mrs. Waddley, as do I. Randolph tells me you were not sickly in youth, so perhaps it was only the strain of your husband's death which injured your good health."

"That is a thought I share."

"I do hope Lady Meriton will be well enough to attend our play on Sunday."

"As do we," Cecilia said honestly.

"Speaking of Randolph, did you know his house was broken into last night?" Elsdon said lightly.

Cecilia's head flew up, her eyes wide. "What?"

"Yes, someone broke into the house. Don't know how they got in, but they escaped by lowering themselves out a window."

"I'm shocked! Did—did they catch the person?"

"No. Randolph came home drunk and scared them off."

"Them? There was more than one?"

"Reggie says he saw two running down the streets, but as he was nearly as foxed as Randolph, he may have been seeing double."

"Was—was anything taken?"

"Not much, some papers and a few trinkets. They probably surprised them by coming in early. They came in before midnight, you see."

"Excuse me, Mrs. Waddley, but the Honorable Mr. Reginald Rippy is below. Shall I send him up?" Loudon asked from the doorway. By his frosty manner Cecilia could tell the butler was on his high ropes. She wondered if his anger was directed toward her for seeing gentlemen unchaperoned, or toward the gentlemen who were calling. Remembering his laxity with Sir Branstoke, she decided the latter.

"You may send him up, Loudon."

"I knew having you to myself was too good to be true for long."

Cecilia laughed. "And are you a greedy man, Sir Elsdon?"

"Very," he replied curtly, much to her surprise. Then he flashed her a broad smile that lit his face, and she thought she must be mistaken. He rose from his chair. "But Rippy is my friend and I know he feels to a disadvantage, so I will say my good-byes and gracefully give him the field."

She made a moue of dissatisfaction. He laughed and chucked her under the chin as the door opened to admit Mr. Rippy.

"I know it," moaned that unfortunate gentleman. "I'm to be cut out again."

Cecilia laughed and rose to her feet. "Nonsense, sir. I believe I am merely learning what it is to be an outrageous flirt."

"Never say so, ma'am," protested Mr. Rippy.

Cecilia and Sir Elsdon laughed, then Elsdon turned, executed an elegant bow and bid them both good day. "And do not be more of a fool that you can help, my friend," he counseled Rippy, patting him heartily on the back as he passed.

Mr. Rippy's lips twisted downward into a pout. Observing his discomfort, Cecilia stifled a laugh and urged him to take the seat vacated by Sir Elsdon. Her glance fell to the bouquet in his hand. "Are those for me?"

"O—oh, yes," he stumbled, handing them to her with a blush surging to his hairline. "And—and I met some grubby little boy outside who was staring up at the house. He asked I give you this." He pulled a smudged and dirty cream bond envelope from his pocket and handed it to her.

"To me?" She turned it over. It was addressed to her with no other mark or seal upon it. "Did you know who it was, or who sent him?"

"Nay, for as soon as it went from his hand to mine he was off like the law were at his heels. And by the look of the grubby little brat, I'll wager the law's often after him, too. Please, don't stand on points with me. You'd better read it now. Might be important."

Cecilia shot him a look of warm thanks. He bristled and beamed in return. Quickly she opened the missive. The message was short, without salutation or signature and written with a well formed hand:

> *Don't question. Sell Waddley's.*
> *And don't look back lest you be Lot's wife.*
> *Another man's palatable spice.*

A puzzled frown furrowed her brow.

"Not bad news, I hope," said Mr. Rippy, uncertainty edging his tone.

"No, not exactly." She laughed. "I'm not quite sure what it is. I think I'm being confused with someone else."

"Happens. Wouldn't think they'd have your name though."

"I don't know," she said, refolding the letter and setting it on the table next to her. She smiled up at him. "But I do not wish to ponder it now. It would just give me a plaguey headache. So, tell me about this play you're in."

"Can't do that. Sworn to secrecy."

Cecilia laughed. "I was told so by Sir Elsdon, but I didn't believe he was serious!"

"Too serious. Don't know why. About the secrecy, that is. But that's what he wants."

"And you'll honor his wishes."

"Gave my word of honor. Man can't go back on his word of honor. What would this world be? Besides, he's pulled me out of some dashed uncomfortable scrapes. Do anything for a friend, would Elsdon. Kind of flighty in the cockloft sometimes, about acting and all. Decent fellow, though. There when the chips are down."

"Gracious, what an encomium!"

Mr. Rippy squirmed uncomfortably. "Now I've gone and done it. Praisin' him when I should be doing my best to cut him out," he said morosely.

Cecilia laughed and reached out to pat his hand reassuringly when the door opened to admit Sir James Branstoke. She drew back and glared up at him.

He strolled lazily into the room. "I told Loudon I would see myself up."

"I do not understand why Loudon should be lost to all propriety where you are concerned."

"We understand each other," he drawled, sitting next to her on the sofa. He nodded politely in Mr. Rippy's direction. "Don't you have a rehearsal or something to go to?"

"I do not believe Mrs. Waddley welcomes your appearance here. I suggest that you leave," said Mr. Rippy.

"On the contrary. Mrs. Waddley and I have an understanding. Why else would Lady Meriton's butler allow me free reign of the house?"

"Sir James!" warned Cecilia in dire accents.

"See, she uses my Christian name," Branstoke said pleasantly.

Cecilia ground her teeth at being caught out so and glared daggers at him. Mr. Rippy rose, his face bright red. "I was on the point of leaving anyway. My regards to Lady Meriton, please." He bowed jerkily and left the room.

"How dare you?" Cecilia asked, her blue eyes dark as lapis.

"We need to talk and we did not need that puppy around to broadcast our conversation."

"So you don't think he'll broadcast the idea that we have an understanding?"

"On the contrary. I'm hoping he will. It may help to save your life. Have you examined those trinkets and papers you filched from your brother?"

"No. I awoke too late and after visiting with Jessamine have had nothing but visitors. But this came in with Mr. Rippy," she said grudgingly, pointing to the note on the table. "He claimed an urchin gave it to him to deliver to me."

Branstoke unfolded the note and read the contents. "Good

God, woman! Things are more serious than I'd anticipated. I suggest you get your things packed and depart for an extended visit to your grandparents, or—perhaps better—I have a small estate near the lake district. You should be safe enough there."

"I am not going anywhere! And I'll thank you to stop trying to run my life for me."

"Don't you know what this note means? Lot's wife turned to a pillar of salt, a popular spice. It is obvious that whoever sent this intends to kidnap you for his brand of spice trade."

"Yes, I know that. That does not alter my decision. I owe it to Mr. Waddley to pursue this matter to the end."

"Did you love him so much?"

"Love him?" she looked confused. "No, no, but he was a good man, he was good to me. Really he was. He was gentle and—and treated me like a queen," she said shakily, a sheen of perspiration glistening on her brow. She plucked her handkerchief from her sleeve and dabbed at her forehead. She stood up and paced the room, wringing the handkerchief in her hands. "He talked to me of business, and people. He treated me well. He was not a demanding man either. He treated me special!"

Branstoke watched her, a hooded, preying expression to his eyes. "I've never heard you address him by his Christian name," he said softly.

"Nonsense. What a silly notion to take. You've not been listening, I'm sure. George was his name. George Waddley," she said, halting in her pacing, her hands fluttering wildly. "Lord and master Waddley. If it wasn't for him, I'd be a charity case. Now I'm a wealthy widow. He was good to me. Really he was. And—and—and I hated him!" she yelled, bursting into tears. "I hated him," she whimpered. She sagged against a burl table then sank to the floor, tears flowing down her cheeks.

Branstoke came over to her, pulling her to her feet. She leaned against him, sobbing. "It was like being in a locked case, a porcelain doll on display. I was never allowed to go anywhere, see anything, except for the once-a-year treat. He took me to the opera. Oh, he brought me books and jewels and fine clothes and anything else I desired, except freedom. I was suffocating in that existence, but how could I not be thankful? He saved my father and brother from debtors' prison, and me from the life of a charity case. How can I be so ungrateful? I have to do something in gratitude!"

"You don't owe him anything, Cecilia. You paid every day of your wedded life."

She looked up at him then, studying his expression, trying to read she knew not what there. She clung to his lapels. "I want that to be true. But now, when I fear Randolph may have led him to his death, my debt increases."

"No, it doesn't. Come, sit down on the sofa and dry your eyes. Do you have any sherry about?"

"No, but Loudon will bring it if I ring."

"Then do so. You could use it, or some brandy if you have it."

She gave a watery chuckle and did as he suggested. "I believe I consumed enough brandy last night. What a fright I must look."

"I doubt you could ever look a fright, but then, I am a smitten gentleman so I may be unnaturally blind," he said lightly, dappled gold light shining from his eyes.

She looked at him in surprise, her eyes dark blue pools of emotion. "Never say so unless you mean it," she whispered, searching his face for truth.

"You rang, ma'am?"

Cecilia started and turned toward the doorway, color surging up her pale face, her eyes sparkling. "Yes. Yes I did, Loudon. We would like refreshments, please."

"I anticipated as much, ma'am, they are right outside the door." He backed out of the room then came back in almost immediately bearing a large silver tray. He set it on the sideboard and poured glasses of Madeira for each of them. "Here you are, ma'am. May I get you anything else?"

"No, thank you, Loudon, that will be all," Cecilia said, ruefully studying the glass he handed her. It was Lady Meriton's best crystal. Trust Loudon to judge people and situations to a nicety.

Branstoke held up his hand in toast. "To never saying anything we don't mean," he said solemnly.

Cecilia felt tears prick her eyes again, but they were tears of happiness. She raised her glass. "To trust." They sipped their drinks and stared at each other, silly smiles on their faces.

"Now do you understand why I wish you to go where you'll be safe?"

She sighed and turned away. His fingers cupped her chin and turned her back toward him. "Cecilia?"

"I'm sorry, James. I can't. This is something I have to see through for myself. I think it long ago became more an exercise to find myself than a sacred quest. I can't run away. I won't go back into a glass case where nothing can touch me. No matter what happens, I have to see this through."

A stubborn expression locked his jaw, and he looked at her in silence for a long moment. "Damn," he swore softly, raking his hair with his hand, messing immaculate waves. Cecilia smiled at the gesture for it was one he used only when particularly exasperated. "At least grant me the right to watch out for you."

She laughed. "You've been doing that without my permission before now, and probably would continue to do so no matter my answer."

A wry smile curved his lips. "But I would like your permission."

"I know when to compromise. I agree," she said.

He pulled her into his arms, her head resting on his chest. A knock on the door interrupted them. Branstoke groaned while Cecilia giggled and slid away from him while granting admittance.

"Excuse me, Mrs. Waddley, but there is an elderly gentleman here to see you. A Reverend Thornbridge, he says."

"Reverend Thornbridge! Mr. Thornbridge's father?"

"So he says, ma'am."

"Show him up, show him up immediately! Oh James, do you think something's happened to Mr. Thornbridge? It's all my fault!"

"Hush. Wait and see what the man has to say."

"Yes, of course. Reverend Thornbridge?" she said, rising to greet him. Only a slight quaver to her voice betrayed her nervousness.

The man who entered looked as if he'd aged years in a night. His skin held a gray pallor, and his blue eyes looked washed and empty. He moved slowly forward to greet Cecilia. "My dear, dear child," he murmured, shaking his head. He tried to smile, but it was more wistful than warm.

Cecilia grew increasingly frightened. "Mr. Thornbridge, is he—is he—"

"David is alive and recovering as well as can be expected," he said, taking her hand in his and patting it gently. "He's told me a great deal about you. You've been a very brave lady." He glanced over at the man standing by the sofa. "May we talk in private?" he asked, looking apologetically at the man.

"I'm sorry," she said, drawing him toward Sir Branstoke, "I'm being terribly remiss. Reverend Thornbridge, this is Sir James Branstoke. He is the one responsible for saving your son's life. He's conversant with Mr. Thornbridge's investigation. You may feel free to talk in front of him."

Reverend Thornbridge's face relaxed into a thankful smile. He grasped Branstoke's hand. "If what she says is true, God bless you, my son."

"Please, Reverend Thornbridge, won't you sit down and tell us what has brought you here?" Cecilia said, gently guiding the older man to sit on the sofa. She sank down next to him, Branstoke sat in the chair.

Reverend Thornbridge took Cecilia's hand between his and patted it absently. "My dear, I have said you've been brave. Now I ask if you have it within you to be braver still."

Cecilia exchanged alarmed, covert glances with Branstoke, but calmly told the old man she would be brave. He patted her hand again and sighed deeply, not knowing how to begin.

"Perhaps we should tell you we believe Mr. Thornbridge's investigation led him to uncover a possible white slavery ring," Sir Branstoke offered, giving the older man the lead-in he needed.

Reverend Thornbridge looked from one to the other, then addressed Branstoke, though his weathered and wrinkled hands kept Cecilia's tightly captured. "According to David, it is not a possibility. It is an actuality. From information he obtained— it pains me to tell you this, my dear, but I must—from information he obtained, Mr. Waddley was not killed because he discovered this sordid affair. It was more in the nature of a falling out among thieves."

Cecilia blanched. "No!"

Branstoke nodded. "I was afraid that might be the case."

"How could you?" Cecilia cried, rounding on him. "Mr. Waddley was good to me. He—"

"Cecilia! He may have married you, but you were kept like

a purchased possession. Like the upper-class *spice* in which he traded," Branstoke said harshly.

Cecilia shook her head, horror in her eyes. "No, no," she murmured, anguished. Yet if what he said were true—

Reverend Thornbridge put an arm around her shoulder. "It was a partnership," he told her softly, sadly, "between Mr. Waddley and some member of society with foreign connections. My son doesn't know who. The women and young girls they sold were primarily flash house residents and their like. Though, on occasion, there were whispers of others of higher position." He turned back to face Branstoke.

"Since Mr. Waddley's death, another manager at the company, a Mr. William Karney, a brash youg man with only one year seniority to my David, has become the Waddley's contact for the shipment of this heinous cargo."

"Does your son have any clues as to the society member involved?" Branstoke asked.

The old man nodded. "He believes it to be either Sir Harry Elsdon or Charles Dernley, Lord Havelock. He says your brother is involved, albeit as of late, reluctantly. But he is not the leader."

Cecilia nodded, a rueful smile touching her lips. "I would find it hard to believe Randolph having the intelligence to mastermind something of this nature. I suppose I should be thankful for small favors."

Reverend Thornbridge nodded, taking his hand from her shoulder to reach into his pocket, pulling out a crumbled slip of paper. "David also believes there is another shipment due to leave within the next ten days. He has identified what orders for finished cotton goods are actually orders for these poor pathetic creatures. They are all stamped with this device." He held out a paper for them to see. On it was stamped a rose with a sword through it.

Cecilia shuddered at the symbolism. Closing her eyes she saw it again. This time on a signet ring. Her brother's signet ring.

Chapter Fifteen

"Jessamine, how many visits like the last do you suppose we'll have today?" Cecilia asked, collapsing in a chair near her aunt.

Lady Meriton, ensconced on the daybed amid a nest of pillows and covers laughed. "Branstoke certainly set the cat among the pigeons yesterday. Mr. Rippy must have made the rounds of all London's gossiping haunts after he left here. Can't you imagine him whispering in some prominent society belle's ear the latest *on dit: Branstoke is taken!* Then when neither of you appear at any party or play last evening, society went wild with speculation. I think our three charming guests who just departed will only be the first of many coming here today to ferret out *the truth!*" she said in dire accents, her narrow eyebrows wriggling dramatically.

"You could avoid this by remaining above stairs and claiming your recent illness continues to lay you low."

"Nonsense! I'm having too much fun! This is just the restorative I needed."

Cecilia made a face at her. "It is all so dashed awkward. Some of the questions those old tabbies asked quite put me to the blush! All I can do is agree he is a frequent visitor here; admit he is allowed to enter unannounced (I swear I'll have words with Loudon about that!); and then admit—in the face of sympathetic—nay, pitying looks—that he has not made me an offer! The entire situation is unbearable. To say nothing of the fact that I have more pressing concerns than assuaging society's voracious curiosity."

"I know, my dear. Frankly, I cannot help but agree with Sir Branstoke. There may be extended safety for you in having his intentions publicly known."

"That's sheer arrogance. There could also be greater risks!" snapped Cecilia. "Furthermore, he has not stated that he has intentions."

Lady Meriton smiled and shook her head. "When do you expect him?"

"Not until later today. He's gone to talk with Bow Street about setting a watch on Mr. Karney. Then he wants to visit with members of that Select Committee investigating corruption and flash houses to see if they might take an active interest in this matter as well." She did not add that she hoped he would come soon for she found among the items she took from her brother's rooms at Cheney House a certain ring and a very disturbing note.

A knock on the parlor door was followed by the entrance of Loudon announcing Lady Amblethorp and her daughter. Cecilia groaned while her aunt, chuckling, instructed him to show them up.

"Ah, my dear friend, Lady Meriton," gushed Lady Amblethorp surging into the room, her hands stretched out before her. "I'm so delighted to see you recovering from that nasty indisposition. We have missed seeing you these past few days, and so I've several times told Janine. Isn't that right, Janine? I said, I do so miss seeing my dear friend Lady Meriton." She pushed aside the covers at the foot of the daybed and sat down on the end. "Now that you're feeling better, we have time for a nice, comfortable coze. Janine, why don't you go talk to Mrs. Waddley. I'm sure you two younger women have much news to share."

Cecilia exchanged wry glances with her aunt, and received an apologetic one from Janine. Obligingly, Cecilia led Janine to a sofa closer to the windows. "You don't need to tell me," she told her young friend, a wry smile on her lips. "You've been sent on a reconnaissance mission. Your instructions are to discover all you can about the truth of the gossip regarding Sir James Branstoke and the Widow Waddley."

Janine blushed, pursed her lips, and nodded. "It is all the talk. London is buzzing with speculation." She looked up and smiled mischievously.

Cecilia was stunned at the transformation it effected in her plain little face. Her eyes sparkled and dimples carved into her cheeks. The expression lent her an attractive gamin prettiness.

"Miss Cresswell is livid," Janine continued. "She is doing her best to discredit Mr. Rippy. Dropping nasty innuendos about him on the side; but no one is paying her much mind. I believe society wants to see Miss Cresswell get her comeuppance. Beautiful though she may be, she is nonetheless a spiteful cat without much else to offer besides her looks. Society is wearying of her."

"She will learn the hard way that beauty does not last. It is style, countenance, and wit that provides a woman with the wherewithal to stay in the forefront of society. She should look to Lady Melbourne or Lady Hertford to see that."

"Yes, but our regent's tastes are a bit out of the norm," Janine said drily.

Cecilia laughed. "True enough. But now, so you will not be embarrassed at asking, I will tell you Sir Branstoke has not asked me to marry him. He has been a frequent visitor here during which time we have had more arguments than pleasant chats. I don't know why Loudon lets him come up unannounced. I suspect he's been bribed, but I do not know. What he said to Mr. Rippy, could, in Sir Branstoke's dry way, be taken several different ways. It is obvious which way Mr. Rippy took it."

Janine looked at her shrewdly. "I believe that is what you tell yourself. I will not press you for confidences you'd rather not give. I will say I am happy for you, though I admit I'd hoped it would have been Lord Havelock."

"Havelock! But that's the gentleman you bear a tendre for—"

"*Did* bear a tendre for. In another time and place. He is not the man now he was then. I was hoping you could help him recover a bit of himself."

"Me? Oh, Janine, my dear. I don't know that anyone could." She bit her lip. How would this fragile young woman take the notion that the man she adored may well be a warped monster? She licked her lips. Now was the time when she could discover when Havelock's cousin disappeared, if she had the courage to ask. "Janine, speaking of Lord Havelock, I was wondering, when exactly did Dorothea Rustian, his cousin, disappear? Was it before or after his house burned down?"

"About a month afterward, why?"

"I was just curious if it had any bearing on his change in manner."

"I couldn't say. After the fire he was unapproachable for a while, stoic, locked within himself. Then too, the family was in mourning and his mother was being perfectly beastly. I believe he disappeared about the same time Dorothea did. He did not return to England until after the official mourning period for his father and brother was over."

The expression on Janine's face was so melancholy that Cecilia felt the lowest worm for bringing those memories out. "He does seem to be increasingly personable. Perhaps if he could be brought to rebuild Havelock Manor, it would lay to rest the remaining ghosts."

"But how to—"

"Excuse me, my lady," exclaimed Loudon, bursting into the room. His face was unnaturally pale, his eyes wide. "There's a man below, just come from Cheney House," he gulped and looked toward Cecilia. She rose unsteadily to her feet. "I'm sorry, ma'am, he says—he says Mr. Haukstrom's dead!"

Cecilia swayed at the bald pronouncement. Janine, a soft cry on her lips, rose to support her.

"How?" she whispered past dry lips.

Loudon looked miserable. "Hung himself, ma'am."

Cecilia moaned softly and did something she'd never actually done before. She fainted.

Cecilia opened her eyes to a sea of faces swimming above her. A sharp ammonia smell waved under her nose mingled distastefully with the lavender water bathing her brow. Her eyes watered and she coughed, batting at the helpful hands fluttering over her. She struggled to sit up. "Please, stop. I'm all right. Give me a moment," she said, her voice husky. She cleared her throat and shook her head to dispel the last of the wooziness. She took stock of her surroundings. She was lying on the daybed hurriedly vacated by Lady Meriton. Loudon stood at the head, wringing his hands. Janine knelt beside her, a lavender-water drenched handkerchief in her hand. Jessamine held the sal volatile. Lady Amblethorp hovered behind her aunt, eyes bright and inquisitive; beyond her, near the door, stood an array of servants openly staring. One man she did not recognize.

"You there, are you from Cheney House?" she asked weakly. Janine helped her to sit up against the pillows over the protests of her aunt and Lady Amblethorp.

"Yes, ma'am," said the fellow, nervously twisting his hat in his hand.

"Come here," she ordered, her voice stronger. The man hesitatingly approached her. She turned to look over her shoulder at Loudon. "A glass of brandy please, and see that the rest of the company here disperses."

At her words there was a scurrying of feet by the door. She closed her eyes a moment to gather her thoughts and waited until Loudon brought the brandy. She took a healthy swallow, to the consternation and surprise of the others, then handed the glass to Janine. Somehow, the two of them had achieved a rapport. It was that hidden strength she once mentioned to Jessamine. She knew she could count on Janine to be of assistance. She hoped it would stand Janine in good stead should her suspicions concerning Lord Havelock prove true.

She looked at the man standing before her. "When and where?"

"Sometime last night, ma'am. He were found this morning by a housemaid. Screamed like a banshee she did, and we all come runnin'. He were dangling from the chandelier in the library, his face all black and mottled."

Gasps came from the others in the room. Lady Amblethorp muttered something to which Lady Meriton snapped back at her. Cecilia ignored them. She raised an eyebrow, thinking. Haukstrom never went near that library of his own. She discovered that two nights ago. "I see. And have messages been sent yet to Baron Haukstrom or the duke?"

"No, ma'am. We didn't know what to do, 'cept cut him down and lay him out," he explained, plainly and painfully looking at her for advice.

She nodded. "Loudon, fetch pen and paper."

"Mama, I think it best we leave now," Janine said, rising to her feet.

Lady Amblethorp started to protest. She wanted to stay and hear all the sordid details.

Janine was unnaturally cool and firm. "Lady Meriton and Mrs. Waddley have much on their minds and much to do." She turned to Cecilia. "If there is anything I can do—"

Cecilia smiled up at the blossoming young woman. "I shall be sure to contact you. Thank you for your assistance and understanding."

Janine nodded, bid Lady Meriton good-bye and escorted her mother from the room. On the steps they met Sir Branstoke dashing inside. Lady Amblethorp made to turn back and follow him but Janine forestalled her. "No, Mother, you shall have to be content knowing Sir Branstoke came hurrying to her side."

Lady Amblethorp looked mulish, but the calm, determined

expression on her youngest daughter's face gave her pause. Meekly she allowed herself to be led away.

Branstoke entered the parlor to find Cecilia acting the general to her troops. She sat on the daybed using Lady Meriton's lap desk as a writing surface. Her pen flew across paper while she issued orders to others in the room. He lounged against the door frame, his arms across his chest, appreciating her. She sanded another note, handing it to a man Branstoke didn't recognize.

"See that this gets to the duke immediately. Take Randolph's fastest horse."

"And the baron, ma'am?"

"I have no idea at what watering spa he is at the present. It may take some time to locate him. I'll send someone else to chase him to ground."

The man nodded, bowed, and turned to go. Cecilia looked up then to see Branstoke. "You heard?"

"Yes, the news is spreading like wildfire throughout London." He walked toward her. "Can you dismiss the rest of your cavalcade? We need to talk."

"Of course. Loudon, I will call for you and the others later. Jessamine, stay please. I've told her nearly everything," she quietly explained to Branstoke.

He nodded. "I anticipated as much. Bow Street is setting a man on Karney. I have not, as yet, had luck meeting with anyone on the committee."

"James, I think we had best examine the library at Cheney House. That is where Randolph was found. He never used the library."

"You suspect murder?"

She looked down at her hands and bit her lip for a moment, then moved the lap desk aside. She rose from the daybed to cross to a carved and painted box on the mantle. She opened it and took two things from inside. She brought them to Branstoke, dropping them into his hand.

The cold metallic shape caught his attention first. It was a gold signet ring. He turned it over. The raised cartouche of a rose and sword was on the flat bezel. A dark eyebrow rose as he examined it.

"It is identical to the stamp Reverend Thornbridge showed us."

"Yes," she said noncommittally. She waited for him to unfold the note. She knew what it said without looking at it. She knew what it meant:

> *The Widow Waddley is not the fool you*
> *or she would have us believe. Stop her.*
> *Lest she meet that fate scheduled*
> *eight years ago.*

At the bottom was stamped the rose and sword.

Branstoke looked up at her, puzzled.

"Eight years ago I married Mr. Waddley," she said softly, "but I don't think that is what the message means. With the stamp on the bottom, I believe I was to be part of their spice trade."

He nodded slowly. "You certainly meet the criteria. Why did Waddley marry you?"

Cecilia shook her head and turned away.

"Mr. Waddley married her sight unseen," put in Lady Meriton quietly. "He expected Randolph's sister to be older and plainer."

Cecilia turned back to face Branstoke. "Remember what Randolph said at Oastley? That he saved my life by marrying me to Waddley? I thought—have thought all along—he meant he saved me from a life of poverty and drudgery."

"When he may actually have been saving you from being kidnapped by him. But that still doesn't make any sense. How would Randolph know his plans?"

"I don't know. Perhaps, with him dead, we'll never know. It was also eight years ago that Dorothea Rustian disappeared."

"Dorothea Rustian?"

"Lord Havelock's cousin. A vibrant redhead, I understand. Havelock also went abroad at the time for an extended period."

"E'gad," mouthed Branstoke. "I know Havelock is one of the two suspected by Thornbridge, but—"

"I know. I haven't seen Lord Havelock in two days. Have you?"

"No, not at all. I think it would be best if you refused any further visitors. Put it about that you're prostrate with grief—"

"For Randolph?"

His thin smile quirked upward on one side. "How about your infamous irritation of the nerves?"

Cecilia frowned, but Jessamine agreed with Branstoke. "Cecilia, whoever is behind this sordid business is vicious and merciless. And they must truly hate women. If Randolph was murdered, it was most likely to prevent him from interfering in plans for you. We cannot take the risk. If what Mr. Thornbridge says is true, the climax of these events cannot be far away. We cannot be too careful."

Cecilia nodded reluctantly.

Branstoke rose to leave. "I'll go to Cheney House before anyone there gets the notion to clean the library. From there I'll try to track down members of the committee and contact Bow Street again. I'll take these with me," he said, dropping the ring and note in his pocket. "Do not look to see me again until tomorrow. Rest assured," he said to Lady Meriton, "I'll leave your house well guarded." He turned to leave.

"James!" called Cecilia after him. He paused at the door to look back at her. "Take care of yourself," she said softly.

He smiled lazily, his eyes shining through the veil of his lashes, and tipped his head in assent.

Cecilia and Jessamine stared at each other, each alone with their thoughts on the implications of the threat to Cecilia.

Lady Meriton sighed. "I wish Meriton was here."

"I'd best write a note for father and set someone on his trail," Cecilia said tiredly, picking up the lap desk and sitting down with it. "Though what good it will do, I don't know. His reaction will most likely be to get drunk for a week. At least it's something to keep my mind occupied."

Lady Meriton nodded. "I'll arrange for a light dinner to be served us here. I doubt either of us will have much of an appetite," she said, rising and walking slowly toward the door. Somehow she felt terribly aged.

The gloom of twilight cast long gray shadows when Loudon removed a scarcely touched dinner from the small parlor. The two ladies engaged in desultory needlework to pass the time little noticed the growing darkness until Loudon silently made the rounds of the room lighting branches of candles. Surprised at the sudden light, they looked up, blinking like owls in the light, before sending a thankful nod the butler's way. The endless ticking of the clock punctuated by the occasional sigh and rustle of fabric were the only sounds to be heard in the small room. Even the outside world quieted, leaving the ladies with loud voices in their heads for company; voices that shouted unanswerable questions and impossible "what ifs."

Cecilia kept glancing up at the clock, judging if enough time had passed to allow the duke or the old baron to be found and return to the city. She knew she saw little hope of seeing them before morning, still she watched the clock and its seemingly infinitesimal forward march of time. Surely garden snails moved faster. She chafed at her inactivity. She felt she should be up and doing something, going somewhere; but she didn't know what. Perhaps she should have gone to view the body. Wasn't that a proper thing to do? Then, while at Cheney House, she could also interview the servants, see if anyone heard anything unusual last night. No, it would be a redundant exercise. Someone—Branstoke or a member of the constabulary—would have asked those questions. She would have liked to search for clues, perhaps find some more notes that would lead them closer to their quarry. Lamentably, she'd promised to stay at Meriton House.

She wondered where Lord Havelock was and what he was doing. As arrogant as the man was, she found it difficult to believe he could be a kidnapper and slave trader. Then again, she found it difficult to believe anyone would so vilely traffic in human flesh! Except, perhaps, for her husband. Though she'd rejected the idea at first, the longer she thought on it, the more convinced she became there was truth to David Thornbridge's suppositions.

Taking his guilt as given, when one analyzed his past comments and actions, there was a certain logic and flow in them. He did keep her like a harem concubine, cut off from the world, yet pampered with worldly things. She was encouraged to read and learn, to develop her wit, to be another Madame Stael or Pompadour. His actions could be seen as a training, preparing her for sale to another. Yet with each passing year he kept her by his side. Surely as she grew older her worth decreased. The taste among gentlemen was for the nubile flesh of youth—of children actually. The jaded hedonism of the age thirsted for untouched, unripe fruit to defile. It provided feelings of power and glory to have such supplicants at their feet. Her value would be declining, wouldn't it?

She thought back to her strange marriage day. She considered Mr. Waddley's reaction when he discovered his bride, his surprise and anger. How naive she'd been to think his anger was for her sake. His anger was at a prospected loss of revenue. He could not ship her off for Randolph saw to it that the notice of their marriage made the columns of the Morning Gazette. Randolph neatly outmaneuvered Mr. Waddley. How was he able to do so? He never struck Cecilia as a man with two thoughts to rub together unless they were dealing with money. Perhaps he felt he stood more to gain with her married to Waddley. Maybe he really did see Mr. Waddley as a purse without bottom. Better that than a one-time payment for purchasing her body and soul. But Mr. Waddley extracted his vengeance. Randolph continued to work with him even after he became heir to the Cheney fortune.

"Franklin is now grandfather's heir," she mused aloud, her needle plunging rhythmically in and out of the canvas.

"Meriton will not be pleased," her aunt said. "I can't say as I am either. It makes him prime vulture bait."

"Have more faith in your son, Jessamine. He's always been a steady youth."

"Yes, but people often change with their fortunes."

Like Lord Havelock? Cecilia silently wondered. "Perhaps you can convince uncle and grandfather not to grant him an allowance. I wager they'd be amenable to that suggestion. That way he won't have an immediate change of fortune. Chances are uncle and grandfather will live to see ripe old ages before Franklin comes into his inheritance. By then he ought to be settled enough to handle it," Cecilia offered drily.

Lady Meriton sighed, her needlework lying idle in her lap. "I suppose you're right. Still, I wish he didn't stand to inherit."

"No more than I do," murmured Cecilia, turning her head away to hide a sheen of tears.

"Oh, Cecilia, I'm so sorry. That was a thoughtless thing for me to say."

Cecilia gave a half-hearted, watery chuckle. "What will be the duke's reaction when he discovers his grandson has managed to blot the family escutcheon worse than he ever did?"

"Outraged, and perhaps a little envious—though not for the subject of his crime. Father has always seen himself as a knight errant rescuing damsels from distress, not putting them *in* distress. He would be livid if he knew the full nature of Randolph's crimes. Must we tell him?"

"I don't know. It will depend on what transpires within the next few days, I would imagine. I also wonder what it will do to my father. Life has been whipping him roundly for his early profligacy. Now he is constantly in pain and is afflicted with a maudlin temperament. His existence revolves around finding a relief from the unremitting pain."

"If I know Baron Haukstrom, he will curse your brother roundly. He will accuse him of dying just to make his life more miserable."

Cecilia nodded, bringing her handkerchief to her face to blot the threatening tears. "I don't know why I should be so emotional. It is not as if we were particularly close."

"Death does that. It removes all the accumulated filth and garbage that colors our thoughts and controls our emotions. Despite all that he's done or hasn't done, Randolph is your brother, he is another human being and as such his death affects you. In some way, it affects all of us who knew him. Don't be ashamed or angry at your tears."

Cecilia lowered her handkerchief and smiled at her aunt. "And how did you come by all this wisdom?" she asked with forced lightness.

"Age."

"Bah!"

From the open parlor door came a discrete cough. "Excuse me, my lady, but there is a young person below desirous of seeing Mrs. Waddley."

Lady Meriton frowned at her butler. "A young person? Can you be a bit more precise, Loudon."

The butler emitted a long-suffering sigh, his hang-dog eyes rolling mournfully. "A young person who goes by the unlikely sobriquet of *Angel*. Miss Angel Swafford, my lady."

"Angel Swafford, here?" asked Cecilia, glancing at Jessamine to see if she was aware of Miss Swafford. She shook her head mutely.

"Yes, ma'am. Shall I send her about her business?"

"No! Send her up, please, Loudon."

Loudon looked at her severely before bowing and exiting the room, his back more rigid than Cecilia had ever seen it.

"Poor Loudon, I feel I have been a sad trial for him since I've lived with you."

"Fustian. Loudon would not be happy unless he could look down his nose at something. Who is this Miss Swafford he has obviously taken a dislike to? Do you know her?"

"It is my understanding that she is—or was—Randolph's mistress. He even has a house for her. I am very curious as to why she should be here."

"Probably to touch you for money. Randolph may have provided a house but most likely kept her short of funds."

"Oh, stop it, Jessamine. Cynicism ill becomes you."

"Miss Swafford, ma'am," announced Loudon in repressing, stentorian tones. Lady Meriton scowled at him and vowed it was high time she trimmed his sails. He sailed too near the wind for her liking. But her frown relented when she saw their new guest. She exchanged quick, surprised glances with Cecilia, then her niece was rising and extending a hand to the unusual vision before them.

\mathscr{C}\hspace{-2pt}\mathfrak{G} Chapter Sixteen

ANGEL SWAFFORD minced into the parlor on ridiculously high-heeled black kid boots. The nature of her footwear, along with the black clocks on the stockings worn with them being immediately apparent owing to the inordinately high hem of her black bombazine gown. The dress was a marvel of stiff black ruchings and furbelows that stood away from the body of the gown like independent sculptures. A black lace veil attached to the wide brim of her bonnet obscured her face from view. A large black net bow vied with similarly colored ostrich feathers to give increased height to the diminutive figure in mourning attire.

"Mrs. Waddley?" inquired a low, husky voice.

Cecilia rose to greet her guest. "I am Mrs. Waddley. This is my aunt, Lady Meriton. I understand you were a particular friend of my late brother?" she said formally, rigidly.

The little veiled woman seemed to collapse inwardly at her haughty tone. Instantly Cecilia knew she'd hurt and intimidated her. Embarrassed at her rudeness, she hurried to make amends.

"Please, Miss Swafford, won't you sit down?" she asked in a friendlier manner, waving her to the sofa where she'd been sitting.

The woman bobbed her head in acquiescence sending long black ostrich plumes swaying. Seated, she reached up to roll the lacy veil upward, laying it across the broad brim of the hat. This task accomplished, she looked up at Cecilia, her pale gray eyes wide open and the color of morning fog. They matched the gray hollows circling her eyes. Bright patches of color in an otherwise pinched white face attested to the abundant use of the rouge pot. Ringlets, curled to frame a delicate heart-shaped face, were richly dyed with henna. The red ringlets and red patches of rouge were the only colors on her. She should have appeared garish, but somehow the entire ensemble seemed to suit her. Primly, she interlaced her fingers and laid them firmly in her lap.

"Mrs. Waddley, I realize it is highly irregular for me to pay a call upon you like this. Please, I beg of you, bear with me," asked the deep, rolling voice that somehow reminded Cecilia of water flowing over pebbles in a stream. It was also a voice that hinted at some culture. Cecilia was intrigued.

"Certainly, Miss Swafford. In what way may I help you?"

A blush crept up the woman's neck. "I am not here for money, if that is what you think." She glanced over at Lady Meriton. "Do you think we might talk alone?"

Cecilia raised a brow. "Lady Meriton is discreet. You may trust her."

The woman licked her pale lips. "I don't mean any disrespect. I know it is not proper. But please, ma'am . . ." She trailed off, looking hopelessly from Cecilia to Lady Meriton.

Lady Meriton folded her needlework and put it away. "I shall be in my studio," she said, rising gracefully.

"Oh, please, Jessamine—"

"No, Cecilia, this woman obviously needs to talk to you. I think we should bow to her desires."

"Th—Thank you, Lady Meriton," whispered the woman huskily, tears welling in her eyes.

"Here, now, none of that. Take my handkerchief and dry your eyes," Lady Meriton instructed briskly, holding out a square of linen.

Miss Swafford took it thankfully, dabbing at her eyes as Lady Meriton left the room.

"Would you care for a glass of sherry or perhaps brandy?" Cecilia asked, rising to cross to a tray of decanters and glasses that Loudon had left in the room that afternoon.

"A little sherry, please," she said meekly. "And please, just call me Angel. It's what everyone calls me. My real name is Mary Jane, but that wasn't stagey enough," she confessed. Prosaically she blew her nose.

Cecilia smiled at the action. She handed her a glass then sat down beside her. "All right, Angel. What is it? I have a feeling it is more than my brother's untimely death that brings you here today."

The woman nodded and sipped the sherry.

"Randy—I mean, Mr. Haukstrom—"

Cecilia smiled. "You may call him Randy if that makes it easier."

"Yes, thank you. Anyway, Randy told me earlier this week

that if anything happened to him, I was to nip over here and talk to you as soon as possible."

"He foresaw his own death?"

The woman looked down at her glass of sherry, seemingly mesmerized by its dark golden color. "I'm not so sure but that death wasn't a release for him. A release from the hell he lived."

"Tell me," encouraged Cecilia softly.

She took another sip of sherry then licked the remnants from her lips. Her hand, Cecilia noticed, trembled slightly.

"About nine or ten years ago, he bought a young girl from her parents to give to a friend as a gift. He was young and it seemed a great joke, a lark; and the girl no more important than a snuffbox—less possibly. His gift was a great success and he was accounted clever for the thought. He preened on such compliments."

"I can well imagine," Cecilia said drily.

"Yes, well, shortly after that, he was approached to provide a similar girl, but this time he was offered money for his efforts. He agreed that time and a second and third time as well. He thought nothing of it. The girls were from the lower classes, their parents desperate for money. He thought it a fair exchange."

"Trust Randolph to be able to rationalize his actions," Cecilia said.

Angel blushed painfully. "He was just like the little boy who didn't understand the nature of his misbehavior, or why he should be punished simply because no one ever told him that the specific action he took was wrong."

Cecilia looked closely at her. "You loved my brother, didn't you?"

She nodded, not meeting Cecilia's eyes.

Cecilia laid a hand over hers. "Thank you for that. I shall not make any more disparaging comments. Please, continue."

"Eventually he was asked to join in a kidnapping. He thought it was to be another drab. To his horror, their victim was from the middle class, a surveyor's daughter. His associates averred that she was no different than the other girls he'd bought. He agreed, but his conclusions differed from theirs. He saw that he was wrong in what he'd done from the first. But it was too late. The money was too good, the evidence against him too damaging should he try to quit the group."

She paused to drain the last of the sherry from the glass and set it on a table. "Then one day, a young girl was described who would be perfect for a discriminating customer in the Mediterranean. She was small with white-blond hair and dark blue eyes. She attended a certain girls' academy in Bath."

"Me," Cecilia interjected.

Angel licked her lips and nodded. "But you see, you were wrongly named. Randy realized that at once. He knew it was only a matter of time before the error was discovered. He convinced Mr. Waddley, whose ships actually carried the girls overseas, that he needed to marry into the aristocracy to raise his credit and to solidify his cover."

Cecilia covered her eyes with her hand and groaned. "I know the rest of this story. You don't need to go on."

"But I don't think you do. Not really all the rest. Like how Mr. Waddley died."

Cecilia's hand dropped like a stone into her lap. "You know about that as well?"

She nodded. "Randy told me everything. His head in my lap, he sobbed his heart out, poor dear. He was tortured by the past. He wanted to make sure that if anything happened to him, someone would know the truth. You see, Randy killed him."

"Randolph did? He killed Mr. Waddley?"

"Yes. Because Randy was convinced he was getting prepared to have you disappear."

"What?"

Angel nodded. "It's true, that's what Randy believed. Only, I don't know if Mr. Waddley really was or not. There's another gentleman involved . . ." she trailed off, uncertain how to proceed. Fear haunted the pale gray eyes that turned toward Cecilia.

She nodded. "I know about him."

Relief swept Angel's piquant face. She sighed. "Then I needn't say much about him. Frankly, I don't think I could. He has always frightened me. His eyes can be so empty at times. I could feel him looking at me sometimes. Contemplating my value. Lucky for me, Randy offered his protection else I'd have been shipped out long ago."

"I understand."

Angel blinked, pushing unshared images aside with a shudder, and continued: "It seems Mr. Waddley was getting too independent-minded. He was making noises like he didn't need the overseas connections any longer. The story of Mr. Waddley sending you away may solely have been fuel to rile Randy to get him to do *his* dirty work. Randy may not have been much of a brother as brothers go, but he held great stock in family."

"Forgive me, Angel, if I have trouble adjusting to your vision of my brother. I have for so long viewed him as interested in money above all else."

"I know." Threatening tears spilled over her bottom lashes and traced dark courses down her pale cheeks. "I asked him why he didn't tell you the truth—about Mr. Waddley and *him*. Randy said you were sincerely attached to Mr. Waddley and would not hear anything bad of your husband."

Cecilia shook her head sadly. "No, I was never attached to him. I felt some measure of gratitude for being saved from a life as a charity case, and I did enjoy the intellectual freedom he fostered by encouraging me to read voraciously; but truthfully, I was confined. Like a doll locked in a glass case. I carried around with me a sizable piece of guilt that I didn't care for him more, and that I was stifled. It reeked so of ingratitude, you see. My meager attempts to discover his murderer have acted like a medicinal restorative on me. They've given me a focus for myself around which I may coalesce. That was the reason I've wanted so to discover his murderer. It was a way to absolve myself." She looked down at her hands in her lap restlessly folding and unfolding a handkerchief.

"We really didn't know each other, did we?" Cecilia whispered mournfully, choking back a veil of tears.

Angel shook her head, her eyes darting up to, then away from, Cecilia's face. Her chin quivered with the effort to fight back a new surge of tears. "I must be going now," she said, her slightly gravelly voice liquid with tears.

"Go? Where will you go? You must stay here with me. Your life may also be in danger. I can't allow that on my conscience. Haukstrom is a big enough burden as it is."

"No, I must go. *He* is already suspicious of me. He knows Randy tended to get pious at home. And, if I do not show up at the theater tonight, he will be suspicious."

"Does he rule your life as well?"

"He is not a man I would cross willingly. If he knew I was here, or what we talked about, your life wouldn't be worth a penny."

"Or your own either, I'd wager."

She shrugged. "I can take care of myself. I always have."

"No, I won't have it. I think you should know that Sir Branstoke has set Bow Street on the case. We are determined to end this heinous trafficking. I want you to stay here until this matter is sorted out."

A flicker of hope leapt up Angel Swafford's face only to be dashed down again. "A part of me would like to, I'm not denying that. But it would be too dangerous for us all if I did. If I do not show up at the theater tonight, he would ferret out my location through one of his many cullies. I have to go to the theater and give a performance—a lackluster one at best, but a performance. Afterward, I can truly claim to be overcome with Randy's death. I will go straight home from the theater."

Cecilia smiled. "Pleading a headache and an irritation of the nerves."

"Well, yes, I think that would be best, but how did you know?"

"It is a ploy I'm conversant with," she said drily. "Instead of going home, why don't you come here? No one would think to look for you until tomorrow."

She nodded slightly. "It might work, though I will have to be seen entering my house first. I shall change, pack a few essentials in a shawl, then wait an hour or so before coming. It would be best if I came in the back way."

"I shall see to it that you are admitted, no matter the hour."

Angel looked up at her with trusting eyes. "I don't know how to thank you." Her low voice sounded unnaturally gruff.

"It is my gift to my brother, late though it may be."

Angel nodded, then sniffed and blotted the tears away with the handkerchief Lady Meriton had given her. "I'd best be going now. I shall be a trifle late as it is. Luckily our stage manager is a congenial old soul. He'll cover for me."

Cecilia rose as her guest stood to leave and escorted her to the parlor door. "Don't worry," she murmured. "It will all work out."

Angel Swafford smiled tightly and blinked back more tears before turning abruptly and hurrying out the door.

It was after midnight before Cecilia was roused from the light slumber she'd fallen into while sitting up waiting for Angel

Swafford to arrive. The noise came from the front of the house. Angel had said she'd enter from the back, and so she had told the servants. Curious, Cecilia went out into the hall to hear what was going on.

Cecilia smiled. It was Branstoke, but he wasn't getting by Loudon as successfully at this hour of the morning.

"It's all right, Loudon, let him come up," she called down the stairs.

She watched the steady, solid grace with which Branstoke mounted the stairs. Trying to see him dispassionately was increasingly difficult the closer he came. Outwardly the mantle of languid posture and dry wit was evident; but she saw beyond the image society accepted. Butterflies erupted in a storm of fluttering wings inside her stomach. Her breath caught in her chest. Inwardly this man was a seething caldron threatening to boil over. There was more energy and life in him than in ten society dandies.

He paused three steps down. He looked up at her, his finely chiseled lips turning up in the wry smile that was uniquely his. Cecilia pressed a hand to her stomach as if to still the wild flutterings.

"I didn't think you'd be to your bed yet," he said softly.

The word *bed* drew forth a kaleidoscope of images in Cecilia's mind. She blushed and stammered. "No, I—I couldn't think of sleeping. Please come up. I have news." She whirled away from him, hurrying into the parlor before him and taking a position in front of a chair.

Branstoke followed stolidly behind. His quick glance took in the tumble of blankets on the sofa and her position in front of a chair set at right angles to its neighbor. He smiled. Cecilia was aware of him as a man just as he was headily aware of her womanhood. He was touched at her determination to keep propriety appeased. With the fires that smoldered between them, it would prove all but impossible if it weren't for the danger that threatened. To ease her mind, he obligingly went toward the other chair. Visibly her muscles relaxed and she waved him to be seated as she sank limply onto her chair.

"Karney is dead," he said without preamble. "Stabbed," he continued, answering her startled look and questioning glance. "The Bow Street runner got to him before he died. He muttered something about someone going to kill them all."

"Kill who all?"

"We don't know. Most likely all the London connections that could identify the leader. Hewitt reports there's been increased lighter activity in and out of the Waddley docks, yet the only ship there is riding high in the water."

"I suppose human cargo is not as heavy as crates of cotton goods."

"No, but it does seem unusual not to take legitimate cargo as well."

"That's true. Mr. Waddley would have had the ship filled with all manner of goods."

He nodded. "It makes good business sense. I did learn something that may ease your mind, however. This spice trade has not gone entirely unnoticed by the authorities. Due to the international nature of this business, the Home Office has been involved. They have an infiltrator in the group. He has been several years gaining their confidence, but evidently he recently has seen some measure of success."

"Who is it, do you know?"

"No. It is safer for us, and for him, if we don't."

"Yes, I see—"

"You said you have some news?"

"Angel came to see me this evening. Angel Swafford."

"Haukstrom's mistress?"

She nodded. "She came to tell me that Randolph foresaw his own death. She told me—she told me—" she gulped, struggling over the lump that formed in her throat, her eyes blurring with tears. "Oh, James, I've been so wrong about Randolph for so many years!" she burst out, tears now streaming down her cheeks.

Instantly Branstoke was at her side. He picked her up out of the chair as if she were a featherweight and sat himself in her place, settling her on his lap. Her head nestled on his shoulder, she cried herself out with a release of tears, finally able to mourn her brother's death. When the torrent passed, she told him, between little hiccups and shudders, all that Angel Swafford had told her.

He stroked her back in comfort, though he frowned in concern. "It's been more than two hours since the end of the play. She should have been here by now."

Cecilia raised her head to look at him. "Do you think she has been prevented from coming?"

"I don't know. I think I'd best go to her house and see."

"I'm coming with you."

"No, you're not."

"James, I should have insisted she stay here. If anything has happened to her, it will be my fault. Knowing that, I can't stay here and do nothing. I have done nothing all day but sit here and worry and wait. If you don't take me with you, I shall follow you," she said determinedly.

Looking at her forward-thrust jaw and the purple glow in her eyes, he believed she would. He leaned his head against the back of the chair and closed his eyes for a moment, hugging her tightly. "All right," he relented.

Cecilia did not give him a chance to think twice. She kissed his cheek then slipped out of his grasp, hurrying to the door. "I'll get my cloak and bonnet and meet you at the door."

Branstoke rose more slowly, already regretting that he had not argued more forcefully.

Branstoke's carriage set them down before a small but very stylish house. "This is an uncommonly good address," he murmured, leading her to the door.

"She is uncommon among the demi-monde. Listening to her speech, I believe her to be gently born."

The house was dark and the front door ajar. Branstoke pushed it open. It creaked only slightly. Inside, Cecilia was about to call out to Angel when Branstoke laid a warning hand over her mouth. He shook his head. She nodded her understanding. They crept farther into the hall, peering into an empty parlor. They started for the stairs when they heard a thump from above. Branstoke motioned her to stay below while he went up to investigate.

Alone in the dark hall, with only the open front door to let in thin moonlight, Cecilia waited anxiously, her ears struggling to catch every stray sound. She shifted from one foot to another, her hands wrapped around the newel post. She strained her eyes to see into the gloom abovestairs. Branstoke had slid silently out of sight.

Suddenly there was a crash, a scuffle of feet, and a groan. Cecilia ran up the stairs, colliding with a figure coming down, carrying something large over his shoulder. She stumbled back against the railing, grabbing for support lest she tumble down the stairs. The figure pushed past her and continued down the stairs and headed for the door. He paused to look up and down the street. When he turned his head she briefly saw his silhouette, though his face was hidden. She didn't stop to identify him, but raced up the stairs in search of Branstoke. In the dark shadows she saw him struggling to get to his feet, a hand cradling his head. She ran to his side, helping him up.

"James! Are you all right?"

He staggered to his feet, swearing under his breath. "I didn't even see who it was. Did you?"

She shook her head. "Only a silhouette. It was too dark to recognize who it was. But he was carrying something over his shoulder. I'm sure it was Angel, James," she said, an aborted sob wracking her body.

"Hush, crying won't help her. We'll have to trust to Bow Street and the infiltrator. I've got to get you home now. I should never have allowed you to come," he said wearily, disgustedly.

"You couldn't have stopped me," she said with a wan smile as they made their way down the stairs.

"Yes, I could have. If I'd been thinking clearly, I would have had you locked in your room. Unfortunately, when I'm around you my thinking becomes a bit fuzzy," he admitted, looking up and down the street for his carriage. He left her side to hail his man.

Left alone for a moment, Cecilia hugged herself, his last words ringing delightfully in her ears. Whatever transpired from this sordid mess, there was one bright spot to help dispel the gloom—her growing relationship with Sir Branstoke. Perhaps she had a chance for happiness after all, she thought, as she allowed him to help her into his carriage. Unmindful of proprieties, she snuggled close to him for the ride back to Meriton House.

Chapter Seventeen

CECILIA WOKE, groggy. She squinted against the light and turned over, pulling the covers over her head. Then a face drifted dreamily into her mind. A face framed with red ringlets and oversized black feathers. A face that held fear in its eyes.

"Angel!" she cried, throwing the covers aside and sitting up.

"Did you say something, ma'am?" asked Sarah, rising from a chair by the fireplace where she'd been mending a chemise.

She looked about, disoriented, as the picture of Angel Swafford faded from her mind. She threw her feet over the edge of the bed and reached for her wrapper. "What time is it?" she asked, stuffing her arms into the sleeves and knotting the sash about her.

"Going on eleven o'clock, I'd say, ma'am."

"Eleven? I've missed services. Why didn't you wake me?"

"Lady Meriton said to let you sleep as long as you would. Now that you're awake, I'm to inform her."

"Could you have some breakfast sent up as well? I'm famished."

"Right away, ma'am," Sarah said, ducking out of the room.

Cecilia was seated at her dressing table brushing her hair when Lady Meriton entered. She looked at her aunt through the mirror. "How could you allow me to sleep so long? I should have been at services."

Lady Meriton sat down in a chair within view of the mirror. "You were physically and emotionally exhausted. You needed your sleep. I put it about that you were prostrate over your brother's death. No one showed the least surprise at that."

Cecilia smiled into the mirror. "My reputation proceeds me, eh?"

"Verily. Oh, and father arrived, as did the baron. I sent them both over to Cheney House where they are more than likely squaring off over the body like two dogs over a bone. I also directed all callers to them. I think I should love to be a mouse viewing the happenings over there today," she mused.

Cecilia laughed and turned to face her aunt directly. "Those two together? You are too bad, Jessamine."

"I know, but I so tire of their posturings. Besides, I felt it should reasonably keep society entertained and out of your realm."

Cecilia nodded. "That's true, and I thank you for that."

"So tell me what happened last night. All I know is what Loudon told me—that you went out with Sir Branstoke after midnight and it was more than an hour before you returned again. What were you about, Cecilia? I shudder to consider the ramifications should that get about the ton. Between the two of us, Loudon and I have assured ourselves of our servants' loyalty. The story shall not get spread abroad from here."

"Admittedly, I'd not considered that. My concern was for Angel Swafford. She never got here last night."

"I know."

"We went to her home to see if she was detained. We were, perhaps, just minutes too late." She told her what happened and also about Branstoke's discovery that the government had a spy in the group. "All I can hope is that, whoever he is, he can save Angel."

"I'm sorry, my dear. I know you feel this deeply."

"Oh, Jessamine, how could I have been wrong about so many things? I feel responsible, for if I hadn't made wrong assumptions and deductions, none of this may have happened. I'm so stupid."

"Nonsense. You had no breadth of knowledge against which to judge the situation or people. Do not hold yourself accountable. Given the information you had, your deductions were quite reasonable."

"I wish I could believe that."

"Don't wish it, believe it. Ah, here's Sarah with your breakfast. Why don't you relax and eat a nice meal? I shall see you downstairs when you are dressed."

Cecilia nodded and rose to cross to a table near the fireplace where Sarah was laying out breakfast.

When she came downstairs less than an hour later, she found Lady Meriton entertaining Miss Amblethorp.

"Janine! Hello, I'm glad to see you," she said, crossing the room to where her friend sat on the sofa. She sank down next to her, taking her hands.

Janine Amblethorp smiled shyly. "I told mama I was going to visit Lucy Farnham. Mother dislikes Mrs. Farnham, so she let me out with just my maid."

Cecilia laughed delightedly. She glanced over at her aunt. "Didn't I tell you, Jessamine, that there was a streak of independence and stubbornness hidden in Miss Amblethorp?"

Lady Meriton chuckled. "Yes, you did."

Janine blushed. "I don't know how it is, but of late I have not been willing to continue this charade of husband hunting. I grow tired of mama thrusting me toward any single gentleman with the least pretensions to civility. I have not *taken,* as they say. All the dances and soirees I could attend will not change that."

"You are too hard on yourself, Janine. But I think you are right to follow your own inclinations," said Lady Meriton. "Smarter than some people I know who push themselves to be what they are not in order to achieve goals that are not for them." She looked pointedly at Cecilia.

Cecilia scowled in fun at her aunt, then sobered and nodded. "I know, Jessamine. Who knows if I had it to do over again what I would do? In my search for answers I've managed to open Pandora's box while at the same time waylaying my own heart. I'm uncertain as to the resolution of either. The question that stalks my every waking moment and haunts my dreams is: Did I cause Randolph's death or Angel's disappearance by my inquisitiveness?"

Janine looked from Cecilia to Lady Meriton and back, confusion written on her face. Cecilia looked over at her and smiled wanly.

"I'm sorry, Janine. That was rude to talk of things you know nothing about. I'm afraid I'm not good company as I am obsessed."

"I don't mean to be rude, or nosy," her friend said carefully, "but I have often observed that a fresh insight on a problem aids in resolution."

"I do not think a fresh insight could solve this situation," Cecilia said.

"It will not change the facts, but it may change how you view them," Lady Meriton suggested pensively. "Let me order refreshments while you consider. She needs to talk," she told Janine.

Janine looked uncertainly from one to the other. "Please, I did not mean to cause a problem. I just thought—"

"It's all right, Janine. Perhaps Jessamine is right. We're so caught up in everything, maybe we can't see things clearly any longer. Though I'm not certain you could be any more objective than we are. But you must promise that what you hear today will not go beyond this room."

"I am not my mother. You have my sincere word on it."

"All right then," Cecilia said sighing heavily. She waited while Loudon served them, using the time to gather her thoughts. After he left, she took a sip of tea, drew a deep breath, and told her how she came to marry Mr. Waddley and what she assumed were her brother's motives for arranging the match. The tale took some telling. There was some Janine did not understand, and much that sickened her, for her life had been insulated against such atrocities. But when Cecilia told her of Mr. Thornbridge's revelations about Lord Havelock and Sir Elsdon, she would not accept Lord Havelock as the guilty party.

"I will grant you he has changed, but nothing could undermine his basic good nature to that extent. No. I refuse to believe it of him. It has to be Sir Elsdon."

"But Janine, Angel Swafford as much as said it was Lord Havelock."

"She didn't name him explicitly, did she? And you said yourself you only saw a dark silhouette of the man who took Miss Swafford. It could have been Sir Elsdon. They are of the same height."

"Janine, Janine, see how hard it is not to allow one's emotions to color one's judgment?"

"He could not have changed that radically! You didn't know him as I did. To change in the manner you're suggesting implies insanity."

"I don't know how anyone could enter into this spice trade, as they call it, without being insane," said Lady Meriton softly.

"It can't be Havelock. I could more believe him to be this government infiltrator than I could the perpetrator of such horror."

"Cecilia, I have a thought. You say you only saw his silhouette. Do you think you would recognize that silhouette if you saw it again?" Lady Meriton asked.

Cecilia nodded slowly, the light of comprehension shining in her eyes. "Yes, I believe I would. Do you have silhouettes of both gentlemen? Preferably ones I have not seen before? That way I can avoid prejudice."

"I believe I do," Lady Meriton said rising and hurrying toward the door. "I'll not be but a few moments."

"And I promise, should it prove to be Lord Havelock, I'll not make objection," said Janine.

"I should never have told you. It's not fair to burden you in this manner. I dislike burdening others in any way."

"No. Don't feel that way. I've lived too sheltered a life. I think, maybe, all of us in society lead sheltered lives. To us, evil and crime are out there somewhere, apart from our world. It's like they're enacted on stage and we sit in our protected little boxes watching it all—untouched by reality. That's not right."

Janine's face shone with an intentness and conviction that startled Cecilia. She'd not thought of the matter in the global manner Janine did. To do so hinted at a growing corruption within the very fabric of their society—regardless of any personal relationship with the perpetrators. She found herself idiotically wishing the entire matter would disappear in a puff of smoke. She chided herself for her weakness, but the wish remained.

"Here," Lady Meriton said, coming through the door. She stopped to close it carefully behind her. "I have brought four pictures. Two are Havelock and Elsdon. The other two are not. Their names are written on the back. I shall place them on this table over here," she said, clearing a space on the cluttered table behind the sofa. "Now, Cecilia, come here and identify Miss Swafford's abductor."

Cecilia came around the sofa hesitantly, nervously. She was followed by Janine who peered around her at the four silhouettes.

She thought she recognized the man instantly, but she took an extra moment to study them all carefully. Finally she pointed to the second one from the end. "That one."

Lady Meriton flipped it over. HAVELOCK.

Janine went white, but steadied herself on the table edge. Cecilia put an arm about her and together they stared at the damning silhouette.

A soft knock on the door pulled their attention away from the black profile. "Begging your pardon, my lady, but Sir Elsdon is here."

"Send him up," Cecilia said peremptorily.

"Do you think that's wise? Though we may believe Havelock to be the leader, that does not mean he works alone," Lady Meriton said as she gathered up the pictures.

"True, but I doubt he'd have more than one in the same social circle," Cecilia said. She led Janine back around the sofa.

"Sir Elsdon, my lady," announced Loudon.

"Mrs. Waddley, I am sorry to intrude on you in this fashion. Hie ho! but it seems the world is falling down around me. I shall never get my play produced. But that is not important now. Dear Mrs. Waddley, I have just come from Cheney House. I went to pay my respects to your brother. While I was there the baron suffered some sort of seizure and collapsed."

"No," whispered Cecilia. She turned to Lady Meriton. "Didn't I say I had no idea what form papa's reaction would take? I should have gone to him this morning!"

"This morning you were in no condition to be of help to anyone," her aunt said, her expression considering, her eyes never leaving Sir Elsdon.

"The place is in an uproar. The duke is yelling at everyone and the baron is asking for you," he said, holding out his hand toward Cecilia. "I said as my coach was just outside, I'd fetch you. But you must come quickly. I don't know if he has much time left."

"I'll fetch my shawl and bonnet," Cecilia said, hurrying out the door.

"Perhaps I'd best go with her," said Lady Meriton.

"Excellent idea," said Sir Elsdon. "Better yet, why don't you pack Mrs. Waddley a portmanteau and follow with it. She's bound to want to stay the night at Cheney House."

She nodded as Cecilia appeared in the doorway.

"I'll see you to the carriage," Janine said, running ahead of Sir Elsdon to Cecilia's side. She put an arm around her and led her downstairs and out the door.

Sir Elsdon's carriage was standing just outside. Quickly, Janine hugged Cecilia and saw Sir Elsdon hand her into the carriage. She stood on the step and watched as the carriage drove down the street and turned south at the corner. Slowly she turned to reenter the house, aware of shouting and scurrying as servants ran to do Lady Meriton's bidding. She asked a passing footman headed toward the servants' quarters to fetch her maid.

Something was bothering her, but she couldn't say what it was. She stood uncertainly in the hallway, trying to puzzle it out. Behind her came a loud banging of the door knocker. With the butler and footmen vanished into the nether regions of the house, she stepped forward to open the door.

On the other side stood Lord Havelock! He grasped her by the shoulders and half-pushed, half-led her into the house.

"Is Miss Swafford here?" he asked anxiously. His clothes were in wild disarray and liberally smeared with dirt.

"Loudon! Stephen! Grab that man!" ordered Lady Meriton uselessly from the top of the stairs. The two servants were not about.

He abruptly raised his hands from her shoulders, but made no move to bolt for the open door. "Wait, Lady Meriton—"

The sunlight streaming in the door was cut off by the broad-shouldered figure of Sir Branstoke. He held a pistol in his hand aimed at Lord Havelock.

Suddenly what had been bothering Janine surfaced in her mind. "The carriage went the wrong way!" she blurted out. She grabbed Lord Havelock's arm. "You're the government agent, aren't you?"

"What?—"

She shook his arm angrily. "You're the one investigating white slavery, aren't you?"

"Yes, damn it, I am! Is Miss Swafford here?"

"But Cecilia identified you as abducting Miss Swafford," said Lady Meriton, confused and increasingly frightened.

"I did. But she didn't trust me and ran. And I'm sorry for hitting you, Branstoke," he said, glancing his way. "In the dark I took you for one of Elsdon's men."

Sir Branstoke lowered his gun slightly and came into the hall. He remembered Miss Amblethorp mentioned a carriage. "Where's Cecilia?" he asked in a dead voice, for he feared the answer with every particle of his being.

Lady Meriton moaned and sagged down on a stair step. Janine's hand gripped Lord Havelock's arm tightly, her nails digging into the wool sleeve. "With Sir Elsdon," she whispered past parched lips.

For a heartbeat, the hall was silent, then everyone began talking at once. Lady Meriton tried to explain what happened, but her words were disjointed and punctuated with asides to Janine that she was right. Finally Branstoke and Havelock abandoned their efforts to get any sense out of Lady Meriton and turned to Janine.

She gulped and clung to Lord Havelock. "H—he said he was taking her to Cheney House, for her father was ill. But I watched them as they drove away. They should have turned north at the end of the block to go to Cheney House. They turned south!"

"South!" exclaimed Branstoke.

"Where could he be taking her? From my information his cargo is to sail this afternoon with the tide," said Havelock. He looked up at Branstoke. "The admiralty is waiting downriver to intercept the ship."

"South, you say," repeated Branstoke. "Damn it, of course! He's not using that ship. It's a decoy! He's headed for the other side of the river!"

"What?" Havelock asked, his eyes intent upon Branstoke, though he kept an arm about Janine.

"I've had a man watching Waddley's. Last night he told me of lighter activity in and out of there to the other side of the river. He said the ship docked at Waddley's looked like it was riding curiously high in the water for a fully loaded cargo ship. Cecilia and I concluded he was only going to take his human cargo which wouldn't weigh the ship down as much. But what if those lighters were transferring the cargo to another ship, to a smaller one, perhaps, anchored across the river? To a type of ship that would not be stopped by the admiralty?"

"You mean something like a hoy, which sails the river between London and Margate?"

"Precisely. It gets by your planned reception committee and meets with a ship anchored somewhere beyond Gravesend. Probably along the coast between the Isle of Sheppey and Margate."

"Yes, if he is suspicious at all—which Elsdon is—that is something he'd do. Particularly as I believe he's leaving the country with this, his last cargo. We'd better get a message out using the semaphore towers. My horse is fresh yet." He looked inquiringly at Branstoke.

"As is mine. If we ride hard, we should be able to beat them downriver for the tide's not turned yet."

They bid the ladies good-bye, assuring them they would do everything in their power to rescue Cecilia. Janine and Lady Meriton watched them ride off in the direction Sir Elsdon's carriage took, nearly causing an accident with a heavy traveling coach that was turning the corner. The driver pulled hard to the side, fighting to keep his startled horses from rearing and tangling the traces. He got them settled, though they still danced a bit, and drove them forward only to stop in front of Meriton House. A tall, angular figure with grizzled sideburns framing an ascetic face descended the coach step and looked up at the house. Lady Meriton squealed and ran down the steps.

"Meriton!" she exclaimed before throwing herself into his arms and bursting into tears.

Cecilia studied the face of the complacent gentleman seated across from her. Sunlight through the carriage windows caught the red-gold of his hair where it curled about his collar. It was odd, she thought in a detached manner, how a man moderately good-looking on the outside could be entirely cancerous and vile inside. He was unequivocally a facile and talented actor and decidedly correct when he claimed that if he'd been born a lesser man he would have been a greater man. That certainty prevented her from berating herself too severely for her predicament. Though she was wrong—again—she felt no guilt, only a strange floating feeling of fatalism.

That detached feeling had overwhelmed her when the carriage turned south, away from Cheney House. She remembered Sir Elsdon studying her with a tense set to his posture. He was waiting for her to discover his lie and either grovel at his feet begging for mercy or fight for her freedom. She did neither. She merely raised an eyebrow and praised him for his acting ability.

He had been for a moment surprised and taken back by her reaction. That pleased Cecilia, and she filed that knowledge away carefully in her brain. Recovering swiftly, he smiled at her in a manner she'd never seen him use. It was more of a leer, and spoke volumes for the depth of his self-confidence. She filed that knowledge away as well.

He in turn had praised her for her perspicacity for which she demurred, saying if she had intuitive talents, she would not find herself in the carriage with him at that moment.

He demurred. He assured her that she would have been right

where she was because that is where he wished her to be. She begged that he accept that they were doomed to disagree, and the conversation slackened there. Cecilia turned her head to look out the window and desultorily followed their journey through the changing landscape.

Now, with the smell of fish, timber and tar redolent in the warm afternoon air, she knew they were approaching the river from a direction she'd never come. The carriage was slowing as it picked its way through narrowing streets. She wondered if she dared try to bolt, then decided to husband her energy for a more auspicious time. Sir Elsdon, though now more relaxed, was waiting and watching for her to make a break. Besides, she didn't see how he could escape the net being cast for him by both Bow Street and the government agent. To do anything untoward would likely result in her early demise or worse, an early induction into the trade he planned for her.

No, it was best to remain calm and clearheaded. Strong emotions would muddy her thinking. Furthermore, calmness on her behalf would likely disconcert him more and perhaps lead to errors on his part. One could only wait, hope, and fervently pray.

Sir Elsdon glanced out the window then turned to address Cecilia. "You surprise me, Mrs. Waddley," he said, pulling a bottle out of his pocket. "You have exhibited none of the reactions I expected on the realization of your abduction. You have not fought and screamed, nor collapsed in a prostrate bundle of pathetic tears and pleas for mercy."

"Indeed, sir. I shall take that as a compliment."

"Nor, curiously, have you fainted or complained of bodily failings as so often society has been audience to."

"It has been my good fortune to have my health improving daily."

"If I were you, I would call it misfortune," he said smiling evilly. He looked at the bottle of brownish liquid that he held. "Almost you convince me that this is not necessary."

She stared at the bottle and wished she'd fought him and tried to escape earlier. It was laudanum. He was going to drug her. She looked from the bottle to his grinning face, tensing her muscles.

"Almost—" he repeated in a soft murmur before his free hand shot out to grab her around the throat, choking, forcing her mouth open.

Cecilia bucked and flailed at him, twisting and turning against his weight as he leaned on her, using his body to anchor her while he guided the bottle to her lips. She jerked her head aside, only to feel his fingers cruelly digging into the soft white skin of her throat. She gouged his face with her nails drawing pin-pricks of blood. He swore viciously and jammed the open bottle between her teeth. She gagged on the liquid, trying to spit it out, but she had no breath. It ran out the sides of her mouth. Tears squeezed from the corners of her eyes. Her eyes blurred and her head began to swim. Spots of gray-blackness danced at the edges of her vision then rushed to close against consciousness. She went limp.

Chapter Eighteen

CECILIA REGAINED CONSCIOUSNESS SLOWLY, her first awareness a fiery pain in her throat and the aching muscles of her neck. She moved fitfully, as if to escape the relentless pain only to discover the slightest movement intensified her agony. A damp cloth touched her brow, her face, and then her neck. She relaxed and listened to the deep, husky murmur of a voice above her head that seemed to accompany the soothing progress of the cloth. In the background she heard soft crying, creaking wood, and the dim echoes of shouting from somewhere above.

She opened her eyes, then blinked as they grew accustomed to a gloomy world. A tangle of dark red curls slid into her field of vision. "Angel," she whispered in a thin, croaking thread of sound. She tried to smile, but only managed a grimace. She swallowed painfully and parted her lips to speak again when a finger lightly pressed against them.

"Hush, don't try to speak yet," said Angel. "Have some water first. Here, let me help you sit up."

It was then Cecilia felt the unfamiliar cold weight about her wrists and heard the clank of chains. Iron manacles around each wrist were joined by a length of chain two feet long. She quickly struggled to sit up, ignoring the wave of dizziness that assailed her. Angel handed her a small jug of water. She drank some thankfully, the tepid liquid remarkably cooling to her battered throat. Each swallow was painful, but less so than the last.

Handing the jug back to Angel, she took stock of their surroundings.

They were obviously below deck on some sailing vessel. Light came in through a small grated opening to the main deck that also let in fresh air. The narrowness of the space convinced her they were not on a large ship. Still, it was a surprisingly roomy hold that would even allow an average-sized man to stand upright. It was empty of all cargo save for the human kind, for with her and Angel were some eighteen to twenty women.

Cecilia sucked in her breath as the reality of the scene filtered into her mind. She scrambled to her feet and, leaning on Angel, slowly picked her way past the straw-filled pallets on which they lay or sat and looked at each closely in turn. The women were for the most part about sixteen years of age, all comely and, judging by their dress, predominantly of middle class or better station. A few were no more than children, the youngest a flaxen blond child of perhaps nine years. It was from her that the crying came that she'd heard. The others were either drugged into a stupor or so frightened and cowed that they sat listless and silent. Accumulating horror robbed Cecilia of strength, and she sank back down on her own pallet, Angel by her side.

She turned to Angel, her mind overwhelmed with questions that she couldn't get past her battered throat. Angel nodded in understanding.

"This—we are Elsdon's spice trade," she said softly, her voice a deep rumble in Cecilia's ear. "We're on a small ship that will take us downriver. Somewhere along the coast we'll be transferred to a larger ship. Elsdon's coming along. He's leaving England: too many deaths, too many suspicions."

"Havelock?" Cecilia croaked out.

Bitterness etched Angel's features. "If I'd trusted him I wouldn't be here now."

"Don't despair," she managed, and swallowed painfully.

"If you're meaning Sir Branstoke and Bow Street, he's wise to them. The big ship's going out clean to fool them."

Suddenly the implications of being on a small ship percolated through to Cecilia and the fear she'd heretofore held at bay swept through her. Her breathing grew rapid and her eyes widened. She clutched Angel's arm.

"I know," Angel said grimly, "it hit me like that too."

Cecilia's frightened gaze swept the small hold. She looked from the blank faces to those turned toward her and Angel, looking at the two of them for comfort. She realized she and Angel were the oldest of the captives and as such, the others would look to them for guidance. She couldn't crumble now. She had to be strong for them, no matter what the future held in store. She closed her eyes a moment, summoning Branstoke's face to her mind. She would draw strength and hope from that image she held of him. It wasn't over yet.

The strident squeal of protesting hinges followed by a flood of bright light preceded a ladder descending into the hold. The sight of immaculate top boots on the rungs followed by an elegantly attired male form warned them of Elsdon's visit.

Cecilia drew a little apart from Angel, not wishing to be seen leaning on another. A haughty mask descended over her dirt-streaked features. She lifted her head high, revealing deeply purpling bruises on the fair skin of her neck.

He walked toward her, a deeply satisfied smile on his face. "Ah, so the final item on our manifest has awoken. Excellent." He reached out one long finger to tilt her chin up. "Tsk, tsk, my dear, I do not like the sight of those bruises on your fair neck. Damaged goods bring lower prices, you know. We shall hope that they fade before we reach our destination."

She moved to bat his hand away but the clank of the length of chain between her wrists warned him of her action and he raised his hand out of reach.

He laughed. "Definitely not the flighty, sickly female. So much the better. Liveliness and fight also increases value. And quite frankly, my dear, at your age, every advantage is necessary to boost the price. Lovely though you are, you are past your prime in my market." He took a few steps toward the flaxen-haired child and hunkered down before her, running a hand down her quivering form. "Now this one, on the other hand, will bring a pretty penny, a very pretty penny indeed."

The child flinched and scuttled back against the curving walls, whimpering.

"Leave her be," Cecilia croaked out, getting up. Behind her, Angel stood as well. A couple women stirred, rising to their knees.

Elsdon turned toward Cecilia, his eyes narrowing. He rose smoothly, his hand delving deep into his pocket to bring out a pistol. He leveled it at Cecilia. The other women drew back.

"I have not that alacrity of spirit,
Nor cheer of mind, that I was wont to have."

His voice was light, yet rung with a power to reach the boxes had he stood on a stage.

A shiver traversed Cecilia's spine, yet she stood her ground. Out of the corner of her eye she saw Angel grasp the chain between her hands, holding it taut so its links could not ring against one another. There was an unholy glint to the woman's pale eyes and a rigidity to her jaw. Cecilia's gaze fixed upon Elsdon, challenging him to break it.

"So, you would still play King Richard?" she whispered huskily, forcing the words harshly past her throat. They had ghostly cadence. "A doomed and defeated man? A curious choice for mentor."

"Perhaps. But I have learned from him. In the end, despite his words:

Conscience is but a word cowards use,
Devised at first to keep the strong at awe:

he was troubled by his conscience. I shall not be. And I have learned what he did not. That gold buys a good many consciences."

"For a time."

"Ah, you are thinking of your brother. It is a sad fact that tools often become too worn for repair and therefore need replacing."

"And Havelock?"

"Yes, Havelock, my Buckingham. Almost he had me fooled. He could be nearly as great an actor as I if he weren't plagued with notions of honor and duty and the other artificial trappings of our so-called polite society."

"Not quite your Buckingham, for he is free and alive," she said, intent on keeping him talking. Angel was stepping carefully around to the side of him. Two other women had grabbed their chains in like manner and rose to their feet.

He waved her words aside. "I shall deal with him later, as I shall your Branstoke and Mr. Thornbridge. Tell me, how did you get those two to do your bidding? Have you been rehearsing for your new role, my dear?" The gun seemed to sink a little, his guard relaxing.

"Not everyone must needs use your methods of deceit."

He laughed. "Are you telling me my empire's toppled for love? That's rich, I vow. Or are you trying your hand at comedy? It won't wash. Remember, I knew your husband and we discussed your abilities—or lack thereof."

Cecilia blushed then paled at his vileness.

"Luckily the customer you are destined for is not so particular in such matters. You shall be the fifth I've sent him. The others are all dead, though one did last as long as two years. He is quite voracious."

Cecilia gagged involuntarily. "You—you monster!"

He laughed heartily, taking a step closer. "Women are commodities. They have value like gems or precious metals. Unfortunately like fresh fruit, they are also perishable."

To the side and a little behind him Angel stood. Cecilia could see her gathering herself for an attack. She stepped to the side, leaning against a beam as if she were sickened. His eyes followed her, away from Angel.

Suddenly there was shouting and the sound of running feet above.

"No!" Cecilia yelled, too late.

Elsdon was already turning toward the hatch and Angel just as she lunged for him. He saw her rush, his pistol jerking up as she threw herself at him, her arms descending over his head as the gun went off.

Screams from the other women drowned out Angel's little cry of surprise and pain as she sagged against him, smearing him with her blood. He cursed and tried to shove her dead body away but her manacled arms were around him, imprisoning him in the circle of her arms. He stumbled awkwardly against a pillar.

Tears of rage and sorrow streamed down Cecilia's face. She would not let Angel die in vain! She came up behind Elsdon as he struggled to wriggle out from under Angel's grasp. She brought her arms over his head, crossing them so the chain formed a noose. His neck was caught in the loop. She pulled her arms apart with all the strength at her command. The chain bit savagely into his neck. He gagged, his eyes bulging. He clawed uselessly at the chain. Two women beat at his arms and legs with the slack of their chains.

"Sir Elsdon! Sir Elsdon!" cried a voice from above. "They're ignoring the big ship! They're ordering us to heave to! Sir Elsdon!" A man's boots appeared on the ladder.

Cecilia howled in rage and frustration as the man bent double to look into the hold.

"Holy mother, they've up and kilt him!" he muttered. Hurriedly he climbed the ladder, pulling it up after him and slammed the hatch shut.

Sir Elsdon squawked once, feebly, but went unheard by the

man. Then he went limp, falling to the floor, dragging Cecilia and Angel's body with him.

Caught under the weight of his shoulders, Cecilia's arms quivered as she eased the pressure around his neck. "The key. Check his pockets," she croaked, her head falling back against the dirty floorboards.

Above them came the sounds of panic: shouting, gunshots, and the splash of men jumping into the river. The smell of smoke wafted into the hold.

"Hurry!" Cecilia urged the two women tentatively touching and poking his body. She struggled to free herself from his leaden weight.

"Here!" one of the women cried, pulling an iron key out of his waistcoat pocket. With trembling hands she unlocked her fetters and those of the other woman who stood over Elsdon. Then she freed Cecilia and rolled Elsdon's and Angel's bodies off of her.

Cecilia climbed painfully to her feet. Dark, acrid smoke curled into the hold through the grating. Cecilia coughed and held out her hand for the key.

"One of you climb onto the other's shoulders and see if you can push that hatch open. I'll unlock the others," she cried against the pain in her throat. Her eyes were stinging from the smoke.

Hands clutched at her to get free, knocking her down. Doggedly she continued. The women who were not drugged scrambled to help those at the hatch. They boosted one of the thirteen-year-old girls out of the opening. A blast of heat entered the hold followed by great billows of smoke. A cry of thanks went up as the ladder descended followed by pushing and shoving as each fought to be the first free of the hold.

"Wait! Stop! We've got to help these women!" yelled Cecilia as she frantically removed the last of the irons from three drugged women. Only the youngest child remained in chains. She was coughing and knuckling her eyes, but Cecilia freed her and managed to get her and one of the drugged women to stand. "Go! Go!" she urged the child, pushing her and the woman toward the ladder. Tears caused by the smoke mingled with tears of frustration. It couldn't end this way. "Oh, James, help me," she murmured as she crawled to the next woman and pulled at her, trying desperately to get her to respond. "Don't let any more die!"

Frantically she poured water on the woman's face and slapped her cheeks. "Please," she cried, sobbing, "please!"

"Cecilia!"

She paused and looked up toward the hatch.

"Cecilia!"

Her face grew bright with hope and joy. "I'm down here!" she yelled, her throat denying her sufficient volume. She swallowed. "Here!" she cried again, louder.

Her call was rewarded with the sound of boots on the ladder.

"Where are you, Cecilia?" he called through the smoke, searching the shadowed hold, his gaze stopping on the entwined figures of Angel and Sir Elsdon.

"Over here. Help me," she croaked.

His head swung around and he saw her kneeling by two prone women. "Havelock!" he yelled up the ladder, "I need your help!" He strode over to her and pulled one of the women up, slinging her over his shoulder just as Havelock dropped into the hold.

"There's another one over here," he told him, jerking his head to the side. With his free hand he pushed Cecilia ahead of him as Lord Havelock brushed past him to pick up the other woman.

Cecilia scrambled up the ladder, every limb of her body quivering from exertion and fatigue though her head felt amazingly clear and alert. On deck she could see that the fire, primarily in the rigging, was being fought by sailors from the naval ship nearby. But the fire was spreading faster than their efforts to put it out. As they crossed the deck, the call was being given to abandon ship. A burly seaman swept Cecilia off her feet and dumped her unceremoniously into a boat drawn alongside. Looking across the water, she saw a boat with a load of frightened women reach the safety of the naval vessel. Havelock and Branstoke lowered their burdens to waiting seamen then jumped down beside them. Branstoke pulled Cecilia into his arms where she clung to him, gulping cooler air while tears of relief slid down her cheeks.

The sailors pulled hard on the oars as the fire spread rapidly across the little ship. They were almost to the naval vessel when a loud boom and crack drew their attention back in time to see the other ship list sideways and slide burning into the river.

Cecilia, wiping the tears away with the back of a grimy hand, said a prayer for Angel Swafford's soul.

The next afternoon Cecilia lay propped in a nest of pillows on the daybed in Lady Meriton's rose parlor, George Waddley's journal lying open and forgotten in her lap. She was staring at nothing, yet in her mind seeing everything. Everything that had happened over the last weeks, over the last years of her life. She felt odd, unsettled. There was a churning restlessness within her.

The horrors of the past—though they might haunt some corridors of her mind—were just that, the past. And the Cecilia Waddley, nee Haukstrom who existed in that past was also gone. Like the legendary phoenix, rebirth followed destruction.

She smiled softly and closed the book in her lap. That old Cecilia, that sheltered, naive Cecilia who feared the world and played parts to exist within it, possessed the truth all the while, yet never saw it. She could only look upon the surface of life for that was how she lived it. She leaned her head back against the pillows and closed her eyes, a smile softly touching her lips.

She heard the parlor door open and close, but still she did not open her eyes, though her smile widened. "I see I shall have to reprimand Loudon for failing in his duties yet again," she said severely even though the smile lingered on her face.

She raised her head and opened her eyes to see Sir James Branstoke leaning against the closed parlor doors, his arms folded across his chest. His eyelids were in their normal lazy, half-closed position. He straightened languidly, drawing a slight giggle from Cecilia. Taking his quizzing glass from his waistcoat pocket, he raised it to peer through the glass at her.

"Will you insist on wearing those infernal caps when we are married?" he asked, studying the lace confection that covered her pale blond curls.

"Are we to be married?" she asked archly.

"We had better be," he said seriously, dropping the quizzing glass and walking toward her, "or I shall not be responsible for the consequences."

"And what consequences are those?" she asked breathlessly, the butterflies careening wildly through her stomach and pressing outward to fill her entire body.

He sat down on the edge of the daybed, appearing to be still studying the lace cap. He reached up to pluck it off her head.

His thin lips curved into a smile. "Shall we take this action to be symbolic of my desires?" He gathered her up in his arms, cradling her against him. "Or are further demonstrations in order," he whispered against her ear, his breath light, warm, and caressing.

She shivered delightfully in his arms and turned her face up to his. "Yes and no," she whispered, straining toward him. Then she paused and reached up a hand between their lips. She leaned back against the pillows, sighing.

"I love you, James. But what are we to do?" she asked seriously.

"Do?"

She waved a hand over her attire. "I am once again in mourning for a year though all I want is to leave the past behind."

"Ah, yes. Social conventions," he said. "I have given the matter thought; we being such society-controlled creatures. We, my darling ninnyhammer, in order to save you from going into a decline, are going to elope."

"Me go into a decline? Am I such a poor-spirited individual?"

"You created the image, not I. I don't see any reason to attempt to persuade people otherwise. Upon consideration I have decided it is the perfect excuse for us to continue to stay out of society's orb. You being so frequently confined to your bed and I, the devoted husband, so attentively attending to your needs," he suggested, smiling raffishly.

"Hmmm," she said, snuggling among the pillows. Then she scowled and sat up, a determined look glinting in her royal blue eyes. "You are making me forget everything. My mind is full of questions. What has happened? How did Havelock get involved? What's going to happen now? What's the world to know?"

He sighed. "I forget you slept nearly twenty-four hours while the rest of us toiled to unravel the skeins of Elsdon's weaving. All right. Piecing this together from various sources, the story goes as follows: Elsdon was on the Grand Tour when Napoleon began playing havoc with Europe. As a consequence he found himself kicking his heels for long periods in backwater locations without access to funds. During that time he met a doge who lusted after a nobleman's daughter pledged to another. He told Elsdon that he'd pay a king's ransom for a night with the girl. Elsdon, young, at loose ends, and lacking funds, took up the challenge and soon supplied the grateful doge with his heart's desire. As in Haukstrom's case, one thing led to another and soon he was in the white slavery trade. One thing he discovered in Europe and the Middle East was that English women were considered great prizes and carried great worth. When he returned to England he decided to see if he couldn't tap into this lucrative market."

Branstoke rose from the daybed and crossed to a side table where Loudon had earlier left a decanter of sherry and some glasses. He poured out two glasses, carrying the second to Cecilia.

"No one knows precisely how he got together with Waddley. Havelock guesses that Waddley had been involved in illegal activities in the Mediterranean that Elsdon knew about from his time there and used them as an introduction. Whatever, about nine years ago they began occasionally filling orders. Slowly their reputation grew among those who had an interest in their products. As their reputation grew, so did the demand. Elsdon began using others to scout for likely women. One of the women they abducted eight years ago was Dorothea Rustian."

"Havelock's cousin."

He nodded. "He went looking for her. People had assumed she'd eloped, but he wanted to know that for sure. He did find her. She was ill, her mind gone. He took her to the best doctors he could find, but she was beyond mental recovery. She lives to this day in an asylum in Switzerland. He set out to discover how she came to be in that condition. That's how he learned about white slavery. When he told the government they admitted some slight knowledge of this practice, but did not know the leaders. They gave him that task." He took a sip of sherry.

"He had suspicions for a long while, but no proof. Elsdon and Waddley were too clever. Then he discovered Haukstrom's involvement. He was quick to identify him as a weak link."

"Actually, I'm surprised Elsdon kept Randolph around and alive as long as he did," Cecilia admitted.

"I believe it was your brother's occasional flashes of brilliance that appealed to Elsdon. The fact that he, too, went out and blatantly procured a woman for another man, much as Elsdon did at the beginning of his career, was something of a bond between them. He also appreciated the way he tricked Waddley into mar-

rying you as a way of saving you. That delighted his Machiavel
lian mind."

"Why did Havelock abduct Angel?"

"He was trying to save her from Elsdon. He was certain she
would either be killed outright or taken as a shipment. Through
Haukstrom she knew too much. Elsdon couldn't afford to have
her around. Unfortunately, Angel didn't trust Havelock any
more than she did Elsdon."

Cecilia shook her head sadly. "Such a waste. What about
Havelock? What's he going to do now?"

"He says he's going to rebuild Havelock Manor and settle
there. However, when I left him this afternoon, he was planning
on visiting the Amblethorps. I understand they were frequent
visitors in his country neighborhood. I believe it was his intention to personally thank a member of that family for the un
swerving faith she carried in him."

Cecilia's eyes widened and she clapped her hands in delight.
"I shall be interested to observe what transpires there!"

"Well, you are doomed to disappointment."

"Why?"

"You're going to have to learn second hand what happens.
You're not going to be around to observe. We are eloping, re
member?"

"So soon?"

He pulled a special license from his pocket. "It has been a fa
tiguing day, but procuring this was my last and most important
errand. Tomorrow morning this will allow us to be joined as
man and wife. Immediately afterwards we are leaving for Scot-
land. Your maid has already begun packing your things. But
I warn you, she has strict instructions to leave everything black
behind." He glanced at the mantle clock and grimaced.

"It is nearly five. Lady Meriton is expecting the duke and your
father here at five. We don't have much time," he growled, gath
ering her in his arms.

She lifted her face to meet his kiss, tingling in expectation.

Their lips touched just as the first peremptory knock touched
the parlor door. They broke apart, the normally urbane Sir
James Branstoke swearing. Cecilia giggled.

"Tomorrow," he said severely.

"Forever," she promised as the door opened.